This item should be returned to a Blackpool
BP   on or before the latest date st_____ h__

To extend the loan perio__
    or phone Cen___

10/04

Somuno

Hr.

W
L

Catherine Barry lives in Dublin with her two young children.

NULL & VOID

When it comes to ending a marriage, there's the easy way, the hard way — and the Catholic way ... For Ruby Blake, there seems to be no happy ever after. Her marriage to Eamonn was a sham from start to finish. Was it a marriage at all? Or one that existed only on paper? To find out for sure, Ruby must apply for an annulment. Her life — and Eamonn's — are taken over by the authorities, as question after question are heaped upon them. Has Ruby got what it takes to see this through? Is their marriage really over? Or could it be just beginning?

CATHERINE BARRY

NULL & VOID

Complete and Unabridged

ULVERSCROFT
Leicester

First published in Great Britain in 2003 by
Pocket/TownHouse an imprint of
Simon & Schuster UK Limited, London

First Large Print Edition
published 2004
by arrangement with
Simon & Schuster UK Limited, London

The moral right of the author has been asserted

British Library CIP Data

Barry, Catherine
    Null & void.—Large print ed.—
    Ulverscroft large print series: romance
    1. Marriage—Annulment—Ireland—Dublin—Fiction
    2. Dublin (Ireland)—Social life and customs—
    Fiction 3. Large type books
    I. Title
    823.9′2 [F]

    ISBN 1–84395–477–X

Published by
F. A. Thorpe (Publishing)
Anstey, Leicestershire

Set by Words & Graphics Ltd.
Anstey, Leicestershire
Printed and bound in Great Britain by
T. J. International Ltd., Padstow, Cornwall

This book is printed on acid-free paper

FOR MAM & DAD

Acknowledgements

Thanks to all my family for continued support, love, encouragement and wisdom.

Thanks to Peter Sheridan, Dave and Patricia Coyle, Jimmy Delaney, Suzanne Erskine, Brian and Gerry McIlkenny, Mary McMahon, Alan Coyle, Charley Stuart, Karen McIlhenny, Patricia Duff, Doreen Shanley, Rose Shiel, Denise Shanahan, Pat Sullivan, Andrea O'Kelly and big Ben for their friendship, support, hilarity and in particular, their loyalty at all times.

Special thanks to David and Geraldine Culhane.

Thanks to Barbara Cullen, an earth angel.

A huge thanks to Gillian, another earth angel.

A special thanks to 'The Irish Girls About Town', especially Tina Reilly, Sarah Webb, Maeve Binchy, Colette Caddle, Catherine Dunne, Annie Sparrow, Marisa Mackle, Cathy Kelly and Martina Devlin for e-mails, texts, letters, phone calls, cups of coffee, dinner parties and mighty whining sessions.

A very special thanks to Malachy Farren and all at Lux Mundi, Fuengirola, in Spain.

My thanks to Caitríona my daughter, for beautifully hand made cards, letters and pictures to help inspire me. I love you, my munchkin.

My thanks to Davitt my son for making me laugh and for saving the computer from being axed on more than one occasion. I am very proud of you. Also Karl O Driscoll for providing chocolate, endless supplies of noodles and good humour. Also thanks to Annette and Keven O Driscoll for being so kind.

A special thanks to Lauren for entertaining me with her special talents for making beautiful cards, pictures, songs and plays. Also to Gavin — 'You're the man!'

Thanks to Darley Anderson, Suzanne Baboneau and Clare Ledingham.

As always, thank you God.

1

Dublin Regional Marriage Tribunal,
Diocesan Offices,
Archbishop's House,
Dublin 9

Nullity of Marriage: Reece — Blake
J.2 254/94.

Personal and Confidential

20 January 1995

Dear Mrs Blake,

We are pleased to advise you that we are now in a position to arrange an appointment for you regarding your application to this Tribunal. Please be good enough to call at the Tribunal Offices, Archbishop's House, Drumcondra, Dublin 9, on Tuesday 14 February 1995 at 9.30 a.m. to meet the Reverend Sean Ebbs.

I would be grateful if you would telephone or write to me, confirming this appointment, *immediately*. If you wish to confirm your appointment by telephone, please contact me on 607810.

You will appreciate that if we are to cater for all who seek our help at the Tribunal, it is most important that each person should attend the specified appointment. I would urge you therefore, to make every effort possible to keep this appointment.

With every good wish,
Yours sincerely,

Aidan Mason
Tribunal Secretary

Ruby held the letter tightly. It had been three months since she had made the initial application to the Catholic Church for an annulment. She hadn't expected an appointment so soon. She wondered if Eamonn had received the same letter. She sat down and read it again, her hand wandering across the kitchen table until it found the packet of cigarettes. She pulled one out with her teeth — her nail polish had not yet dried and the Church was not going to ruin her nails as well as her marriage.

She took a deep drag and studied the words slowly, taking each one in. She blew the smoke on her nails as she exhaled. It had started too soon. She needed more time to think.

Think about what? she wondered. There was nothing more to think about. The marriage was over and had been for almost two years now. It was only right to set the ball rolling. She had already appointed a solicitor to look after the divorce, but somehow an annulment seemed more profound.

She picked up the phone and dialled Eamonn's number. It rang for ever. Didn't he know he could set the answering-service to pick up after six rings? Eventually the recorded message came on. Ruby listened to Eamonn's voice, soft, confident, strong.

'Hi, you've reached Eamonn, I'm not available to take your call right now, you can try me on my mobile, or leave a message after the long bleep.'

Ruby listened to the long bleep and the silence that followed. Her voice abandoned her. She hung up, pulled out her inhaler and took two puffs. She picked up the receiver and dialled again.

A deep voice answered the phone.

'Archbishop's House, how can I help you?'

'Thank you, my name is Ruby Blake, I'm phoning to say — '

'Your reference number, please,' the voice interrupted.

'Reference number?' Ruby stumbled.

'At the top of the page, madam,' the voice said.

'Oh, yes, I see it,' Ruby replied, and read it out. 'Thank you, I just wanted to say — '

'Putting you through now, madam,' the voice cut in.

The line crackled and she heard a woman's voice. 'Hello, Mrs Blake.'

Ruby waited for another interruption.

'Hello? Mrs Blake, are you there?' the voice asked.

'Yes. I just wanted to confirm my appointment for Tuesday the fourteenth of February,' she said sharply.

'Nine thirty a.m., Mrs Blake.'

'Thank you,' Ruby replied, and hung up. She smudged her nails on the telephone directory. 'Bloody hell!' she screamed.

Why do I have to get so angry? she thought. After all it was she who had initiated the whole thing. No half-measures. If it was over, then let it be really over. She had married within the Church; the union would be ended within the Church. Ruby hadn't the faintest idea why annulments took so long. Some weeks ago she had heard a radio phone-in about them: one poor unfortunate had been waiting five years. What had they been doing? Reinacting the scene of the crime? Living it day by day? Did they move in with couples, just to get a better picture? She couldn't understand it.

It all seemed frightfully boring and tiresome. Anyway, that wouldn't be the case with her and Eamonn. It was clear-cut: no mysteries, no children, no extramarital affairs. She was sure Eamonn would co-operate, and it would all be over in a couple of months. With that in mind, she reapplied her nail varnish and made an appointment to see the hairdresser. Her highlights had begun to fade. She always made sure her hair was perfect . . . She frowned at her impeccable standards. Why couldn't she let go, just for once, of the stupid little things that upset her? Like how she had to have her perfume bottles in order, starting with the smallest one at the end of the line. Any discrepancy irritated her beyond belief.

It hadn't always been like that. There had been a time when she couldn't have cared less about such things. She tried to remember when it was. The answer eluded her.

The telephone rang. She let the answering service take it, and heard the beep-beep of the taxi outside. She was looking forward to a few drinks and had decided to leave the car at home. A dab of perfume, and she was on her way. Without doubt, the best part of a night out with the girls was getting ready: now it was over, Ruby was anxious about meeting them. She hadn't had enough time to think things through, or prepare her excuses. It was becoming more and more difficult to agree on a night when they were all free. Ruby was available every night now, but she never told them that.

Inside the bar, she surveyed the chattering mob, and spotted hands waving at her from a corner. They were all there: Brenda looking around frantically, Judy talking loudly on her mobile phone, and Marjory — no, Marjory wasn't there yet. But Marjory had never been late for anything in her life . . .

'Hi, stranger.' Brenda beckoned to the seat beside her.

Judy waved at her, as if she was a passing waitress.

'Some things never change.' Ruby nodded at Judy.

Judy stuck out her tongue like a bold child.

'Where's Marjory?' Ruby asked. 'I hope she hasn't backed out again.'

'She promised she'd come, but with the final separation papers arriving, well, I wouldn't be surprised if she backed out at the last minute. This really isn't in her best interests, is it? I mean, smoky atmosphere, alcohol, snogging couples and all that kind of thing. I tried to suggest somewhere a little quieter to Judy but you know . . . ' Brenda sighed.

'Hi, Ruby, about time.' Judy placed the mobile phone on the table beside her drink.

'Why don't you put that thing away for the rest of the evening? It's so impersonal having that bloody *William Tell Overture* blast in my ear every five minutes.'

'Sorry. I'm expecting an important call. I'll put it away as soon as it comes. Where's Marjory?' She flung back the remains of her Bacardi and Coke. Before anyone could answer, she grabbed a passing waiter and ordered some more drinks.

'I was just saying to Ruby that she probably backed out at the last minute. Why the hell couldn't we have gone for a quiet meal instead?' Brenda said.

'I couldn't eat a thing.' Ruby was relieved they hadn't arranged to do that.

'What in God's name is that rock doing hanging round your neck?' Judy roared.

'It's not a rock, it's a stone,' Brenda said. 'It has special healing powers.' She held it in her palm, and rubbed its smooth surface.

'Uh-oh, not another of your wacky alternative therapies.' Judy wagged a finger at her.

'I like the idea of alternative methods,'

Ruby put in. 'If it makes her feel better I'm all for it. What healing powers is it supposed to have, Brenda?'

They both fondled the stone.

'Look at the pair of you, mauling a stone,' Judy exclaimed. Then she reached out her hand and touched it. 'Nice texture,' she agreed.

'I have one in my bag for Marj if she shows up.' Brenda looked anxiously at the door.

'She'll show up all right. I was talking to her on the mobile only thirty minutes ago. Told me nothing, as per usual. Jesus, I bet she'll turn up in her daughter's jeans again.' Judy giggled.

'I envy her being able to get in to them,' Ruby remarked. 'How does she do it?' She wiped the rim of her glass with a tissue, then sipped delicately. Judy had observed the wiping of the glass, and nudged Brenda.

'How is she anyway? I mean *really* how is she?' Judy asked Brenda, who usually had all the important details.

'She's probably still very raw. Just don't start with the singles jokes, OK? Try to remember that she's still very hurt over losing Sam.'

'Yeah. Traumatised,' Judy sneered. 'Who wouldn't be after living with him?'

'I read somewhere about the after-effects of

a marriage breakdown. Did you know, for instance — ' Brenda began.

'Marriage breakdown is nothing new — hey, it's fashionable.' Judy smiled drunkenly at her friends.

Ruby's face burned. 'We don't know the full story,' she said calmly, determined not to show any sign of emotion. She lit a cigarette and puffed at it furiously, holding her palm underneath it to guard her skirt from fallen ash.

'Correct,' Brenda agreed. 'Who knows what goes on behind closed doors?' She looked at Ruby.

'My thoughts exactly.' Ruby stared back at her.

'What?' Brenda asked.

'Nothing.' Ruby shrugged her shoulders. She wanted to tell them about the annulment, but Marjory's problems took precedence this evening. It seemed unfair to Ruby to unleash this bit of news on top of everything else.

They ordered some more drinks and chatted amicably. Judy stole most of the conversation with tales about who was with whom, and who wasn't. She was the brightest and prettiest of the girls. Her model-like figure was the envy of them all, and she had hair down to her waist. Tonight it fell over her shoulder in a thick plait. Her ice blue eyes, full lips and endlessly long legs made men stop and stare openly.

Finally, Judy turned to Ruby, who was nervously picking at her nails. 'Well, how's Eamonn?' She leaned over Brenda and motioned to the barman again.

'How should I know?' Ruby replied flatly.

She was admiring Brenda's chestnut curls, remembering how they had piled them on top of her head on Ruby's wedding day. Brenda had objected to the stylish change — that had been down to her innate modesty. But how beautiful she had looked without the slightest effort — and she never seemed to notice it. Not like me, Ruby thought. I can't leave the house without checking my bag three times to make sure it's all in there. The tissues, the makeup, the right perfume, the correct change in case I need to use a public phone, even though I have a mobile. I certainly couldn't go anywhere without knowing my coffee and sweeteners were in it.

The three girls had been bridesmaids at her wedding. Judy, Brenda and Marjory were her best friends. They had shared her most precious moments. Why had it become so difficult to tell them the truth? It wasn't as if they wouldn't understand. They were used to Eamonn and Ruby being separated. It was yesterday's news. Why should an annulment make the slightest ripple? But she couldn't say the words aloud. The annulment felt so final, the last-chance saloon. To say it would mean it was happening. Ruby wondered why that bothered her so much. Logically it was the next move, but her feelings told her differently . . . Damn those feelings.

She chose one at random. An easy one. She decided it was her pride. Admitting it meant admitting defeat. Ruby didn't like defeat. She didn't like failure. A lull in the conversation threatened to consume her. She considered a visit to the ladies'. She wanted to check that there was no ladder in her tights. There never was, but she always had to check.

★ ★ ★

'What's up with her?' Brenda said, her eyes following Ruby across the floor.

'I never noticed anything. Is there something you know that I don't?' Judy asked.

'I don't know. I just feel something . . . '

★ ★ ★

Ruby returned, feeling foolish. Her tights were perfect and, anyway, she always carried an extra pair, just in case. She launched into small-talk. 'Hey, Brenda, did you do that astronomy course yet?'

Ruby thought that Brenda was the most sensible of the four girls. When there was trouble on the horizon, everyone phoned her. She was good for advice, a great listener and wonderful to talk to. Unfortunately, she never practised what she preached, which amazed Ruby.

'Yeah. Well, almost. I did half of it. Actually, I met a really cute guy and he asked me out on a date.'

'C'mon, gory details.' Ruby was delighted with the turn of conversation.

'Well, there's nothing to tell. Really. I didn't go.' Brenda sighed.

'For God's sake,' Judy slurred.

Ruby glared at her. 'Why didn't you go, Brenda? You have to take a chance sooner or later. What are you afraid of?'

'Nothing. I just wasn't interested. That's all.'

'You said he was cute,' Judy pushed.

'He *was* cute.' Brenda drew a circle with her finger on the side of her glass. The others all knew that she just couldn't summon up the confidence to date someone.

'You could have brought the rock thingy — that might have helped,' Judy joked.

Brenda giggled and Ruby grinned reluctantly.

12

'What about you? Still seeing George what's-his-name?' Brenda asked.

Judy's face burst into a spontaneous smile.

'You needn't answer that one,' Ruby said.

'I'm blissfully in love.' Judy sighed.

'Of course you are. You have the perfect relationship. He's married so he can't live with you. That suits you down to the ground. A nice midweek romp, and he's gone from your bed in the early hours. You never have to deal with reality. If you were forced to live with each other and deal with household bills, nappy rash and broken-down appliances you'd kill each other,' Brenda remarked.

Ruby laughed. It was true. Nonetheless, Judy was luminous with joy, and if she was happy, that was all that mattered.

'Hey, go easy on me . . . ' Judy trailed.

Just then, they spotted a woman coming towards them. It didn't look like Marjory — but it was.

'Wow, Marj! You look amazing,' Ruby whispered, 'What have you done to your hair? It's beautiful, so different.'

'I've never seen you look so well, Marj,' Brenda said. 'You look even thinner, if that's at all possible.'

'If you lose any more weight you'll disappear,' Judy said, staring at her friend's tiny frame and minuscule waist.

'Thanks. I have lost a little weight.' Marjory beamed, as if she hadn't a care in the world.

All three girls continued to stare at her, until Brenda moved up and made room for her. 'Here, sit down. Judy, order her a drink. Look, Marj, if you don't feel up to it and you want to go home at any stage just say so, OK?'

'I'm fine. What would I want to go home for? I've only just got here, for God's sake. What's the matter with you lot? Where's my drink?'

They all stared at her in astonishment.

Marjory wedged herself on to the seat. Ruby was dumbfounded by her calm demeanour: not long ago she had been silent, brooding, but now she looked peaceful and serene. Ruby guessed the final papers must have eased her up. If the separation agreement was responsible for this transformation, she wanted one too. The conversation continued.

Brenda was lecturing Marjory on self-esteem and assertiveness, but Marjory looked like she could give a course on it. Ruby felt jealous. She pulled out her compact and sneaked a look in the mirror.

Marjory seemed different — aloof and distant, but that was not unusual: she had always been the quietest and most reserved of the quartet. Tonight she looked radiant and there was a quiet confidence about her that they had never seen before. Her new short haircut enhanced her perfectly rounded face. It drew attention to her piercing green eyes, surrounded by long black curling lashes, a feature they all envied. Ruby was intrigued. For a long time, Marjory had seemed trapped in some self-inflicted prison from which she rarely tried to escape. They had understood: they knew that in time she would get over it. Perhaps the final papers had closed that chapter once and for all, and she felt free now to start living. Perhaps they had meant she could start being herself again.

Certainly, the Marjory who now graced their presence wasn't what any of them had expected. Ruby couldn't figure it out.

The waiter returned with a fresh round of drinks, and left complimentary tickets for the club next door.

'Don't even think about it, Judy. Marj isn't up to that at the moment,' Brenda said.

'I'd love to go!' Marjory interrupted. 'I haven't been to a club in ages, and it's not often I get a night away from the kids. Come on, Ruby, you never go anywhere these days.'

Ruby didn't hear her. She was building a mountain of torn-up beer mats. 'Yes, sure, OK,' she said finally, not lifting her head.

'I'll just go and powder my nose, back in a min,' Marjory said, and jumped up.

'What the hell is wrong with her? You'd swear she'd just won the lotto or something. Something's not right. No, wait. I think I know what's going on,' Brenda said.

'Let's have it, then, Dr Ruth,' Judy slurred.

'No. Listen. Haven't you heard of the outer mask? Marj is in denial. The pain of the separation procedure must have been so traumatic that she can't hack it right now and she's pretending it didn't happen. I've heard of this thing before. At the psychology class the guy said — '

'Ah, shut up, will you?' Judy interrupted. 'She looks pretty fucking cool to me. Not a hint of agony. In fact, I've never seen her look better. Come to think of it, I never thought short hair would suit her. Maybe there's a new man on the scene.'

'No,' Ruby said quietly. 'It's not that. It's something else.'

The others turned and looked at her.

'I didn't say I knew what it was,' Ruby said, and shrugged her shoulders.

★　★　★

Inside the nightclub, a large crowd swayed to the incessant rhythmic beat. Judy was the

16

focus of every man's eye. They slipped past, glancing at her furtively. One almost fell over his feet. However, the girls were used to it, and Judy didn't bat an eyelid. Marjory sipped a gin and tonic and nodded in time to the music.

'That must be her fifth already. Maybe she's going to freak out or something. You know, flip — like they do in movies,' Brenda whispered in Ruby's ear.

'Oh, don't be so dramatic. Hasn't it occurred to you that she just might want a nice normal night out? She's been like a hermit for months. Maybe she's tired of talking about it. There's nothing wrong with that. You know Marj. She'll talk when she's good and ready.' Ruby wondered if she was thinking of herself as she delivered this piece of armchair psychology.

At one a.m. Judy was snoring loudly on the table, her half-empty glass toppling unsteadily in her hand. The smile on her face spelt 'George'. The following weekend, he had promised to take her to Paris, just the two of them. She was certain he was building up to commitment. She closed her eyes and imagined them holding hands under the Arc de Triomphe, dining in the romantic candlelit restaurant on the second floor of the Eiffel Tower, looking down on the city lights . . .

Ruby was looking at Marjory, who seemed to have stolen the only piece of talent in the place. Now she waltzed past on the arm of her mystery man, fluttering her fingers at them. What was it about Marjory that men loved? Ruby watched her intently. It was then that she realised what had happened to Marjory. It was then that she saw what was really in her smile, her confidence, and her new beauty. It was freedom. Freedom had given her a new lease of life.

Ruby wanted freedom too. What kind of freedom, she still hadn't figured out. For now she was willing to feed off Marjory's.

She watched her throw her head back in laughter and imagined that one day she, too, would be back in her own skin, her own mind and her own life.

★ ★ ★

Eamonn Blake listened to the telephone ringing in the hall. He put on his Sennheiser headphones and leaned back into his armchair. He didn't care who was phoning. He was determined not to be disturbed. Puccini's *Madam Butterfly* blasted into his eardrums. He leaned forward to adjust the volume. He had spent a small fortune on the Aiwa hi-fi system, and Mission speakers, but the tone wasn't right.

Irritated he threw the headphones on to the floor and went to answer the phone. Just as he reached it, it stopped ringing and the answering-service picked up. He waited. Then lifted the receiver. No message.

Beside the phone, the letter from the Archbishop's House lay crumpled in a ball. He picked it up, fired it at the bin and missed.

He rubbed his forehead. He had a headache now. Since when had the Catholic Church's views mattered to Ruby? Annulment, my arse!

That woman! This was just another of her ploys. Another way to tell him she was moving on. Another twist of the knife. Any more twists, and he'd keel over. It was pathetic. An annulment? It was a joke!

He knew Ruby hadn't the faintest idea what an annulment was about. Nor was she interested in finding out. God, she was infuriatingly predictable! Was it her arrogance, her foolishness, or her stupidity that he hated most? He couldn't decide. Ruby didn't understand the ways of the spiritual world. The nearest she had come to spirituality was when she got five numbers on the lotto and uttered the words 'Sweet Jesus'.

He remembered when her grandmother

had died. At the funeral, a single tear had made its way down her face. She had pulled out a tissue and wiped it away, thoughts of spoiled makeup infinitely more important to her than her granny's passing. It had been the first time for months that Eamonn had witnessed Ruby show any softness or vulnerability. Even then, her face was more important than her feelings. How he had longed to smear her lipstick across her jaw. How he had yearned to smash her head against the wall just to get a reaction. How he had prayed that she might cry properly. He wanted to know that there was a human being somewhere underneath that frozen exterior.

Calm down! he told himself. He put his head into his hands and sighed. He knew he was being harsh: it wasn't the whole truth — he wouldn't have married her if it had been. It was just the way she was going about things. An annulment. Why? Why now? He retrieved the anger. It got him through. It helped him cope with his other feelings. Like an oasis in the middle of a desert of pain. Water, water . . .

Now, as he contemplated the proceedings, it dawned on him that this was Ruby's chosen assault course. The final attack. It was out-and-out war. His anger got the better of him and he dialled her number. It rang and rang. Eventually he heard the answering-service message.

'You've a bloody nerve!' he roared down the line. 'You haven't seen the inside of a church since our wedding day! Want to play Spiritual Trivial Pursuit, eh? Well, you'd better do your homework, girl! You'll need more than clever anecdotes to win over those guys! They can't fathom their own humanity let alone anyone else's!'

He slammed down the receiver. The ball of paper lay beside his foot. He picked it up, smoothed out the creases, then placed it on the table before him. Perhaps if he stared at it long enough, the situation might spontaneously fix itself.

He sat there for an age contemplating whether he should phone again and leave a second message. But what difference would it make? They were separated. Ruby was still going to apply for an annulment. He returned to his headphones and buried himself in music. The front-line could wait another day.

2

Tuesday, 14 February, 10 a.m.

Ruby found the waiting room intimidating. Bland background music would have been better than the forced silence. Feet shuffled, throats cleared. Old magazines lay open on the table, torn and dog-eared. A meagre two-bar electric heater tried its best to warm the room but was rendered ineffective by the opening and closing door.

'You could hang meat in here,' commented a fat lady.

'Yeah. Could be dead for months and you wouldn't go off,' replied another.

People filed in and out. Like soldiers going to war. The walls were cream-coloured, or had been, Ruby supposed. They had turned a nasty yellow with age. One small window offered a view of rooftops, dipped in an early-morning smog. People vied for the seat beside the window. Funny how they do that, thought Ruby. As if the view might elevate them from their discomfort. Heads turned, eyes searching outwards, trying to escape their shame. Shame knows no shame, she thought.

Ruby hid behind dated issues of *Hello!*, not retaining a single word — or wanting to. This was the game: to appear to be deeply immersed.

A woman was called and discarded her magazine, leaving it open at the page that had held her rapt for so long. Ruby peeped at it: a Tampax advertisement. The game was exposed: nobody was here to read.

Everyone shifted up a seat, uneasily but swiftly, eager to get back to their all-important magazines. Excuseme's and coughs filled the room. Then it settled down again. The waiting. Feet tapping, arms folding. Thumbs rolling. A man with a hat smiled briefly at her. She felt herself flush. The fat woman adjusted her coat buttons, then studied the toes of her shoes, twisting and turning them in a slow monotonous circle. A smile began to creep on to her face then faded: she was in deep thought now. Pondering. Wondering. Sad. There were tears in her eyes, Ruby was certain of it. The woman reached inside her coat pocket and pulled out a much-used paper hankie. Ruby would never have carried such an appalling item. Hers were menthol, extra strength, and came in a neat foil container. She patted the bulge in her bag. It reassured her somehow.

The woman wrangled with her tissue, then blew loudly.

The coughing started again. Ruby could hear footsteps outside. Voices. Muffled crying. Thank-yous. Reassuring words.

'Be sure to keep your next appointment.'

The voices trailed away. Footsteps. Two sets. Going in different ways. Signifying the divide.

An impeccably dressed man attempted to start a conversation with the man in the hat. 'They're awfully slow,' he ventured. 'You'd think they'd see you when they said they'd see you. Ah, but, Jaysus, they never do, do they? Christ himself would have lost his patience by now,'

The man in the hat nodded a polite acknowledgement.

'Here's my appointment card,' the man tried again, shoving the card under the other's nose. 'Nine a.m., it says. I was here at nine now it's past ten, if I miss my bus at eleven I've had it.'

More coughing. More shuffling. His lone voice echoed through the room like a bass drum. He was happy to continue, regardless.

'This time I decided to be cute, you see, left the house a half-hour earlier. Thought they might slot me in, you know? Still shagging here, amn't I?' He broke into a loud guffaw and the man with the hat crossed his legs abruptly.

Ruby was watching this with curiosity and some amusement. She smiled at the man in the hat over her magazine. The fat woman turned to the lone talker and responded. Soon they were chatting away. She seemed receptive to the one-way conversation.

Ruby was glad of the distraction: it allowed her to focus on her own thoughts. The fact remained that she was there too. How did I get here? Ruby wondered. Do I really know what I'm doing? The dismal room and its contents faded as the memories came forth. She was right back. Seven years ago, on this very day, she had married Eamonn. How ironic! She had loved him then with a naïve passion. The passion experienced by every bride. She was innocent. Pure. Unspoiled. Filled with love and eternal devotion. There was no other man for her, she had been certain. Eamonn was the only one. At the altar, he had taken her shaking hand and, with his new handkerchief, gently wiped her damp palm.

No other act of love had been more poignant. Unconditional. Unrehearsed. If only they could have stayed in that state of uncomplicated bliss, reality would never have stood a chance. Reality, with its ugly, brutal truth. It had sliced its way through their lives with a menacing predictability, pulling them apart, instead of closer, until the day arrived when handkerchiefs were that something you washed, along with the shirts and socks. Dreams were something they had in the middle of the night. The dreams they had had . . .

★ ★ ★

Inside the interview room, Ruby sat staring nervously at the floor. Father Sean Ebbs seemed a pleasant enough man, offering tea and biscuits. Ruby asked if she could just have boiling water. She surveyed the rich surroundings. The furniture was old, expensive: antique bureau, leather-backed Queen Anne chairs, large oil paintings of the Last Supper, and a suffering crucified Christ.

Tea arrived, with fine bone-china cups and a second pot of boiled water. Ruby was impressed. Usually people commented on her unusual requests. Father Ebbs hadn't. She felt free to take things a step further.

She reached into her bag and pulled out an assortment of objects: a tiny silver spoon, an old Valium bottle filled with decaffeinated coffee, and some sweeteners. She never went anywhere without them. At least then she was certain of what she was putting into her body. There was no need to worry about infections she might pick up — except for the cups, of course. That was why she always wiped them before drinking. She dropped a spoonful of coffee and two Canderel tablets into the cup, swirled them round, and wiped the edges with a tissue. Only then did she grasp the dainty handle and sip the contents. I could get used to this, she thought.

Father Ebbs seemed to ignore the ritual. He ruffled some papers before him and fiddled with a long lead connected to the back of an old tape-recorder.

'I apologize for the delay, Mrs Flake, it's this taperecorder, you see. It's very old, very old indeed, as you can see, almost as old as myself!' Father Ebbs was evidently convinced he was a comedian.

Ruby found nothing remotely humorous about him. He was in his early forties, she guessed. His warmth was somewhat feigned, and he had that distinctly 'Catholic' air about him: 'I know it all, thou shalt not question anything.' The eleventh commandment that Ruby had learned at school. He had a head of black unruly curls that had a mind of their own: they plopped down on to his forehead when he leaned forward. Ruby noticed the streaks of grey. His belly pushed against the bureau, but he had an amiable face, oblong with deep-set eyebrows that met in the middle. Ruby thought him pleasant-looking when he smiled. He should smile more often, she concluded.

After further fumbling with the lead, Father Ebbs seemed open for business. Ruby took out a cigarette.

'Oh, I'm afraid smoking is not permitted in here, Mrs Flake,' Father Ebbs murmured.

Ruby paused, decided to let it go. She didn't want to get on his wrong side. 'I apologize,' she said, and put the cigarette back into the packet. 'It's my nerves.' She drew in her breath, with a slight wheezing sound.

'Indeed.' The priest nodded understandingly, as if he had made it a lifetime's vocation to study nicotine addiction. 'Let us begin, then, shall we?' He cleared his throat and reached for a Rich Tea biscuit. Then he slurped his tea.

Ruby was horrified. A priest without manners? Disgusting.

Father Ebbs dunked his biscuit into the tea and a large piece dropped into the cup, whose contents spilt over into the saucer. He fished out the biscuit with his fingers. 'Let me explain to you what we are about to do today,' he said, soggy biscuit gathering at the corners of his mouth. 'We try to make it absolutely clear from the onset, Mrs Flake, what an annulment means, what it entails, and how it comes about.' He wiped his mouth with his sleeve.

'The name is Blake,' Ruby said.

'You see, an annulment of marriage means that the marriage has to be proved null and void. In other words, it must be found on reasonable grounds not to have existed. Not to have happened. Not to be valid, so to speak.'

Ruby listened.

'The object of the Tribunal is to prove that a marriage, in the real sense of the word, never took place. The grounds vary. The process is long and sometimes upsetting. Do you follow me so far?' he queried.

Ruby followed the dirty sleeve down to the armchair, where it came to rest, caked in dried biscuit. She nodded.

'So our job here today, Mrs . . . em . . . is to find out if you have grounds for an annulment. Without grounds your case has no substance. So we must examine the particulars to see if we have a case to work with.'

Ruby wondered if she looked like a flake.

'Do you understand?' Father Ebbs repeated.

'Yes, I think so.' Now Ruby felt uncomfortable. She was finding it hard to listen. She noticed that the nail on her left forefinger was chipped. It annoyed her and made the longing for a cigarette even worse.

'I am going to ask you a series of questions, which you will answer to the best of your ability. Please take your time before you answer. I will then repeat what you said into the tape-recorder as best I can. If you do not agree with what I'm saying into the tape-recorder, please feel free to interrupt me.'

'On the subject of repeating, could I just say that my name is Blake, not Flake as you keep calling me, Father?' Ruby said.

'Forgive me, Mrs, em, Mrs Blake, I have no head for names,' he stuttered.

You have no head at all, Ruby thought. 'Thank you, Father. I'm ready to begin. However, I must tell you that I feel quite confident that I do have a case based on non-consummation.'

'I see,' said Father Ebbs, rubbing his chin. 'That will be a matter for the Tribunal to decide. I have to say, some grounds are difficult to prove. For instance, they might include lack of judgement, lack of due discretion, or incapacity to assume the obligations of marriage. There are also the impediments to consider as well as *ratum non-consummatum*. I feel obliged to tell you that you will be questioned on all grounds.

That includes matters relating to your relationship, including your sex life, and this may cause some embarrassment.

'Let us start at the beginning, shall we?' Father Ebbs picked up a small microphone.

'When where you married, please?' he asked.

'Ironically, seven years ago today, Valentine's Day 1988,' Ruby replied.

Father Ebbs switched on the tape-recorder. 'Question: when where you married? Answer: seven years ago today, the fourteenth of February 1988.'

'How old were you?' he continued. 'Twenty-eight,' Ruby replied.

Father Ebbs repeated question and answer into the tape-recorder. 'Could you tell me a bit about yourself, your family, where you were born?'

'I was born in Dublin, I am the eldest child, with three brothers. I was thirty-five in January just gone, I have a full time job in advertising sales, and I have worked all my life. We have no children. Is that OK?' All of a sudden Ruby felt stupid. What did he want her to tell him? That Eamonn couldn't get it up? That their marriage had lost its spice years ago? How much she had longed for a child? How lonely she was? Did he want an awful Woody Allen-type childhood story?

31

'You're doing fine,' Father Ebbs reassured her, and repeated the question and answer into the tape-recorder.

Ruby felt as if the *Sunday World* was interviewing her about some murder trial. She felt as if she was being scrutinized. Guilty until proven innocent. She fiddled constantly, moving objects on the bureau, lining them up like soldiers.

'Can you tell me how you met your husband and under what circumstances you were wed?' Father Ebbs proceeded cautiously.

'Well, I met Eamonn at a concert. My boss had received some free tickets to the National Concert Hall. He asked me to accompany him. To fill the extra two seats, he brought two friends. One of them was Eamonn.' Ruby found herself smiling reluctantly.

'Go on, please, Mrs Blake.'

'Well, you see, we both love music. Peter Skellern was playing piano with Richard Stilgoe, and it was a wonderful night. I liked Eamonn immediately. We seemed to have an abundance of things in common. We just hit it off. We dated for about nine months before we got engaged in November. We were married two and a half months later.'

Father Ebbs repeated everything into the tape. 'Were there any unusual circumstances surrounding the wedding, any rows, arguments, upsets?' he asked.

Ruby racked her brains. To her disappointment she found herself replying, 'No. Nothing of relevance comes to mind.'

Father Ebbs paused. 'Was there any discussion prior to the wedding about sexual difficulties, impotence?' he said quietly.

Ruby blushed. She had thought that the clergy would not be interested in the sex end of things; now she realized her own naïveté. However, to prove her case they would have to know something. Father Ebbs looked like he wanted to hear in any case. 'No. There were no problems, no discussions. I loved Eamonn. It was as simple as that.'

Father Ebbs repeated question and answer into the tape-recorder.

The process had begun to irritate Ruby. There were long pauses between each question, which left her feeling isolated and exposed. She shifted uneasily in her chair. The room had become a prison and her longing for a cigarette had reached fever pitch.

Father Ebbs seemed to sense her unease: 'Would you like to take a little break, Mrs Blake? There is a room straight across from here where you can have a cigarette if you like.'

For once Ruby was grateful to him. After all, he was only doing the job she herself had instructed him to do.

'Yes. Thank you.' Ruby let herself into a room adjacent to the waiting area.

The man in the hat was sitting in a corner looking out of the window and puffing furiously at a cigarette. Ruby grappled with her leather shoulder-bag, tipping its contents out on to the floor. The man bent to help her gather it all up.

'Here, have one of mine.' He extended a packet of Silk Cut.

'No, thanks. Don't know how anyone smokes them. Like air. I'd prefer a good strong Major, if you don't mind.'

'Don't mind at all,' the man replied, eyeing the inhaler that had rolled under his feet.

Ruby drew heavily on her cigarette, basking in its immediate sedative effect.

'Total addict, like myself,' the man commented. Ruby smiled for the first time that day. The man had quite a stubborn face, she thought. Strong bone structure, and soft sky blue eyes. Then he grinned, and his face was transformed. He was a good deal older than her, she guessed. Perhaps ten or fifteen years. What had brought him here?

'It's my only vice.' Ruby smiled back, and

exhaled a plume of smoke. The man handed her the inhaler.

She sighed with each drag. He puffed. Their smoke filled the air with unspoken words and feelings.

Ruby stubbed out the half-finished cigarette in a shell-shaped brass ashtray, and immediately lit another. The man did the same. When she had finished, she stood up and smoothed down her suit. She placed the inhaler in her mouth and took two strong puffs. She picked up her bag and slung it over her shoulder. The man watched in amusement as she dropped the inhaler into it. 'Well, no rest for the wicked,' she said.

The man in the hat burst out laughing. Although Ruby could not know it, it was the first time he had laughed in three years.

★ ★ ★

Back in the interviewing room Father Ebbs waited patiently. He hated his job. He hated it so much that words failed to describe it. He was tired of the endless stream of pain that came and went through the oak doors, day in and day out.

He was well known for his mediation skills and had been appropriately chosen to work on annulment cases. He was expected to

35

carry the heavy burden of others' sins, shortcomings and failings, and did it to the best of his ability. There were days, though, when his humanity took him over. He wanted to be spared the sexual confessions of a beautiful woman. He wanted to be spared torturous thoughts of something he could never have. Today he did not want memories to surface of past regrets. He did not want to remember his hurried, rash decision, at the age of eighteen, to spend his life as a priest. His father and mother had encouraged him. What a blessing it was to be 'called' to the priesthood, they had said. Not for the first time, Father Ebbs wondered if he had mistaken the call? Had he imagined it, in an effort to please his parents?

Mrs Blake returned to the room, bringing with her a breeze of cigarette smoke. He sniffed the pungent mixture of perfume and nicotine as she sat down, a good deal more composed now. He took stock reluctantly of the woman before him.

She was of average height and build. He noticed the cut of her immaculate blue suit. Her skirt, just above the knee, displayed well-proportioned legs. Her black shoes were polished. She was extremely pretty, with shoulder-length bobbed blonde hair. She continually pushed it behind her ears, making sure every strand was in place. A natural blonde, he guessed, if there was such a thing nowadays. He noticed her perfectly manicured hands, her large, soft brown eyes in the naturally dark-skinned oval face. Then he saw the dimples in each cheek. She was cute, angelic-looking. Father Ebbs averted his eyes. Then he closed them tightly. He had seen enough. He drew on his only defence: disassociation. He cut her off like a useless limb and slipped into Hitler mode. It was the only thing that worked.

'Tell me about yourself, Mrs Blake,' Father Ebbs asked, when she was sitting down.

Ruby pondered the question. What exactly did he want to know? 'Well, as I said, I work for a newspaper, in advertising.' She stalled.

'Do you enjoy your job?'

'Yes. Well, I used to. Lately, though . . . Well, actually, I wish I'd done something else sometimes.'

'What would you have liked to do?'

'I don't know,' Ruby answered, feeling foolish. 'That sounds so silly,' she added, chewing her lip.

'Not at all.'

'Perhaps gardening, maybe art, I'm not sure, really. I never thought about it before. I've not had time to think about anything for a long time, only the — ' Ruby broke off.

'I like gardening myself,' Father Ebbs pushed on, without comment.

Ruby gave a half-hearted smile. It felt more like a women's coffee morning than an interview for an annulment. Next thing he would be exchanging pavlova recipes with her.

'How long are you and your husband separated?' he asked suddenly.

'Two years,' Ruby answered.

'Do you feel quite certain that there is no chance of a reconciliation, Mrs Blake?' He scribbled away, having repeated her answers into the tape-recorder.

'Yes, I don't feel there is any chance now.' She emphasised the 'I'.

'Why say you that?' he asked, without looking at her.

Ruby found it difficult to answer. It had never occurred to her that she might not know. I have to have an answer. What's wrong with me that I can't answer a simple question?

'I guess I feel I've tried everything to make it work.' Again she emphasised the 'I'.

'I take it from your tone that you do not feel your husband has tried hard enough.'

'I suppose you would have to ask Eamonn that,' she said.

Father Ebbs jabbed the pencil on the paper

38

for the final time, indicating a full stop. 'Perhaps we have done enough for today, Mrs Blake. We have made a good start. We will let you know presently whether or not we think you have a case.' He closed the file and stood up.

Ruby was flummoxed. How could they possibly decide that when all they knew was how old she was, when she had married, her name and address? 'Has my husband agreed to co-operate?' she chanced.

'I'm afraid I can't answer that.'

'I see,' she said, exasperated. 'Is there anything else I can do at the moment, Father Ebbs?' she asked. Perhaps there was something that might hurry things along.

'You might find time to write a report of your wedding. It will help you remember when we need to know the details,' he said.

'I'm sure I can do that.' She smiled, and bade him goodbye. She was glad that the session was over.

She excused herself and took the lift downstairs. The man in the hat was sitting quietly in the reception area, on the first floor. He stood up to greet her as she passed.

'Excuse me?'

Ruby turned.

'You left your cigarettes behind.' He offered them to her. Ruby noticed that the third finger of his left hand was bare. Perhaps he was unmarried.

She took the cigarettes and thanked him politely. He opened the door for her to go out, then followed close behind.

They emerged into a full car park. Ruby tried to remember where she had parked. The man shuffled uneasily from one foot to the other. The wind was bitingly cold. He pulled up his collar.

'Can I give you a lift somewhere, perhaps into town?' Ruby found herself asking.

'Thank you. Anywhere near the city centre would be great.'

Ruby led the way to her car, a modest Opel Astra that contained several air-fresheners: three hung from the mirror and another three were pasted on to the dash-board. Ruby unlocked the car and sprayed a mixture of scented pot-pourri and forest-fruits into the back. The man got in and coughed.

Ruby turned on the ignition, and the radio blasted. She lowered the volume and pulled away from the Archbishop's House.

'I apologise for my rudeness.' She smiled at her passenger. 'I'm Ruby. Ruby Blake. It was my first time.'

The man nodded. 'You'll get used to it. I've been going for three years now. It hardly causes me a ripple. Sorry. I'm Robert

— Robert Ryan. Nice to meet you, Ruby. Nice name.'

The stress of the interview had eased now. Ruby was comfortable in the knowledge that the first hurdle was over, but the mention of three years baffled her.

'Do you mean you have been attending that place for three years and you still haven't finalised your annulment?' she asked.

'Never mind finalising it, it could be another two before they decide. Of course, there's no guarantee they'll find in my favour.' He flicked at a fir-tree freshener that dangled in front of his eyes. 'Yes. There's nothing more meaningless than the score at half time, I suppose,' Ruby joked.

'I see you like your car to smell nice.' He smiled.

'I'm sorry. I'm not used to passengers.' She felt awkward.

'Did you attend Father Ebbs?' Robert asked.

'Yes.' She paused. 'I'm a bit confused about the whole thing, to be honest,' she admitted.

'Why?' Robert asked.

'Well, I was told on leaving that they would contact me when they decide whether my case deserves further investigation.' Ruby found herself laughing.

'What's so funny?'

'Well, I can't fathom it. I mean, how could they make such a decision after asking me five questions? How do you sum up seven years of marriage in one short interview?' She drew on a cigarette, while trying to manage the steering-wheel at the same time.

'Oh dear. The questions have started already.' Robert smiled again and looked out of the window. 'Ruby — can I call you Ruby?'

She nodded.

'There's your story, there's *his* story, and then *there's the truth*,' he said flatly.

Ruby glanced at him. 'I'm certain I don't know what you're talking about.'

'Oh, but you will, in time. Life is like that, Ruby, isn't it? Full of surprises.' He was still smiling.

Ruby pulled up beside the Coombe Hospital. 'I'm not good on surprises,' she confessed.

'Then you have my commiserations.'

Ruby was confused. 'I'm afraid this is as far as I can take you. I have a few errands to run in town,' she said. 'It was nice meeting you, Robert Ryan. I probably won't have the pleasure of bumping into you again.' She shook his hand, hoping that her case in the Archbishop's House would be dealt with immediately and she would not have to make any more visits.

'I doubt that very much, Ruby Blake.' With that Robert got out.

Ruby found herself looking in the rear-view mirror until he disappeared into the bustling O'Connell Street mobs. What a strange man, she thought.

3

Ruby had a list. She couldn't remember when she had started to make it. She guessed it must have been when she was around twenty, and her one and only romantic encounter had ended on a tragic note. Her boyfriend of the time had dumped her without so much as a glance over his shoulder. Ruby had gone through her personality with a fine-tooth comb to root out the offending character defect. Trouble was, she hadn't found it: she hadn't the faintest idea why he had left her for someone else. But, being a woman of logic, Ruby had felt compelled to get to the bottom of it. She couldn't let it go. She had to find out the whys and wherefores. At first she had jotted down just one or two qualities she would like in a man. It was practical, a sensible inventory. After all, she intended to marry some day, and sooner rather than later.

As the years had passed, Ruby's list had become longer. She perused it more often, added and subtracted new needs or wants as they surfaced. She wanted someone strong, but not silent. Someone affectionate. Someone who had a sense of humour, as well as a sense of self. Someone who wasn't afraid of hard work. Someone with honesty and integrity. Someone tall and handsome, if at all possible. Someone who was cultured and well-mannered. Someone who would remain loyal to the last. Loyalty meant everything to her.

Where would she find someone like that?

It was around this time that Ruby was invited to an evening at the National Concert Hall. She would accompany her boss and two of his friends. She had no romantic intentions towards him, she found him dull, but she was not stupid enough to turn down his invitation. The great day might be just round the corner. A chance encounter might be waiting for her. Time was running out. She had set her hopes on snagging the right man by the time she was thirty. Now she was twenty-seven.

Somehow, she felt partly responsible for still being single. She wasn't without feeling, but she couldn't express herself. But that night Ruby didn't care. She was tired of the endless parties, the prospective partners boring her to death. Tonight she was only interested in hearing the velvety voice of Peter Skellern. She'd loved his music for years. He serenaded her senses, and now she was going to see him in concert. She longed to hear her favourite songs. It irritated her that no one else seemed to know about him or appreciate the 'real' songs he transformed into lyrical masterpieces. Old, romantic songs that made her swoon. Every time she put on the tape, she was transported to another era. She imagined Fred Astaire, and Ginger Rogers in his arms. She loved old-style romance, but she knew it did not exist anywhere other than in her fantasies.

She had long given up the idea of finding it in Leeson Street at four a.m. when some drunken fool was gurgling into her ear about a wife who didn't understand him. Ruby had tired of the search for love.

She took little care with her attire that evening, even though she was going to the National Concert Hall. The dress code was not important. She was only meeting Rob Cunningham, her boss from the newspaper. Rob wasn't the finest conversationalist in Ireland, and Ruby was grateful for that. She just wanted to slip into her seat and be carried away on the voice of an angel.

She arrived in the foyer and ordered a drink at the bar, and another for the interval. Just then, Rob breezed in, followed by two men. Two more witless morons, she thought.

'Ruby, sorry I'm a bit late. Let me introduce you to my bank manager John Dunn and his assistant Eamonn Blake.'

Ruby remained seated and extended a hand to the strangers. Eamonn shook it. It was a firm handshake, Ruby liked that, and he looked straight at her. She blushed.

The bank manager was as expected: he breathed too close to her once too often, which announced to her that his dinner had been garlic-drenched. Eamonn Blake stood tall, taller than the other two men. He had an air of supreme confidence.

Tall and handsome.

Ruby felt a trickle of excitement and was furious that she looked like a dog's dinner. They sipped their drinks as John Dunn made conversation for all four of them. He asked someone a question, didn't wait for an answer, then turned to the next person and did the same thing.

Eamonn Blake remained silent, smiling at Ruby over Rob's shoulder. Ruby smiled back.

Inside the auditorium, Ruby exchanged seats so that the bank manager was seated on the outside beside Rob. Then she began to take off her coat. Eamonn reached behind her shoulders to help.

Well-mannered.

Ruby smiled again. She was impressed.

He folded her coat inside out and carefully placed it under *his* seat. That was a *very* good sign. She peered down at his shoes. They were black leather, expensive, shining. His suit was spotless, not too showy, with a beautiful lemon shirt and matching tie. Ruby examined his nails: they were clean and well polished. Eamonn Blake was impeccably groomed. She stole a sideways glance at his profile. His face was solid and square, nose straight and chin proud. His wavy hair, a mousy brown, was short and tidy. Then she remembered the best bit of all: he was a bank employee, which meant success and stability. She was nearing the finishing line.

Security.

There was only one more hurdle. Ruby wasted no time: she was going for gold. 'I didn't think there would be so many people here,' she remarked innocently. 'Not many people know of Peter Skellern. It has always bewildered me. Such a talented man.'

'I only came to hear him. I wasn't interested in Richard Stilgoe.'

'So you know of Peter Skellern, then?'

A cultured man?

Ruby almost curled up in his lap and purred.

'Do I know him? I'm afraid I'd bore you to death if I started talking about him! I love his music. I've been a big fan. Especially of 'Astaire', which has just been re-released. It's my favourite.' Eamonn grinned.

It was her favourite too. How scrumptiously perfect!

Only one other item and she was on the home stretch. 'I had a boyfriend once who threatened to leave me if I didn't start to listen to something more modern.'

'I hope you had the sense to change *him* for something more modern?' Eamonn gave her a sly sideways glance.

Ruby had already chosen the wedding dress. In her mind's eye she could envisage the sparkling diamond engagement ring. She had met the man she wanted to marry. She found it hard not to stare. The evening passed in a dream. She was hardly aware of Peter Skellern, for all his musical brilliance. She just could not take her mind off the fact that she was seated beside her future husband. She was so happy she wanted to burst with joy. It never entered her mind that Eamonn might not have the same interest in her.

She needed a plan, a strategy, and her mind worked feverishly as she calculated every step of the way. She only had this evening to make her mark.

The interval came all too quickly. Ruby hadn't had enough time to come up with a fail-proof plan. She excused herself and went to the ladies' room. She stepped up to the mirror and regarded herself. What did it matter? It was better that he saw her as she was. There was no need to go pouring on makeup. Nonetheless she set about making herself a little bit more presentable. A little lipgloss, some mascara. She talked aloud to herself. 'I'm fine as I am. I'm fine as I am,' she wheezed. Her asthma was taking a turn for the worse — it always happened when she got too excited, or upset.

'A little more blusher, that's it, there. I look fine.' She looked down at her Levi's jeans. If he really liked her, he wouldn't care what she had on. Still, she would have preferred to be in a little black dress.

'Why tonight, of all nights? He likes Peter Skellern! I can't believe it!'

She curled her hair behind her ears and smacked her lips. She would have to depend on charm and clever conversation to carry her through the rest of the evening. How was she going to corner him so that she could talk to him alone? Just for once she found herself hating Peter Skellern and wishing they were in some quiet little restaurant. Perhaps a drink after the show? Yes, that was a good idea. Rob would probably suggest it anyway. And if *he* didn't, Ruby would! Eamonn Blake was not getting away easily. By the end of the night, Ruby swore she would have wormed her way into his heart.

Eventually the show ended. Much to Ruby's annoyance, Peter Skellern gave three long encores. For the finale he chose 'The Way You Look Tonight'. Eamonn seemed mesmerised and rose to each ovation.

Back in the foyer Rob was deep in conversation with John Dunn. Ruby knew why he had invited the banker to the concert. He might have been boring, but he was not stupid. He was trying to change his small newspaper into a tabloid and he needed financial backing.

Ruby turned to Eamonn. 'Do you fancy a quick drink?' they blurted out simultaneously.

Then they burst out laughing at their boldness. It was plain sailing after that.

★ ★ ★

The evening flew by. Suddenly the barman was calling last orders. Ruby tried not to show her disappointment, but she couldn't bear the thought of having to leave.

As if reading her mind Eamonn chanced his arm. 'Perhaps a bite to eat in the bistro down the road would be nice. Unless you're tired.'

Ruby paused, as if she was considering it. It took every ounce of self-discipline she possessed not to shout out her availability. 'I'm not tired,' she replied.

They bolted out of the pub, leaving Rob Cunningham and John Dunn with no alternative but to watch the dust from their feet.

Eamonn gripped Ruby's arm to cross the busy street. It was nearing midnight and droves of young people huddled on street corners, wondering whether to head home or go clubbing.

Ruby felt her arm tingle as Eamonn led her across the road. She was looked after, safe. She gazed up at her new minder. All she had ever wanted was someone to look after her. Now here he was, her knight in shining armour. More handsome than she could ever have imagined. More dashing then she had ever dreamed.

They found a quiet table. Ruby's stomach was doing somersaults — the last thing on her mind was food. The small bistro was perfect: couples were grouped at the chequered tablecloths, passing intimate glances and whispering soft words.

Ruby spotted a pair caressing feet beneath the table. For the fifth time she tried to read the menu. It was useless. 'You choose.' She handed it to Eamonn. A waiter appeared at their side.

'Is it French or Italian?' she asked Eamonn.

'A bit of both.' Eamonn smiled. He looked to the waiter for help.

'Correct, sir.'

'We'll have *mozzarella pomodoro* as a starter.'

'What's that?' Ruby asked.

'Slices of tomato with mozzarella cheese and basil dressing,' he replied. 'For the main course we'll have *saltimbocca alla Romana*.'

Ruby stared at him. They both broke into fits of laughter.

'OK! Roughly translated that is escalope of veal stuffed with ham cooked in butter and white wine, and generously sprinkled with Parmesan cheese.'

He might as well have been talking Swahili. Ruby's stomach churned at the thought of putting anything into her mouth, let alone swallowing it. Eamonn was educated, elegant, understood etiquette, yet, he wasn't afraid to show he didn't know everything.

Honesty, even dignity.

Pretty soon Ruby had forgotten about her Levi's. Eamonn made her feel comfortable, at ease. She wanted to sit there for ever. At one a.m. she yawned: she hadn't wanted to appear tired but her body was telling a different story. Eamonn behaved like the perfect gentleman: he took the bill and paid it by Access. Ruby noticed he left a rather large tip. Well, wasn't that what he was supposed to do?

She stood awkwardly at the door — she had forgotten how she was supposed to get home. Eamonn escorted her to the pavement and, without asking, led her to a taxi rank. 'I can always give you a lift, if you'd prefer, of course?'

Ruby was in a quandary. She didn't want him to see where she lived — not that there was anything wrong with Sutton: it just seemed too soon. A certain sober logic had kicked in. And her yawns were presenting themselves now with an alarming regularity.

'I'll get a taxi, if you don't mind, but thanks for the offer anyway. Thanks for the meal. It was lovely meeting you.' Ruby wanted to get away now, to the privacy of her own thoughts.

How would she secure a further date with Eamonn? She hadn't extracted enough information: she didn't even know where he lived. But she knew where he worked: if the worst came to the worst, she would open an account there. She would offer to do Rob's accounting. She would take out a loan if she had to. She would go to any lengths to keep this man in her life.

Eamonn helped her into the back of the taxi and handed the driver some money. Ruby sat upright, terrified at the prospect of things being left as they were.

'Can you do me a favour?' Eamonn leaned into the car and handed her a small white card. 'Can you call me when you get home? You'll probably get home before me, so just leave a message on the answering-machine. I want to know you got there safely. OK?'

Ruby had to order herself not to reach up and kiss him tenderly on the lips. She took the card and cradled it to her chest, as if it were as valuable as the *Book of Kells*. 'Of course.'

Eamonn closed the taxi door then reopened it, and closed it again, this time with a bang.

'In with a chance there, love.' The driver laughed. 'He has it bad, that fella does.'

Ruby didn't hear him. She had fallen in love at first sight. She leaned back in the car and closed her eyes. Eamonn. Eamonn. Eamonn Blake. Ruby Blake.

What a wonderful ring it had to it. It was perfect! Ruby Reece-Blake. That was even better. No. Ruby Blake. Eamonn. Eamonn and Ruby Blake. Mr and Mrs Eamonn Blake.

Mrs Ruby Reece-Blake. She dreamed of holding him. She dreamed of touching his wavy hair and wondered if it extended to his chest. She dreamed of caressing the back of his neck. She dreamed of laying her head on his chest. She dreamed of seduction, surrender.

She lifted her legs and crossed them, letting out a soft moan. The taxi driver turned on the radio. It played 'When I Fall In love' by Nat King Cole. Ruby knew it was a sign. A sign from God. It was a match made in heaven.

The minute she let herself in she telephoned. Sure enough the answering-machine came on. She left a brief message and hung up. She was going to do everything right. She had to be perfect from the start. She was not leaving herself open to another abandonment. She threw herself on to her bed, smiling and repeating his name over and over . . .

★ ★ ★

The following morning, Eamonn turned in for work as usual. He was a little early. He had woken up before the alarm had gone off and sat staring at it until it was a few seconds before seven a.m.

He felt strangely energetic for one who had had only four hours' sleep. The bank seemed eerily silent without the staff. He typed in the four-digit alarm code and began to set up the office for business. In the main foyer he got the Rombouts coffee going, and set out paper cups, a full bowl of sugar, and a jug of cream. He turned on the time safes next, and switched on each computer terminal as he made his way across the office. He approached the vault and released the alarm. He eyed the camera overhead and waited patiently until the timer reached zero and the doors unlocked. He stepped inside, and the door closed immediately behind him. The closets were alphabetically marked. Beside them sat a line of smaller safes.

Inside each were several brown envelopes, all different shapes and sizes. They were clearly marked with black felt pen, and sealed with brown masking tape.

Eamonn pulled up a chair and his folder, and began to check each one, making sure that the date and contents were correct for each safe. Ciara, another employee, appeared on the camera screen outside. She pulled a face and Eamonn released the lock to let her in.

'You're early,' he commented, without raising his head.

'So are you. You needn't start on them — I told you I'd have them done by this evening,' Ciara replied.

'Well, this goddamn inspector is calling,

and I don't know when. I don't want any foul-ups, like the last time, or the boss will blow a fuse.'

Eamonn knew he could rely on Ciara to do an expert job, but this morning he needed to concentrate on something gritty. He let out a reluctant yawn.

'Late night? Anything exciting to report?' Ciara nudged him as he pulled out more envelopes.

Eamonn smiled. 'Yes. I met the woman I am going to marry.'

4

Eamonn turned off the tree-lined Drumcondra Road. The large gates displayed a cross in the middle. He drove through the arches and up the long driveway to the Archbishop's House. He noted the blue signposts: 'Slow', 'No dogs', 'Private Property'. Little rolling hills, oaks bending in the stiff wind, narrow woodland walkways dotted here and there. It was peaceful and serene, hard to believe he had left the chaotic traffic just seconds ago. He parked his car and wandered about for some minutes, looking for direction. He saw a white sign on a door: 'No rear entry'. He contemplated putting it on his back. Considering the Church's bad press of late, it seemed like a good idea.

Eventually, he went in. A small brass plate on the wall read 'Marriage Tribunal, 3rd floor'. He stepped into the lift and pushed the button. Soon, he was sitting in the waiting room, reading, in *Woman's Way*, 'Ten Ways To Keep Your Man On His Toes'. He sniggered to himself and wondered if Ruby had read it.

Some thirty minutes later, he found himself sitting in a plush leather-backed chair before Father Sean Ebbs. After the introductions and explanations Eamonn was in the hot seat. He was convinced that the priest would telephone that morning to tell him the whole thing had been called off. That Ruby had come to her senses. They had been separated for two years, which was what she had wanted. It was not what Eamonn had wanted. He had gone along with it at first to pacify her. When there appeared to be a total stand-off, he had approached her to try to come to some sort of agreement. It had only seemed to make things worse. What had happened? Where had it all gone wrong? Had women some secret built-in telepathic system that alerted them to a failing relationship?

Sure, they had had their differences, but when Eamonn had returned one evening to find her wardrobe empty and a cold letter on the mantelpiece, he thought she had taken it too far.

He wasn't ready to end his marriage, let alone accept that he hadn't shared seven years of his life with Ruby. He thought that if he fought his case hard enough, the Church would see that she was in the wrong.

Father Ebbs wasted no time in explaining to Eamonn that that was not the way it worked. It was not a question of right or wrong but where and when.

Putting up a fight might only help Ruby get what she wanted. Eamonn would have described himself as a knowledgeable man. He had a degree in theology under his belt — a fat lot of good it was doing him now. How could anyone tell him his marriage hadn't happened? It bloody well had! He had the broken heart and solicitor's bills to prove it. Now some idiot in a collar was trying to tell him *he* knew better. And the final insult: 'Well, I hate to tell you but your marriage never existed. Goodbye and thank you.' He was armed to the teeth with his only weapons: truth and honesty. If he had never married Ruby, he was a monkey's uncle.

'Mr Blake, you are aware that your wife has made an application to this Tribunal to have your marriage annulled,' Father Ebbs said matter-of-factly.

'I understand. If I don't participate what will happen?' Eamonn asked.

Father Ebbs repeated the question and answer into the microphone. 'The annulment proceedings will take place without you, Mr Blake. However, it may slow down the process if you don't co-operate. On the other

61

hand, it is our duty to allow a certain amount of time to elapse before we can proceed. We must be certain that you have been given every opportunity to have your say. If you decide today that you do not wish to participate we will still write to you until such time as we are satisfied you have made the decision not to participate. Regarding the annulment itself, your presence or lack of may have little bearing on the outcome.'

Great, Eamonn thought. Now they don't even need me to decide. Hey! Annulments by post. How convenient! His anger surfaced. 'Look, Father Ebbs, I'm sure you are a good man and a professional, but I have to tell you straight away that I'm against this annulment thing. I never heard anything so ridiculous in all my life. I believe that only God himself can decide whether my marriage existed. I cannot accept that it is null and void. I was with her for seven years! I find this whole thing laughable. I can assure you that she will not turn up for the second round. If it gets that far. Even if she turns up for the first. Or has she been here already?'

'I'm afraid I can't answer that.' Father Ebbs sighed, sounding bored, which made Eamonn feel worse.

'Mr Blake, I can only advise you, for your own peace of mind, to comply with the appointments. If the Tribunal finds in your wife's favour, you may regret not having said your piece.' Father Ebbs coughed loudly into the tape-recorder. He drew in his breath further and barked like a dinosaur.

Eamonn winced: he must have strayed into Jurassic Park. 'I take your point, Father. I'm rather perplexed at the moment. I can't even see what grounds we could possibly have for an annulment.'

Father Ebbs chewed on the end of his biro nonchalantly, revealing absolutely nothing.

'Well, to get us started, I have a few simple questions. You are not obliged to answer any of them, Mr Blake.'

Eamonn wasn't going to waste his journey. He did not know if Ruby had attended or what she had said, but he would get his twopenceworth in, no matter what.

'How old are you?' Father Ebbs started.

'I will be forty at the end of April.'

(Question, answer, record.)

'How did you meet your wife?'

'At a concert.'

Father Ebbs waited.

'Should I elaborate?' Eamonn asked.

'Only if you want to.'

Eamonn remained silent: for once in his life he was afraid of his own honesty. Then he related the evening's events.

'Would you like to tell me your feelings on meeting Ruby for the first time?' Father Ebbs went on.

Eamonn chewed his lip. It was a habit he and Ruby shared.

'I felt quite taken with Ruby the minute I clapped eyes on her. Truth be known, I was smitten from the word go. I remember thinking, So this is what it feels like when you look into someone's eyes and know they are your soul-mate, your other half, your destiny. I expected to feel something different. Perhaps overwhelming joy or great emotion. I didn't feel any of that . . . ' He paused. 'What I felt was a kind of homecoming. Like I had known her all my life but hadn't bumped into her for a while. I know it sounds like a cliché, but that's what I felt. At home,' he finished.

Father Ebbs jotted some notes. 'When were you married?'

'The fourteenth of February 1988.' Eamonn made no reference to the anniversary.

'Were there any problems leading up to the wedding, any arguments, stresses, unresolved conflicts?'

Eamonn thought for a minute. 'Yes. No. Only a small thing. Hardly worth mentioning,'

'Please, do go on.'

'Well, there was a bit of arguing about the guest list. At one stage Ruby threatened to call the whole thing off. I thought it was a bit over the top, to be honest. She seemed so upset over what I considered to be a small detail. You see, we were working to a reasonable budget but the list was getting longer and longer. Ruby's aunt from Australia. Uncle Harry from Timbuktu. I remember thinking, What next? A distant extra-terrestrial cousin from Mars?'

Father Ebbs laughed.

'Does any of this have any relevance?' Eamonn asked.

'Not really, Mr Blake. But feel free to mention anything that comes to mind, whether it is important or not does not matter. All of it helps me to build up a case.'

Father Ebbs repeated the question and answer into the tape-recorder. Eamonn noticed he left out the humour. No need to throw the Tribunal into hysterics. They needed their wits about them, which at the best of times were suspect to say the least. Eamonn imagined the line of geriatric priests filing into the courtroom. They would all discuss the nuptials of Ruby and Eamonn never having met them, never having experienced sex, emotion or the deep, bonding ties of marriage. It seemed absurd to talk to this stranger. His future lay in Father Ebbs's hands. The priest's fingernails were filthy. That spoke in volumes.

'Can you tell me a little about your background, Mr Blake?'

'I'm a banker, have been for fifteen years. I come from an ordinary family. Four brothers, two sisters. Mum and Dad are still alive and still married, I might add. I love music and literature. I graduated from All Hallows' college with a degree in theology. I love my wife. I want this ordeal to stop.'

Eamonn put his head in his hands and drew a sharp breath.

* * *

Father Ebbs liked Eamonn. A degree in theology would help him to come to terms quickly with things. It also permitted Father Ebbs to take some things for granted. The man before him was spiritually educated. Of that he was convinced. It was nice, for a change. He had a fresh attitude — a rare quality. He had nothing to hide. His love for Ruby was evident. At the moment, it was clouded with anger and hurt pride, but Father Ebbs could see it clearly. Eamonn told it how it was. And he knew too that, like many before him, Eamonn assumed that the priest knew nothing. But Father Sean Ebbs knew it all. If the walls could talk they'd be on *The Jerry Springer Show*. He repeated Eamonn's words into the tape-recorder and leaned back in his comfortable chair. 'Mr Blake, were there any discussions before or after the wedding that precipitated eventual future problems of the sexual kind?'

★   ★   ★

Eamonn tried not to flinch. The priest wasn't wasting any time, and Eamonn liked his choice of wording. The man wasn't an idiot, after all. It took strength of character to mediate in a dilemma such as his and Ruby's. It took all of Eamonn's courage to answer honestly.

'Ah. There were no discussions as such. However, many things are not said. Many things *were* not said. So, the fact that they were not expressed aloud or aired openly doesn't mean anything to me. Looking back, I can see now that we should have talked more openly about such matters.'

Father Ebbs turned on the tape-recorder. It made an obnoxious whining sound with a little squeak every time it made a full circle. It was grating on Eamonn's nerves.

'Question: were there any discussions around sexual difficulties that might have caused problems in the future? Answer: No.

There weren't any,' said the priest.

'That's not what I said,' Eamonn interrupted.

'Excuse me?'

'I said there weren't any discussions. You didn't record the correct answer. There is a big difference between your answer and mine! Sometimes there is more in what's *not* being said.' Father Ebbs was getting confused, he desperately wanted his tea. The whining started up and he tried again.

'Answer: there were no discussions as such, but I sensed we were both unable to discuss things at the time.' He stopped the tape and raised an eyebrow at Eamonn.

'Perfect.' Eamonn nodded.

★   ★   ★

Eamonn left the Archbishop's House worse-tempered than when he had arrived. If he didn't believe in the annulment why was he attending? He found it difficult to keep the steering-wheel from veering in Ruby's direction. He wanted to call on her now and talk this whole thing over. Being separated was one thing; having his past obliterated was another.

He punched the car stereo and turned up the volume as far as it would go. He jumped from one station to another. The radio poured out an incessant stream of love songs. He turned it off abruptly, slipped in a CD and pressed Play. Jon Bon Jovi filled the car. Perfect, Eamonn thought. That'll keep the bitch at bay. Soon he found himself inching his way through the city-centre traffic. He decided to stop and do some shopping.

He drove to the third floor of the Ilac shopping centre car park, resenting the extortionate fee. He took his time, browsing through Moore Street, ambling along Henry Street and eventually arriving on O'Connell Street. The city centre was unusually busy for a Tuesday afternoon.

He did his best to ignore the glaring evidence of Valentine's Day, which explained the crowd. He was assaulted by chocolate boxes, heart-shaped balloons and an array of stuffed toys. Red dominated every shop window. Red roses. Red hearts. Red. Red. Red. Like a red rag to a bull, the constant reminders bombarded him. The street traders were out in force. They had gathered in droves at the foot of the Jim Larkin statue. Potential customers flocked in semicircles, eager to purchase flowers. The street traders competed loudly, each doing their level best to outcry their rivals.

Eamonn studied the selection on offer:

pink and red carnations, proud irises stiffly bearing the breeze, and roses, of course, hundreds of them, red, yellow and pink. Their heady scent assailed his nostrils. He drew out two large bunches of red ones, and sniffed and sneezed.

'You bleedin' animal!' a short fat woman attacked him verbally. 'Snots or no snots, you can fuckin' buy them now, do you hear, mister?' She dug her hands into a dirty apron and adapted a bull-like stance.

Eamonn rooted in his trouser pocket. He grappled with the roses and his loose change. Eventually, he handed the woman a crisp twenty-pound note.

'For Jesus' sake, have you nothin' smaller? I'm not Howard fucking Hughes, you know,' she barked at him.

Eamonn started to fumble again. This time he performed a perfect acrobatic display as he balanced the flowers on one extended knee.

'Ah, Jaysus, forget it.' The trader tut-tutted. 'Give me the twenty. Mickey? Have you change of a twenty?' She held the offending article up to the sunlight, inspecting its authenticity. She folded it, shook it, flapped it about like a dead fish and, when wholly satisfied that it was the genuine article, handed it to Mickey.

'Do you want to make Jaysus love with it as

well?' Mickey handed her back the change.

A few customers tittered. Eamonn felt like the lord mayor with all the attention he was receiving. The trader dumped the roses into a Dunne's Stores plastic bag, and sealed the top with a knot. Eamonn shoved the roses under his arm. The thorny stems stung his armpit and the excess water dribbled down his sleeve. He spotted a newsagent on the corner of Henry Street, went to it and stepped swiftly inside.

He purchased two large sheets of pretty red satin wrapping paper. Outside, he sat on the wall of the Floozy in the Jacuzzi. Carefully, he discarded the plastic bag and drained the stems. He went to great lengths to wrap the flowers neatly in the shiny new paper.

All of a sudden, they resembled a bouquet that might easily have been bought from an expensive florist.

All in all, the entire purchase had set him back a mere five pounds. They weren't white roses, the ones he really wanted, but Eamonn was well pleased. He sat on the wall, flowers under his arm, enjoying the temporary sunshine that had unexpectedly burst through the grey February skies.

★   ★   ★

71

Across the street, Ruby stood on the corner, shrouded by the divine intervention of Bewley's coffee-shop canopy. She watched, fascinated. A twisted knot in the pit of her stomach told her that Eamonn's roses weren't destined for her. Her imagination ran riot.

5

Not long after the National Concert Hall rendezvous, Ruby and Eamonn had become an item. Everything seemed to fall easily into place. They dated two or three times a week, increasing the frequency of their meetings as time passed. Ruby was ecstatic, could not believe her luck. When she socialised with her friends, which wasn't very often now, all she could talk about was Eamonn.

Marjory, Judy and Brenda waited for the inevitable first row, but it never came. They celebrated and rejoiced in Ruby's new-found happiness. But it wouldn't have mattered what any of them thought: Ruby had made up her mind. Eamonn was perfect marriage material and she longed for the day when he would propose on bended knee and she would demurely accept.

In late November, he did exactly that, with a sense of purpose and dignity. From that day on, time flew past on angel's wings and Christmas week was upon her in a jiffy. At the newspaper offices, on O'Connell Street, Ruby daydreamed. She doodled on a piece of paper, sketching various versions of her wedding dress. Eamonn hadn't phoned and it was almost one p.m. He usually called at some stage during the morning. She stopped staring at the phone and continued with her work.

She was bored: the records assistant was off sick and she had had to fill in at the last minute. She stretched out the newspaper in front of her on the desk and began measuring the display ads. First the length then the breadth. Then she recorded the date, the issue, the size of each on the index cards before her. How did anyone do this for a living? she thought.

Suddenly, her phone rang. Ruby grabbed it. 'Hello?' she said, hopefully.

'Ruby, it's Judy. Look out of your window.'

She obeyed. Judy was standing in the phone-box across the street, waving like a madwoman. Brenda and Marjory were packed in beside her. She could hear their laughter down the line.

'You pack of idiots, what the hell are you doing?' Ruby laughed.

'It was Brenda's idea,' Marjory yelled. 'Can you take lunch?'

'Well . . . I'm waiting on a call from Eamonn.' Ruby hesitated.

'Come on, he can leave a message. We'll go local.'

Ruby relented, donned her coat and went

to meet the girls. The city centre was crowded with shoppers. They made their way down Abbey Street shouting over the noise.

'Marjory, where are the kids?' Ruby asked.

'My parents are bringing them to see Santa Claus in Clery's, so I called Judy. Then we rang Brenda.'

'We thought it would be nice, before the wedding, you know, just to meet up for a while,' Brenda put in. They stopped outside a local pizza place.

'This will do,' Ruby said, not wanting to venture too far off the beaten track.

'Relax, will you?' Judy laughed.

'Hey, Madame Christine's is somewhere along here.' Brenda's curls bounced back and forth as she looked for the sign.

'Not today,' Ruby said. 'I'm not going to see any fortune-tellers, Brenda.'

'Oh, please, let's go!' Marjory begged.

'It's all a load of hogwash. It's a money-making racket.' Judy pulled Brenda away from the door.

'It's not, I swear!' Brenda cried. 'My sister has a friend in work, right? She went to see this woman and everything she said came true!' Brenda was already rooting through her pockets for money.

'Look, the Mystic Megs can wait,' Ruby objected again.

'Madame Christine,' Marjory corrected her.

'Look, let's have a cup of tea and then I'll turn it upside down and I'll do a reading for you. I'll tell you all you want to hear and I won't charge either,' Judy pleaded.

Brenda frowned like a scolded baby.

'C'mon, it will be fun!' Marjory persisted.

Ruby was still hesitant: she didn't like fortune-tellers at the best of times. She was soon to be married, and didn't relish the idea of her happiness being spoiled by some old widow's prittle-prattle.

Judy shook her head, and her long hair fell down her back like a waterfall. She gathered the ends and tucked them into her fur-lined collar. 'OK. Three against one wins,' she ruled.

'Hey, I never agreed!' Ruby protested. She was hauled in by the others.

They entered the dirty, dank-smelling building and followed crude yellow arrows towards a door. They knocked lightly, then heard feet shuffling slowly towards them. The door opened and a jewellery-clad arm beckoned them to step inside.

'This is so childish,' Ruby remarked. 'What's that awful smell?'

'Oh, lighten up.' Judy prodded her arm playfully.

'Now, which of you ladies would like a reading from the tarot cards?' the woman croaked.

Brenda stepped forward, her grey eyes sparkling with curiosity.

'You must cross my palm with silver first,' the old woman snapped.

Brenda put ten pounds on the table. 'Of course that's an old figure of speech,' the woman said. 'Silver, that is, an old saying.' She stared at Brenda, who seemed none the wiser as to what she meant.

Ruby laid a second ten-pound note on the table.

'It's thirty for the lot,' the old woman said.

Judy reached into her bag and stuffed a third note into the woman's bony hand.

'Now, draw three cards,' the woman demanded sharply, grabbing the money and stuffing it into a jar beside her.

Brenda did so and the old woman turned them face up. 'Mmm . . . Yes . . . I see . . . I see. A mysterious dark stranger.' She looked at Brenda with wild eyes. 'This stranger is . . . ' She paused.

'A mysterious dark stranger?' Judy whispered to Marjory. She was eyeing the old woman with suspicion.

'Sssh!' Ruby warned her.

'You will cross paths with this man, in

unusual circumstances,' the woman droned.

'Oh, great, how general can you get?' Marjory whispered in Judy's ear.

'There will be difficulties. I'm not certain where the difficulties lie, perhaps in family background, religion?' The woman leaned forward, locking eyes with Brenda, willing her to acknowledge some part of the information for her to latch on to.

Brenda shrugged.

'No. Wait . . . I'm getting something now.' She tried a different tack.

'No, *you* wait,' Judy interrupted. 'I think I'm getting something too. Yes. I'm sure of it . . . It's coming . . . Wait for it. Yes! I have it! You're a con! This place smells like a toilet and we're out of here!' She grabbed Brenda by the arm and pulled her out of the chair. Marjory made a grab for the money.

'Wait!' the old woman cackled. 'You. The blonde one.'

Ruby pointed her forefinger at her chest.

The woman beckoned her forward.

'Yes, you,' she repeated. 'Are you with child, my dear?' she asked.

'What? No!'

'Did you lose a child?' The old woman continued, her mouth turned down.

'No, I did not,' Ruby said, a little frightened.

78

'A niece? A godchild?'

'No,' Ruby repeated.

'I see a child as clear as day. She stands behind you as I speak.' The woman nodded as she looked over Ruby's shoulder.

'That's enough.' Judy dragged her away.

'She follows you everywhere.' The woman smiled.

Ruby stared at her, mesmerised. Marjory put the money down again and they all walked towards the door, the old woman following them.

'As God is my judge, there is a child beside you at all times!' The door slammed behind them.

'Hey! I was enjoying that!' Brenda objected.

'Oh, Brenda, you don't believe in all that crap? Dark mysterious stranger, a child behind Ruby! Anyone could make that up. Didn't you see her guessing? Hoping you would nod so she'd know she was on the right track?' Marjory laughed.

Ruby felt a shiver run up and down her spine like someone had walked over her grave. 'She gave me the creeps,' she said.

'Sorry. It was just a bit of fun.' Brenda looked shamefaced.

'Ruby, is there something we don't know?' Judy asked, half laughing.

'Don't be ridiculous!' Ruby burst out laughing.

'What the hell was she on about?' Brenda asked.

'Look, I swear I don't know!' Ruby protested.

'Let's forget the whole thing, right?' Marjory suggested. 'I'd kill for a decent burger right now,'

Inside the restaurant, the girls were shown to a table. They were lucky that none of them smoked, or they would have been waiting considerably longer.

Ruby hated cigarettes and had vowed at an early age never to get started. As a teenager she had been diagnosed with asthma. She was restless and agitated. The fortune-teller had unnerved her, but Ruby put it down to pre-wedding nerves. The big day was consuming her every waking moment.

The others seemed unperturbed and made small-talk. 'I'm getting sick and tired of turkey and ham. Why can't they serve something nicer at business functions? If I have to face it again this evening, I'll throw up.' Judy made a face.

'Where are you going anyway? You're always jet-setting around the place. It's Christmas week — aren't you going to stay with your folks?' Ruby asked her.

'I haven't decided yet.' She played with her dessert. Her friends knew, although she wasn't telling them, that she was leaving her options open for George, in case he could get away at short notice.

Judy ran her own cosmetics company. It had been a success from the word go: her beauty products sold by the zillion, and she never seemed to stop working. She was always either promoting a new line, or checking up on stock in her stores. Failing that, she was knocking them dead in the boardroom with her razor-sharp business mind or scheming up something new. The girls imagined her hectic lifestyle to be glamorous and exciting. Just listening to her globetrotting, name-dropping, party-whirling agenda exhausted them.

'You can join me,' Brenda said, pulling several bottles from her bag.

'I can't. It's business as usual. You know that. It's the busiest time of the year for me. This is when I make my profits. What, in God's name, are all those?' Judy asked.

'Vitamins, evening-primrose oil, garlic capsules, Star of David and St John's wort,' Brenda said. She took one from each bottle and threw them back with some water.

'They're a waste of money,' Judy scolded.

'That's choice coming from you. You ought

to know better. These things are all the rage. You should look into buying some for your sales-ladies. I bet you'd make a killing. And they work,' Brenda insisted.

'They certainly can't be doing any harm,' Ruby said.

'The evening primrose oil is good for PMT,' Brenda told them.

'Says who?' Judy asked.

'Says every magazine in Ireland.' Ruby giggled.

'In that case, pass the bottle,' Marjory joked, and they all laughed.

Ruby noticed an oily salad leaf on her skirt and wiped it off. It left a streak but she didn't care. 'How are the geriatrics, Brenda?' she asked.

'Still geriatrics.' She stuffed a piece of lemon meringue pie down her throat.

'I don't know how you do that job,' Marjory confessed.

'It's easy,' Brenda answered. 'I only work nights at weekends now. It's great. I have the days to myself. Besides, they're not that bad, really.' She chomped.

'It's a gift.' Ruby smiled.

'You don't need to be gifted to do it, just patient,' Brenda returned.

'I still wouldn't do it for all the money in the world. Remember when you told us about that old woman Kathleen who packs her bag every night and makes for the door thinking she can go home?' Marjory said.

'Yeah. What about the old guy who insists you're starving him?' Judy chortled.

'Then there's the incontinence. Yuck!' Ruby chimed in.

'Can we change the subject?' Judy shouted. 'I'm trying to eat my mince pie! Suddenly it looks like — '

'Don't say it,' Marjory warned her. They all stared at the object in horror.

'I've chosen the wedding dress.' Ruby tried to divert their attention.

'When can we see it?' Brenda asked.

'I'll have to have a final fitting. We can make an evening of it, have dinner,' Ruby suggested.

'What about the bridesmaids' dresses?' Judy asked excitedly.

'Being made, as we speak.'

'I've already seen the material,' Marjory said. 'It's fabulous.'

'We still haven't talked hair and makeup,' Judy said.

'I'm not doing either,' Brenda objected.

'Yes, you are,' Ruby insisted.

'It's OK for you, Judy. You could go in a sack and look wonderful,' Brenda moaned.

'There's a price to pay for all this glamour,

you know. It's hard work,' Judy said seriously.

Brenda didn't look as though she believed her.

'Brenda, you're going to be just as beautiful,' Ruby told her.

Brenda blushed at the compliment. 'How are you and Eamonn bearing up?' she asked, wanting to change the subject.

'Well, I *am* a bit nervous — silly, really.' Ruby sighed. 'Both sets of parents meeting for the first time, you know' she added.

'Hey, what's there to be nervous about? You won't even be aware of them.'

Ruby managed a little smile. 'I don't know what to expect,' she confided. 'Meeting your partner's mother is a nerve-racking experience. What if she doesn't like me?'

'She'll love you. Then again, his father might despise you. You can't win, eh?' Marjory chuckled.

Ruby hadn't thought of that. She was determined to make a good impression, no matter what. Even if his mother turned out to be the original Quasimodo, she was adamant that she would behave impeccably.

'There's nothing to worry about. I asked the astrology teacher to do a personal reading for Ruby and Eamonn. They are the perfect match. Miss Capricorn meets Mr Taurus!' Brenda said triumphantly.

'Is Eamonn a Taurus?' Judy asked.

'Taurus makes good money.' Brenda wagged a fore-finger.

'Taurus, the bull,' Marjory warned.

The waiter arrived with the bill. Ruby picked it up, read it and put it down. She slid it over to Marjory. 'Capricorn the miser,' she quipped.

'You can say that again.' Marjory grinned.

Ruby took out her credit card and placed it on the saucer. 'Just kidding. This one is on me.'

They all had a good, hearty laugh.

★   ★   ★

As they chatted Judy was quiet, listening as the other girls played mother-hen to Ruby. She thought how lucky Ruby was. How she would have done anything to trade her exquisite good looks for Ruby's unique beauty. They would never have believed that men rarely made a pass at *her*.

How lonely she felt inside. Despite having George around, and loving him to bits, Judy knew that the relationship was open-ended. It wasn't a real commitment. Not like the one Ruby and Eamonn were about to make. She admired their courage. Her thoughts were interrupted when Brenda piped up with the mother of all questions.

'Hey, wait! Who am I walking down the church with?'

'Let me guess . . . ' Marjory winked.

'*A dark mysterious stranger!*' they chorused.

Brenda's chestnut curls bounced as she gave in to an explosion of laughter.

6

Dublin Regional Marriage Tribunal,
Diocesan Offices,
Archbishop's House,
Dublin 9

Nullity of Marriage: Reece — Blake
J.2 254/94.

Personal and Confidential

10 May 1995

Dear Mrs Blake,

After careful consideration of your application, it has been decided that your case merits further investigation.

This will be undertaken as soon as possible and, in due course, a member of our staff will be in touch with you.

In your own interest, I want to stress that this decision does not mean that you can take for granted an eventual Declaration of Nullity.

I enclose herein, for your kind attention, a document relating to the expenses involved in the nullity case and I should be glad if you would read over this document carefully.

I am forwarding a copy of this letter to your husband in today's post.

With kind wishes,
Yours sincerely,

Aidan Mason
Tribunal Secretary

Ruby re-read the letter from the Archbishop's House. Since her last visit she had not been able to think of anything else, and had had a violent cleaning blitz in an effort to keep busy. She had started on the kitchen, pulling out the washing-machine and the fridge. She swept out the debris and cleaned the lino. She tore open the cabinets and presses and scrubbed them. Then, armed with bleach and disinfectant, she attacked the bathroom. She sponged down the shower cubicle until it gleamed.

She washed her whites by hand and arranged them neatly on the line. Not satisfied, she unpegged them, shook out each piece of clothing, and replaced them, making sure they hung evenly. At the end of the line, she noticed an irregular peg. She only used wooden ones. This one was red. It ruined her peace of mind, not to mention the orderliness that she was used to: it stood out like a sore thumb. She reminded herself to do something about it, and added it to her shopping list. The list reminded her of Eamonn, and how he had detested them. 'Lists are boring,' he used to say. She thought they were useful: they helped her to organise her thoughts.

Now, more than ever, she felt sure she was taking the correct steps. Outside Bewley's coffee shop, she had been surprised by her reaction. She had never been jealous until now — Eamonn had never given her reason. She recalled how he had sent her flowers every week in the first year of their marriage. Then they had stopped coming.

Her stomach had done a double-somersault when she saw him purchase some that day on O'Connell Street — partly the memories, partly jealousy. She was shocked by the latter. She had thought the two years of separation had dealt with all those old feelings. So she cleaned. And cleaned. And cleaned some more.

She felt like a prisoner. If she could get out on parole now and then she would survive. She had tried hard to dismiss her emotions, reminding herself that it was she who had initiated the closure of their marriage, but she was still in a cage, the only difference was it was a bit wider now . . .

She took out her shoes, and set about polishing them, one pair at a time. They shone so brightly she could almost see her reflection in them. She lined them up like soldiers displaying their kit for inspection. She spotted a cobweb and got out the Hoover. She vacuumed the ceiling, and killed a million spiders.

All the time, her inner voice kept nagging. She had no right to feel jealous, she thought. It was none of her business any more. She repeated the mantra until her head spun. *I have no right to be jealous! I have no right to be jealous!*

She attacked her chores with renewed energy. She would physically exhaust the feelings! She would work away the frustration! Eamonn was entitled to see other women now. Yes, she thought, he deserved a little happiness. God knows, he had had a miserable time of it. She knew she needed to talk to someone about it, but pride refused her permission. Now every woman with whom she came into contact seemed more beautiful, younger, healthier, richer, more intelligent, more desirable than she. At thirty-five she was starting a new life, but she felt older than her years and was constantly critical of her appearance. Laugh lines had exploded on her face. Lately she had found herself wandering through department stores, snapping up the latest anti-wrinkle creams, searching the cosmetic aisles for an antidote to her new-found enemy: time. She hadn't enough of it some days, and too much on others. Today she had too much. Too much time to think.

She sometimes perused her body in the mirror. She had stretchmarks on her belly and thighs. All her friends had told her that they had too: it was inevitable, every woman got them. But they had an excuse. They all had children, and Ruby didn't. Her thighs had always been heavy. Now they had spread outward and were more noticeable than ever. No matter how much she dieted, her thighs insisted on demanding more than their fair share of space. She enrolled at expensive gyms, but when she went, young beauties bounded gaily from one exercise class to another. The slender, tanned instructors made her feel worse.

Ruby sat in the newspaper sales office trying to feel proud of herself for having somehow combined the positions of wife and working woman. But the truth was like a cancer eating away at her insides: she had failed at her marriage. There were plenty of failed marriages in the world, but Ruby's was the only one that mattered. Her newly separated friends joined associations like Gingerbread and Minus One. She couldn't entertain the idea of dating someone else.

Two years had passed, but the pain was still unbearably raw. She ran her hands across her desk. She could still smell the bleach from that morning's housework.

Her hands looked wrinkled. She was annoyed that the rubber gloves had split. She dabbed on some nail hardener, and waited for it to dry, then added rubber gloves to her growing list. She picked up the week's statistics sheet, taking note of the fact that her sales for that week were up again. She grappled with the figures noting that she had surpassed her expected quota three weeks ahead of schedule. The manager had asked her to tackle a new project on cosmetics. Ruby made a mental note to call Judy at the end of the week and haul her on board. Her friend could use a bit of free advertising and the manager would be impressed. Her ever-increasing workload made her happy. No time to think. She blew on her nails and stretched them out in front of her. When she was certain they had dried, she called Marjory.

'Hi, Ruby.'

'Marj, are you about to run out the door?' Ruby enquired.

'Not for another half-hour. What's up? Are you OK?'

Marjory's kind tone disarmed Ruby. 'Well, no, actually. Marjory, can I be frank? There's something bothering me. You see . . . I've applied for a Catholic annulment.'

'I knew there was something on your mind.' Marjory paused. 'Christ, I'm glad you phoned. Who knows about this?'

'Nobody. Just you and me so far . . . and Eamonn, I think.' Ruby twirled the phone cable.

'Why didn't you tell me before?'

'I don't know. I guess I wanted to manage it alone. Isn't that what we strong, independent women are supposed to do?' Ruby said.

'Ideally, yes.' Marjory laughed. 'Are you sure you want to do this? Look, I know you and Eamonn have had your problems — who hasn't? Why don't you try a marriage guidance counsellor first? This is very final. God. I can't believe it!' Marjory sounded upset now.

'C'mon! You know us. A counsellor? We tried that. I made the appointments with the Catholic Marriage Advisory Council, but we only went once. It wasn't for us. What more can one do? We can't communicate any more. Besides, there's something else ... ' Ruby hesitated, wondering if she could trust Marjory to keep her mouth closed.

'What?'

'Oh, nothing. It's silly, really.'

'Tell me. I promise to keep it to myself,' Marjory said softly. 'I've been through this whole thing, you know.'

'OK. We've only had one appointment with the Tribunal, so far. At least, I have. I don't know if Eamonn was called yet. Anyway, I was on my way home when I stopped off in town to collect some messages. I saw him . . . buying flowers . . . ' There was a great big lump in Ruby's throat.

'Go on,' Marjory urged.

'I think he's seeing someone else. I can't bear the thought of it. I keep seeing images of him with someone else. It's horrifying.'

'Ruby, you've been separated for two years,' Marjory reminded her.

'I know! It's so bizarre! Why am I suddenly filled with jealousy? I don't understand myself.' Ruby quavered.

'I understand. When I heard Sam was seeing another woman I thought I'd die. I didn't want him. I didn't love him. But I didn't want anyone else to have him either because that made me feel like I'd failed.

That's all it is, Ruby. A reminder of the breakdown. You're not in control of him any more. You're still trying to fix things. Let it go.'

'I can't,' Ruby said defiantly. Why did Marjory have to use the word 'fail'?

'C'mon, Ruby, you don't even know why he was buying flowers. You don't know for definite he's seeing someone else, do you?' Marjory asked.

'No, I suppose I don't. Do you?' she asked, alarmed. Her free hand swept non-existent dust from her desk.

'Look, I know Eamonn a little bit. The last thing on his mind right now is another relationship. I'm sure of it.'

Ruby wondered how and why Marjory could be so certain.

'Look, why don't you and I meet up and have a good old talk about this? I can guide you, help you along the way. Maybe I can make the road a little easier, fill you in on the next steps. I still can't help thinking you're being a bit hasty. Do you really understand what an annulment means?' Marjory probed.

Ruby was annoyed. Father Ebbs had already proved himself an ace interrogator and she didn't want another. Why was everyone treating her like she was an idiot? A buzzing fly nosedived from the ceiling. She reached down to her drawer, pulled out a can and sprayed.

'Ruby? What are you doing?' Marjory asked.

'It's these damn flies.'

'They're only flies.'

'Don't you know what germs they carry? They're disgusting things. You wouldn't believe me if I told you how they eat their food . . . '

'Flies are the least of your worries,' Marjory assured her.

'You're right,' Ruby replied, resentful that her friend was always so grounded. And practical. But it didn't stop her trying to kill the fly. She *had* to kill it.

'Look, Ruby, if there's anything I can do, anything at all . . . ' Marjory trailed off. Ruby recalled her new calm and confidence when they had met up in the pub. She still couldn't figure it out.

'Ruby? Is there something else?' Marjory asked, amid the long pause.

'No, nothing. I was just thinking. You look superb with your hair short. I can't help noticing how well you are these days. So free! You seem so different since you split up with Sam. Especially now that you're no longer married legally.'

'Ruby! I *am* still married! It's not that simple. Sam and I have been apart for years. I've done three years' counselling — that's why I'm so well. Have you forgotten how bad it was when Sam and I first split up? It wasn't the separation specifically, more a combination of things. Look, let's meet up and I'll explain.'

Ruby had already decided Marjory was taking sides — Eamonn's side. Why wouldn't she? Anyway, there was no comparison between Marjory's break-up and Ruby and Eamonn's. The circumstances were entirely different. Ruby thought of Eamonn.

She swatted at the irksome fly, whose buzz-buzzing suddenly stopped. Mission accomplished. She scooped it up with a manila envelope and popped it into the bin. Then she sprayed some air-freshener around the room.

'I'll think about it, OK?' Ruby said finally.

'OK,' Marjory said, and hung up.

Ruby opened the Lever Arch file she had bought especially for the annulment proceedings. She clipped the two letters from the Archbishop's House inside it and dated them. The second page of the second letter attracted her attention and she started to read it.

7

Nullity of Marriage: Reece — Blake J.2. 254/94.

Please read this document carefully.

Expenses involved in a nullity case.

At this stage, we wish to mention to you the question of expenses.

You will understand that proceedings of this kind necessarily involve expense; competent staff have to be engaged; an efficient office has to be run; frequently, medical and other such professional assistance has to be engaged.

In order that you will know what is involved, we wish to tell you now that, as your case has been accepted for further investigation, the sum of £500 will be requested towards the Tribunal expenses. This figure does not include such professional fees as may be incurred, e.g. medical consultations, psychological assessments, etc.

Psychological assessments?

We are therefore asking of you, by way of initial contribution, the sum of £50 and we should be grateful to receive this amount at your earliest convenience.

As far as the balance is concerned, we wish to let you know that, if you prefer, we will be glad to receive this in whatever instalments would suit your convenience, rather than as a single sum at a later stage. Should you decide to adopt this method of payment, we would strongly suggest that you commence these instalments as soon as the initial contribution of £50 has been paid. Please let us know your wishes in this regard.

Finally, we want to make it perfectly clear that the progress of your case, or its outcome, does not in any way depend upon your ability to pay all or any of these expenses.

If you are genuinely unable to pay all, or any part of the costs, the Church will gladly come to your aid in meeting whatever deficit is involved. We feel, however, that in appreciation of the Tribunal's efforts to solve your matrimonial problem, you yourself would wish to pay whatever you can discharge of this debt.

This document is issued: Ms Ruby Reece-Blake.

Date: 10 May 1995

She filled in a cheque grudgingly. In Ruby's opinion, the Church was wealthy enough. 'Pay: Dublin Regional Marriage Tribunal £5 only.' It would do for now. She signed it, put it into an envelope, addressed it and slipped it into her bag.

* * *

Eamonn had just finished reading the letter from the Tribunal for a third time. He had had a hectic morning at the bank and was in no mood for this. He had been certain that Ruby would drop the application. Now not only was his marriage being scrutinised, his bank account was getting a going over too.

He dismissed himself from the office for lunch, and headed home for a break. The weather was warm and sunny, but it did nothing to lift his sagging spirits. In the apartment he tried to drown his thoughts with Albinoni's Adagio. It seemed a trifle depressing. On another day, it would have relaxed him.

He munched a salad sandwich and searched through his CD collection for something a little lighter. His video cabinet spilled open. Eamonn flipped through the collection. He hadn't watched any of them. A stubborn tape remained wedged at the back.

Eamonn wound his hand through the compartments and tugged at it until, eventually, it came free. He pulled it out and stared blankly at the cover: 'Ruby and Eamonn's wedding day, 14 February 1988'. Slowly he slipped it into the recorder and pressed Play. Nat King Cole's silky vocals rang out: a shot of Ruby zoomed into focus.

Eamonn felt sick. He put his sandwich on the floor and watched as the images flowed across the screen. He and Ruby looked so innocent, so sweet, and so naïve.

Eamonn remembered seeing her when he turned at the altar. My God, she was a stunning bride! Those gold highlights in her natural blonde hair, her big brown eyes, her cute dimples, beautiful indentations which enhanced her smile.

He leaned against the chair as he watched. It was history: their dreams, their hopes, and their love. It had happened. It was as real as if it had happened yesterday. No one can erase this, he thought. I have proof! I am watching my own wedding, yet someone is trying to tell me this never happened. Not only that, they want me to pay for it too! Emotionally, and financially! He laughed at the insanity of it all.

The camera zoomed in on their wedding rings. He glanced at his hand: it was still on his finger, as shiny as the day he had first worn it. He would wear it till the day he died. She had put it there. Only she could remove it. No Church was going to tell him it was invisible or that the tape he was now watching didn't exist. He began to search the apartment. He knew there were photos somewhere.

He found the album under the bed. He blew off the dust and wiped the cover with his sleeve. Their names were engraved on the front.

The photographs had been pasted inside, with a caption under each. Ruby had spent weeks arranging and rearranging them, as if they were priceless objects. Back then her writing had been a spidery scrawl, like a child's. She had even made mistakes and boldly crossed through them, not caring how it looked. It was a testimony to her free spirit.

He reached under the bed again and pulled out the suitcase. In it, he found her dress and her shoes. Some confetti, which had been embedded in the veil, dropped to the floor. How could she have left behind such treasured possessions?

Eamonn gathered together the cards, the telegrams, the wedding invitations, the photos and the video. He took two black sacks from the kitchen drawer and flung in the offending articles, but only stopping short of dancing on them. Then he dragged the sacks to the front door. He released the car boot with the remote control. Ruby's dress had fallen out of the sack, and Eamonn struggled to stuff it and the train back in. Eventually he threw the dress on to the back seat.

The next-door neighbour peered out curiously between the drawn curtains. Eamonn felt as if he had committed a murder. He certainly felt as if he could. He thought about taping *Coronation Street* over the wedding video and sending it to Ruby in the post . . .

The phone rang in the hall, then stopped. It rang again.

Eamonn ran tripping over his shoes, catching it on the last ring. 'Hello?' he shouted, breathless.

'Eamonn, it's your father. Have you gone crazy?'

'What?'

'Mrs Norton has just phoned me to say you've lost your mind. Something about being in the garden and hauling wedding dresses around? Eamonn?'

Eamonn dropped the phone, leaving Anthony to talk to himself. He charged up to Mrs Norton's door and banged on it with his fist. She did not answer so he opened the letter-box and peered inside. He could see the distinctive slippers of nosy Mrs Norton jutting out from the sitting room.

'I know you're in there, you cantankerous, busybody Muppet! Open the door!'

Mrs Norton remained still.

'Next time I want to murder my wife in private, call the newspaper she works for! If you don't I will!' He gave the door one last thump and stormed back into the house.

He could hear Anthony screeching down the phone: 'Eamonn! Eamonn! Are you there? Arlene? Come here! He's lost his marbles altogether. Eamonn?'

Eamonn lifted the phone from the table and slammed down the receiver. He walked to the car, jumped inside, and sped away. Mrs Norton would never know how close she had come to being in another black sack.

He drove recklessly, not knowing his destination. He glanced at the speedometer, which was rising steadily. The crumpled dress began to call to him. He bit his lip. Still it called to him. He released his pressure on the accelerator and the car slowed. He indicated to the left and pulled in to the kerb. The dress was whispering to him of old love. He pulled it off the back seat, then, lovingly, he folded it with tears in his eyes. He smoothed the creases as if he were petting a loved one, paying particular attention to the tiny beaded pleats around the waistline. When he was satisfied that it had been restored to its previous glory, he held it to his face and breathed in. Old love. It smelt of old love. Beginnings, hope, excitement, thrill. He shut his eyes tightly.

★   ★   ★

Marjory Hand lived in a three-bedroomed terraced house in Fairview. Her two children, Jessica and Ben, attended the local school. She had found contentment without Sam, but suffered pangs of loneliness. Sunday seemed to be the worst day, when Sam collected the children and Marjory could not avoid the nagging inner voice. For a long time, she had simply survived from one day to the next. Still, things had improved and she was grateful for the peace that now reigned in her home.

Marjory had been a friend of Ruby, Brenda and Judy since their schooldays. She had been the first to leave school, not of her own choice: her father's premature death had forced her to enter the workplace before her time. She had resented this but had vowed to return to school later and complete her education. However, she had met Sam in her late teens and fallen head over heels in love.

Within months they had been married. Marjory had looked forward to returning to school, and now that she had a husband to support her, it seemed within her reach. But two children later she was no nearer her dream to sit the Leaving Certificate examinations than she had been at school.

Sam hadn't taken to family life. He spent most of his time travelling between the pub and the betting office, leaving Marjory to deal with the house and the children. Marjory's dream died among the washing-up liquid and dirty crockery ever present in her kitchen sink. After some years of misery, she threatened Sam that she would leave with the children if he did not mend his ways. Sam assured her he would. The next day he spent the best part of his wages at the pub and lost what remained at the bookie's.

Marjory followed up her threat. She packed her bags and took away the children, rendering her and them homeless. Her friends had rallied round offering support. Each helped in her own way. Brenda was the first to offer accommodation. The others encouraged her to seek a barring order in court. After a two-month wait, the judge ruled sympathetically and Marjory moved home, minus Sam. Eamonn had made enquiries at the bank about employment prospects for her. This resulted in a part-time secretarial position in one of the local branches. Marjory had always made clear her gratitude to him for his kindness.

Running the home, raising two children alone and her job kept her too busy to contemplate another relationship. Besides, the longer she lived alone, the more comfortable it had become. She doubted that someone would come along to change that. Anyway, the kids had to come first. That was her choice. Besides, the only other man she had ever wanted was unavailable. Or had been, until now.

She sat reading an old magazine on a kitchen chair. She could hear Ben upstairs: he was making sure that she did. He stomped about his room with exaggeratedly heavy feet and now and then opened the door to slam it. He switched on his portable television and turned up the volume full blast. Then he thumped about again. Marjory watched the ceiling in the kitchen as flaky particles detached from it. She chuckled to herself as she listened to the temper tantrum. She was not giving in. Not this time. She licked her thumb and turned another page. Then a chunk of plaster landed in her lap.

'That's it!' she said.

She jumped up and made her way towards the stairs. As she passed the front door, she caught a glimpse of a car outside. The engine was still running. A man was inside it, his head on the steering-wheel. She recognized him immediately. It was Eamonn. She opened the front door and walked to the car. Eamonn looked up, sheepishly.

She approached him, hands behind her back. 'Hello, stranger,' she said, through the open window.

'Hi.' Eamonn looked at her uncertainly.

'What on earth are you doing?' She gave a half-smile.

'I don't know.' He gave a half-smile back.

'Would you like to come in for a cup of coffee?' She gave him a full 360-degree smile, exposing her perfectly straight white teeth. Her green eyes sparkled against her jet-black hair.

'If it's OK with you.'

'Sure!' Marjory was positively thrilled.

Eamonn got out of the car and followed her indoors. 'Where are the brats?' he asked, as he sat down. Marjory had come to expect Eamonn's visits. She knew he loved her kids. Especially Jessica: she was the apple of his eye. He and Ruby were godmother and godfather to them both. Birthdays were never forgotten, and at Christmas time, they rained presents on the pair like it would never come again. However, Ruby had cut down on her visits since the marriage break-up — Jessica seemed to remind her of what she was trying to forget. Marjory understood: Ruby found Eamonn's devotion to Jessica hard to bear.

'Jessica's probably next door, terrifying the neighbours' hamster.' Marjory filled the kettle.

'Why don't you buy her one?' Eamonn suggested.

'I hate them, you know that.' Marjory shivered at the thought of a mini-rat in the house.

'Where's Ben?' Eamonn asked.

'Grounded.' Marjory raised her eyes to the ceiling, which was still taking a pulverising.

'What has he done this time? What can be so bad that you grounded him?' he enquired.

'He stole twenty pounds from the milk money.'

'That bad, eh?' Eamonn fiddled with his cuffs.

Marjory knew his body language well. She had made a point of studying him and Eamonn only fiddled with his cuffs when he was getting ready to go into battle. He stood up and made his way up the stairs.

'Don't bother, Eamonn, you're wasting

your time,' she said.

'I want to talk to him for a minute,' he said sternly. He drew himself up to his full height. Just over six feet. Another tell-tale sign of approaching controversy! Marjory laughed. She knew full well that Eamonn couldn't be angry with Ben for more than two minutes, even if he'd murdered the hamster next door. She also knew that Ben paid more attention to Eamonn than he did to anyone else. She appreciated that Ben, at ten, was beginning to change, and tried hard to ignore his ever-increasing mood swings.

But sometimes, like today, he pushed her too far. It was not the stealing that had upset her: it was more that he had told a barefaced lie. He had denied stealing it so vehemently that at one stage she had almost believed him. When she had threatened to take his Super Nintendo away from him, he had cracked. Marjory had sent him to his room and grounded him for two days.

★ ★ ★

Eamonn pushed against Ben's bedroom door. It was locked. He smiled as he read the scribbled note stuck to it: 'Warning! Keep Out!'

110

'Ben? It's me, Eamonn,' he said.

There was no response.

'Ben! I have something for you!' Eamonn seduced him.

He heard the lock click. Ben stood before him, almost at chin level. 'When, in God's name, did you get to be so tall?' he said, astonished, his steely-father role forgotten in a jiffy.

Ben gave a half-hearted smile and opened the door wider. Then he looked at Eamonn's hands and his face fell.

Ben's room was a den of iniquity: it was chaotically untidy with mountains of clothes in every available space; the obligatory four-day-old pizza slice waved from under the bedclothes. The smell of rotten socks threatened to knock them both out cold.

'What's the story?' Eamonn gazed at the mess with a beady eye.

Ben lowered his eyes.

'Your mother has just told me you stole from the milk money. Is it true? I find it hard to believe you would do such a thing.' Eamonn frowned at him, but it was a poor show of authority. He couldn't get angry with Ben, no matter what.

Ben acknowledged his guilt.

'You did it? I'm shocked!' Eamonn said softly. 'Your mum needs every penny she can

111

get, you know that, Ben. She can hardly make do with what she has. Now, I don't need to lecture you on the evils of thieving, do I?' he asked.

'I put it back,' Ben mumbled.

'You did?' Eamonn asked.

'It was only a loan. I needed it to buy back my Super Mario Brothers game.'

'I see. Well, I'm glad to hear it. However, it doesn't excuse your behaviour. Ben, are you listening to me?' Eamonn said.

'Yes,' Ben said sulkily.

'I hope this is the end of it. You promise not to do such a thing again?' He used his soft voice to encourage a little shame in the boy. He spotted a quivering lip. Eamonn hated that. 'Enough of this nonsense,' he said, and pulled the boy to him.

'I said I was sorry,' Ben looked up at him with his green eyes: he was a carbon copy of his mother.

'Good, that's a start. Any more bad reports and I'll have to tell your friends you still watch *Thomas the Tank Engine*.'

Ben smiled. 'Can I sit in the car and use your CD player?' he asked. The crisis was forgotten in three seconds.

'What's wrong with your own CD player?' Eamonn asked.

Ben shuffled.

'Don't answer that.' Eamonn stood up, afraid he would be roped into another confrontation. 'We'll have to ask your mother,' he added, and patted the boy's back.

Jessica appeared in the doorway.

'Uncle Eamonn!' She ran to him and bear-hugged his legs.

Eamonn's face lit up. 'Hello, little madam, I hope you're being a good girl?' He kissed her cheek.

'Uncle Eamonn, can I sit in the car too, please?' Jessica begged.

'What's the fascination with the car?' Eamonn turned to Marjory, who was now leaning on the doorframe.

'We don't have one.' She laughed. The children turned their eyes to her, knowing she had the final say.

She nodded. 'OK, but Ben, do not, I repeat *do not* attempt to turn on the ignition.'

Eamonn jangled the car keys to show her they weren't in danger.

'Thanks!' they squealed, and raced downstairs.

'When did he get to be so tall? Come to think of it, when did you get to be so small?' Eamonn towered over her. Marjory barely made five feet in high heels.

'He gets it from his father.'

'As long as that's *all* he gets from Sam,' Eamonn said.

'You still haven't told me why you came over.'

They had returned to the kitchen for their coffee. 'Is something wrong?' Marjory was careful not to press him.

Eamonn stared at her, straight in the eyes. Then he pulled the letter from his inside pocket and handed it to her.

Marjory took it and read it quickly. 'Oh, God,' she said. 'I can't believe she's serious about this.'

'Exactly!' Eamonn said defiantly. 'I can't believe it either.'

'Have you tried talking to her?' Marjory suggested.

'You're kidding, right?' He eyed her with suspicion. 'Ruby hasn't talked to me in two years. You know what she's like when she thinks she's right. A dog with a bone! She can't let go of anything without leaving clawmarks on it! A dog with a fucking bone!' he mumbled to himself.

'Maybe I could talk to her?' She moved to his side. 'Maybe it's just a phase, maybe she'll think things through and realise she's wrong.' She laid a hand on his shoulder, let it linger.

Eamonn didn't notice. He continued, 'I can't understand this. Something has brought

114

it on. It's gone beyond a joke.'

'I think she's confused, Eamonn. I really can't see her going through with it. She'll drop the application when she finds out what it's all about,' Marjory reassured him.

'*What is it all about anyway?*' Eamonn scratched his head, genuinely perplexed.

'Eamonn, have you been seeing anyone?' Marjory asked suddenly.

'What?' He looked at her with amusement.

'Well, it's just that a little dickie bird saw you buying flowers on Valentine's Day.'

'I don't remember buying any flowers.' She watched Eamonn rack his brains. 'Does this little bird have blonde hair and a penchant for house-cleaning?' He raised an eyebrow.

'Perhaps.' Marjory tapped the side of her nose. She could see that Eamonn was still thinking about the flowers. Then the light went on.

'Hold on a minute. Yes. I remember now. I did buy flowers on Valentine's Day. They were supposed to be for . . . ' He blushed.

He turned to Marjory, whose face had gone a whiter shade of pale.

'What?' he asked. He followed her eyes to the door.

Jessica stood there giggling. She had on Ruby's wedding dress. It was tucked into her knickers and the veil was perched crookedly on top of her head. 'I'm a princess!' the little girl declared.

'Jessica!' Marjory screeched.

Eamonn stared at her. 'Oh, God,' he muttered.

8

Ruby had begun to recall the details of her wedding day. The exercise was agitating, but she was determined to get it out of the way. Alone in her apartment she started to scribble. On 14 February 1988 they had been married in the local Catholic church at three p.m. Ruby recalled it had been a Sunday.

They had had to perform cartwheels to get the priest to marry them on that particular day. Ruby had insisted the ceremony was held on 14 February: it was St Valentine's Day. They *had* to be married on St Valentine's Day. The priest insisted that it was a *Sunday*: they did not do weddings on a *Sunday*. Anthony Blake offered a generous contribution towards the poor box for the 'inconvenience'. The priest humbly accepted the gesture, but only because it was for the suffering underprivileged, mind you.

Ruby had gone to the hairdresser's that morning with Marjory, Brenda and Judy, who were the bridesmaids. Later she gazed at herself in the full-length mirror as the girls fussed with her veil. Her dress was ivory silk with an embroidered bodice, into which the girls had struggled to pour her. Pearl buttons adorned the back and sleeves. The skirt billowed outwards and rustled along the floor as she moved.

Underneath she wore a silk bra and matching pants, stockings and suspenders. She had wanted to feel comfortable *and* look a million dollars, but she couldn't have both: the underwear pinched, but it was a price she was happy to pay. She simply had to look perfect. Her hair had been gathered into a bun with little curls around her face. The twelve-foot veil was causing problems for everyone, especially the bridesmaids, who frequently stepped on it, tugging at Ruby's diamond tiara.

As she wrote, she had a sudden urge to look at those photos again. She wanted to see their faces, their happy faces, full of love and great expectations. She smiled to herself at the thought of the girls fussing and pulling and tugging at her.

'You look so beautiful!' Brenda had kept squealing.

I did look beautiful, she thought. She had let a professional makeup artist from Brown Thomas do her face. Not too heavy on the foundation, as suggested. She had settled for a natural look.

She had glowed with excitement.

Marjory had handed her the bouquet of pink roses, which toppled down on to a backdrop of ivy.

'Now look,' they had said, standing behind her. They all peered into the mirror, smiling.

Ruby's mum dashed into the room, holding two tins of paint. She was trying to find a suitable place to hide them in case she had visitors after the wedding.

'Mam! Don't bring them in here!' Ruby screamed. Doreen Reece turned on her heel and went out again. Recently there had been a panic after Ruby had suggested the Reeces might invite Eamonn's parents round some day. Doreen had ordered her husband, Richard, to paint the house immediately: the job had not been completed and half-empty paint pots lay strewn here and there.

At 2.50 p.m. Ruby had stepped outside the house to rapturous applause from well-wishing neighbours. They clapped and cheered her on. Some came to hug and kiss her and Ruby had been terrified they would destroy her hair or makeup. It took an age to manoeuvre the dress and train inside the car. Ruby's father had instructed the driver to take a detour and travel the scenic route. They had driven towards the bull wall, up Raheny Road, through Raheny village on to the Howth Road, then did another full circle. She tried to remember what she had been thinking about on the journey, but she couldn't. She tried to remember her feelings. They were easy to find. She smiled to herself at the memory of love. As if to take her back to the present, her right hand fiddled absently with her wedding-ring finger. The empty space seemed all-consuming.

No semblance of eternal love there, she thought ruefully. How could I have been so sure? Hadn't he lied to her on that very day? How could he have thought that the letter from Marjory could be trivial to her?

She lit a cigarette and gazed out at the sea view. She took two puffs of her inhaler and brought herself back to the journey to the church. Emotions dealt with temporarily, she continued writing.

She remembered glancing at her watch. It had been 3.10 p.m. — a suitable delay. When they reached the church, Ruby had caught a glimpse of the best man in the doorway reading *The Best Man's Organiser*. At the sight of the oncoming Mercedes he had run inside. Ruby had only met Stan Mulhearne briefly. Two hurried drinks had hardly acquainted them, but he seemed a nice guy. He had been to college with Eamonn, and although they weren't bosom buddies,

Eamonn couldn't think of anyone else to do the job. As it turned out he had been a great choice. Ruby wondered what had happened to him.

Outside the church, a crowd had gathered. A strong gust had blown up and she held tightly to her veil. The photographer insisted on taking some photos outside, but the wind played havoc with her dress. Eventually the best man, still clutching his book, ushered them all inside.

Ruby fixed herself at the end of the church and looked up the long aisle. It seemed to go on for ever. She was extremely nervous now. She spotted Arlene, Eamonn's mother, at the top of the church. She was wearing a gigantic straw hat, complete with peacock feather that kept poking Anthony, his father, in the cheek. The organist was playing Acker Bilk. Then the music stopped, and he pounded the opening chords of the Bridal March.

The congregation stood up and looked expectantly towards the door for their first sight of Ruby. She turned to her father. 'Any last words?'

'Yes. How about 'get moving'?' he replied.

Ruby laughed, and took a step forward. Marjory, Brenda and a tall, languid Judy followed her holding the train above the ground. The pews were decorated with white lilies and pink ribbons. Ruby was pleased: the florist had not forgotten her orders. It was her perfect moment.

Then Eamonn turned to greet her. She saw the explosion of pride on his face.

They took their places at the altar. Ruby thought she would burst with joy. He looked so beautiful. Resplendent in tails, his height was accentuated. His dark skin complemented his soft blue eyes. He looked like a proper Mr Bingley!

The priest delivered a lengthy sermon on love, honour and loyalty. Ruby had refused to take the vow of obedience but the priest managed to squeeze the word in during his pontificating. They exchanged rings and the congregation burst into spontaneous applause.

Ruby had been certain she would cry, but her eyes remained dry. They received communion. She smelt a hint of alcohol on the priest's breath. She longed for a drink herself — her mouth was dry too.

Inside the sacristy, the parents gathered. The video man held his camera steady as the happy couple suspended a pen together over the register. 'Can the two mothers come together behind the couple? Yes, that's it. Perfect.' He smiled. Now Ruby recalled how Arlene Blake had held her head at a ridiculous angle, as far away as she could from Doreen's. Then, as soon as he had finished the shot, Arlene had walked to the other side of the room and played with her hat. Ruby remembered her mother's embarrassment. There had been a silly row or two over the guest list, who was coming, and who wasn't. Whenever Ruby submitted the list, the Blakes always added someone else, so that his family side had more.

The list had gone backwards and forwards with Ruby at the head of the negotiating table. Eamonn's brother insisted that his daughter should be a flower-girl. Ruby had never even met the child. Anyway, she had countless friends who had children too. Some child would have felt left out. They decided it was only fair to all concerned that there would be no flower-girl. To make up for it, all the children were invited to the reception.

Ruby was determined not to let the mothers' coolness spoil the day. The ceremony had gone off without a hitch, and outside the cheering guests showered them with confetti, most of which was carried away on the storm-like winds. After photographs had been taken outside the church, Ruby and Eamonn climbed into the car where a bottle of chilled champagne awaited them.

They drove to St Anne's Park, to have

more snaps taken. The wind wouldn't abate and Ruby found it hard to stand still.

They were greeted in the reception area of the hotel with a red carpet and sherry. Ruby recalled the wedding banquet. The meal was served swiftly and efficiently, starting with the top table and moving outwards towards the hungry guests. Flowers adorned the tables and the wedding cake, three tiers high, was a delightful centrepiece. The drink flowed; voices and laughter rose. When the meal was concluded, Stan Mulhearne got to his feet and tinkled the side of his glass with a spoon. 'Ladies and gentlemen, can I have your attention, please?'

Some of the guests took a while to quieten down: peals of laughter could be heard from the back where Ruby had placed the younger guests.

He gave a humorous speech. Ruby was delighted when it became apparent that he had done his homework: he got all the names right, gave appropriate thanks to those who played a big part in the wedding, and even remembered the priest's name, Father Kehoe. Speeches concluded, it was out to the surrounding gardens for more photographs.

Eamonn was swept away from her for most of the evening. Ruby dutifully did the rounds of long-lost relatives, smiling, waving, greeting. She was tired, and looked forward to getting away. She longed to be alone with Eamonn.

The band played a perfect blend of old-time and present trends. They did a set of sixties, seventies and eighties music. Young and old alike were thrilled. Eamonn and Ruby took to the floor first, to get the ball rolling. Soon the room was full of bopping bodies. Father Kehoe was whooping it up on the sidelines and making the best of the free drinks from the bar.

Now Ruby couldn't contain a chuckle at the memory.

The evening had dragged on. Ruby remembered wanting so much to be alone with Eamonn. Every time she tried to talk to him he was dragged away by a guest. Children were napping contentedly under the tables and in the reception area. Old people snored in their chairs. The day was ending. Ruby remembered how it had all been over so quickly.

She recalled the last hours with an uncomfortable knot in her stomach. She had taken advantage of a brief interlude of peace to sit down at a small table on the edge of the dance floor and remove her shoes. Eamonn had taken to the floor with Marjory, at

Marjory's request. Ruby watched them dancing, smiling and whispering. She observed Marjory's close proximity to Eamonn's ear and that Eamonn was listening intently to whatever she was saying. Then Marjory handed him a small envelope, which he accepted. He kissed her cheek. Ruby could see his mouth form a thank-you. When the music had stopped, she went to talk to him but was interrupted by her mother, who wanted her to meet yet another distant relative. Ruby recalled feeling uneasy about the envelope. She had wanted to know what was in it. It seemed strange that Marjory had given it to Eamonn and not to her.

However, the remaining party had formed an archway, with a decidedly drunken Father Kehoe at the end. Eamonn and Ruby made their way slowly down it. Her mother greeted her at the end, tears welling in her eyes. She pulled Ruby close and kissed her forehead. Ruby hugged her dad, who remained unemotional and strong.

She had watched Marjory smiling at Eamonn as he opened his arms for a hug. Their eyes had held a certain intensity that had worried her. The hug had lasted a lot longer than she had expected, and they separated a little drunkenly. Eamonn was swaying from side to side. Ruby stared at Marjory. Everybody was drunk! What was the point in taking a hug seriously? But she *had* taken it seriously, and she hadn't known what was in the envelope.

Ruby was brought back to the present moment by her chest. She had begun to wheeze. She dropped her pen and paced the floor, took in some small breaths, deepening them with each pace. Fear and revulsion rose in her. Why had he hugged Marjory? Drunk or not, surely he had known what he was doing and how odd it had seemed? Or had he? Why had Marjory done it? Why not?

Marjory had hardly been trying to steal him. She had been married herself. Ruby paced up and down, reassuring herself for the millionth time that she had blown the incident out of proportion. Eamonn had never been disloyal to her.

The wheezing abated slightly. She made herself some decaffeinated tea, added Canderel tablets, then washed her spoon a dozen times before stirring. Clad in rubber gloves, smelling of disinfectant, she sat down and continued to scribble.

The guests had dispersed, some moving on to the nightclub next door. Suddenly Ruby had wished she could go too. What was wrong with her? This was her wedding night, the night for which she had waited a lifetime!

Eamonn stood at the top of the stairs jangling their keys. He really was quite inebriated. 'Your parlour awaits.' He lunged at Ruby, just managing not to keel over.

'You're pissed,' she remarked.

'No, I'm not,' he slurred.

'What was in the envelope?' she asked.

'What envelope?'

'The envelope Marjory gave you,' she reminded him.

'Huh? Oh, that . . . ' He paused. 'A card, of course, to wish us well.' He hiccuped. A card to wish *us* well? Ruby thought. Why had she given it to *him*, then?

Inside the suite, the bed was covered with beautifully wrapped presents. The mantelpiece was covered with half-finished drinks.

'Who was up here?' Ruby asked, moving the presents from the bed to the floor.

'Just about everyone.' Eamonn had spied a bottle of champagne and a card by the window. 'We had nowhere else to put the presents. I gave Marjory the keys. Wow! Look at all this stuff.'

Ruby was annoyed that strangers had had access to their private suite. She could smell Marjory's perfume. She had left her scent, like a dog does when it pisses in a garden, claiming ownership to its territory. The card had been enough, thank you.

Ruby recalled feeling very annoyed about it.

Eamonn opened the champagne. He filled two glasses to the brim and lowered his in one gulp.

'Greedyguts.' Ruby had smiled, to hide her irritation.

They sat on the bed drinking and reading the gift tags on the presents. Ruby went to explore the bathroom. The bath was enormous, with big brass taps. White towels perched on the heated rail, inviting her to use them.

How she had loved messing up hotel bathrooms in those days! she recalled. She hadn't had to worry about cleaning up. Now when she travelled, which wasn't often, she always cleaned the hotel room after her stay, despite knowing a chambermaid would do it. She couldn't bear the thought of someone talking about how untidy she was, whether it was a chambermaid or the milkman.

She concentrated on remembering the bridal suite, the bathroom and its splendorous luxury. She had felt hot and sticky from the day's events and longed to soak her aching limbs in the inviting tub. She remembered undoing the dainty pearl buttons and sliding out of the dress, being careful to hang it on the back of the door. Her veil had detached itself when she had thrown her bouquet over her head to the screaming guests. She carefully removed the mountain of hairclips that held the tiara in place. Her hair was stiff with lacquer.

She peeped through the gap in the bathroom door: Eamonn was still opening cards and reading them. 'I'm just going to pop into the bath,' she called to him. He raised his hand in acknowledgement. Ruby was glad of the door. It was a small boundary, but a boundary nonetheless. She needed some moments of privacy, just to ready herself.

She ran the bath, which took an age to fill. The bathroom filled with steam. She added some oil, and donned a shower cap, then slipped into the warm, soothing water and lay back in the peace and silence.

What an incredible day it had turned out to be. Nothing had gone wrong, really. Nothing major. No catastrophe. No inescapable, irreversible disaster. Except for Marjory. She was not angry with Eamonn. He had been as drunk as a skunk. But Marjory should have known better. Ruby dismissed the incident. It was wedding-day stuff. What did it matter? She was married to Eamonn now! She thought back to the beginning when they had met. She smiled to herself. It had been only a year ago, and the twelve months had passed in a whirl of excitement.

She still couldn't believe her luck. She raised her hand and examined the two rings on her third finger. The spanking new wedding band looked exquisite, and complemented her engagement ring. She was so happy she could hardly contain herself. She lifted the champagne glass that sat on the stool beside her, and basked in their success. They had made it. They had arrived. She was now Mrs Ruby Blake. A married woman. Eamonn Blake's wife.

The thought frightened her a little. Would she make a good one? Then she remembered the night was not yet over. Her stomach jumped at the thought of sleeping with Eamonn and waking up beside him. She had stood up, pulled out the plug, then turned on the shower to hose down any remaining suds. Now Ruby recalled using every single towel and tossing them about with wild abandon. Why not? It wasn't often she had the chance to behave like a spoilt diva! Then she had reached for her toilet bag and leisurely smoothed on a a scented body lotion. She reapplied her makeup, released her hair, and put on the silk stockings, suspenders and bra again.

She ran her hand along the inside of her thigh, feeling its smoothness, anticipating Eamonn's touch with a longing now that was almost impossible to bear. Checking herself in the mirror for the last time, she felt sexy and childlike. A dab of perfume, and her preparation was complete. She pushed the door ajar and leaned naughtily against the wall.

Eamonn lay sprawled across the bed, with nothing on except a bright red pair of boxer shorts. His head hung awkwardly over the edge, bobbing at each breath. Mouth agape and dribbling, he expelled loud, guttural snores. She couldn't believe her eyes. It was their wedding night and he was fast asleep, snoring his head off. She relaxed and sighed.

Then she remembered the envelope. She looked about for his trousers, which were flung haphazardly on the floor. She tiptoed over, gathered them up and took them into the bathroom. She glanced back to check that Eamonn was still fast asleep.

She locked the door and sat on the edge of the bath. I really shouldn't be doing this, she chastised herself. Eamonn has told me the truth, so why am I so suspicious? The white envelope peeped out of his back pocket. Ruby took it in her hand and opened it. As soon she saw that it was not a card but a *letter* her heart began to thump.

Dear Eamonn,

I just wanted to wish you and Ruby the very best in your married life. As I have always thought of our relationship as a special one, I hope that being married will not change that now! I have never forgotten your kindness towards the children and me, not only in times of trouble in the past, but also presently. I appreciate and respect our special friendship greatly and can only hope that it continues to flourish, as does your marriage.

With love always,
Marjory.

X X X

Ruby was horrified at the content of the letter. She was horrified that Eamonn had lied to her. Yes, lied to her. Why had he lied?

Why had he said it was a card when it was so much more than that?

Now she recalled her hand trembling as she read and re-read the letter, digesting every word. What had Marjory thought she was at, writing him a letter and handing it to him on his wedding day? What did she mean 'special relationship', and what did that imply to Eamonn? If it had been a harmless card he would have shown it to her, but he had chosen not to.

He had withheld this letter from her for some reason, which bothered her greatly. She had never before known Eamonn to be dishonest, not once, not ever.

Yet her wedding night had been marked indelibly, not by the specific content of the letter or by the fact that Marjory had written it — Ruby realised with hindsight that she should have been just as angry with her friend. She wondered why she had not challenged Marjory about it or taken seriously the question mark that hung over their friendship.

No. Eamonn's actions had upset her more. She was married to *him*. It was *his* behaviour that took precedence. It was the inexcusable blatant lie that he had told her when she had asked him what Marjory had given him. Drunk or sober, it had been unacceptable, unforgivable behaviour, and Ruby would never, ever forget it.

She put her pen down and sighed. 'What a way to have begun my married life,' she whispered to the air.

9

Dublin Regional Marriage Tribunal,
Diocesan Offices,
Archbishop's House,
Dublin 9

Nullity of Marriage: Reece — Blake
J.2 254/94.

Personal and Confidential

20 May 1995

Dear Mrs Blake,

Thank you for your recent contribution towards the expenses involved in your nullity case. If at any later stage you are able to contribute further to the expenses incurred, we would be grateful.

We have arranged a further interview for you at 9.30 a.m. on Thursday 25 May. We look forward to seeing you then.

With every good wish,
Yours sincerely,

Aidan Mason
Tribunal Secretary

Father Sean Ebbs was feeling unwell. He had arrived late, irritable and out of sorts. He had been suffering from a continuous cough for the last ten days. Today he was feverish. Bill, the caretaker, had let him in. Bill had worked for the House for over twenty years.

'Good morning, Bill.' Father Ebbs nodded. Bill was hovering over a large plant that sat on a table in the interview room. He had been tending it for weeks.

'What do you think, boss? Isn't she coming on lovely? Look at the heads on those flowers.' Bill shook his head, pleased with his efforts.

'Wonderful. Bill, you're doing a marvellous job, as always!' Father Ebbs lied, through his teeth. He hadn't the heart to tell the man the plant was a fake. Bill had been ministering to it for so long now. Anyway, this morning he was unable to confront anything more than a cup of tea.

'Are you all right, Father? Looking a bit peaky, you are. How about a cuppa?'

'That would be nice,' Father Ebbs agreed. The day had not begun and he was already exhausted. He went past the waiting room, not wanting to look in. From the corner of his eye, he caught a glimpse of the waiting hordes. A busy day seemed imminent. He had never been sick before he was transferred to the Archbishop's House. He wondered whether if he had not taken up the position he would still be feeling the growing sense of dissatisfaction.

He took out his morning missal, and tried to concentrate on the prayers. He mumbled the meditations, but they didn't feel part of him any more. They just looked like meaningless words on a page. He squeezed his eyes tight shut and tried again, but the words failed to hold his attention. He stared long and hard at the picture on the wall: the Last Supper. It did nothing. There was a vacant space where there had once been a sense of purpose. Father Ebbs wondered when it had started.

*   *   *

Ruby arrived a few minutes late. She sat down in the waiting room and realised she needn't have rushed. The room was packed to capacity: she would have to wait her turn. The man in the hat was there again. She squeezed in beside him. The fat woman was also there. She leaned over to Ruby. 'I've been here so long I think my birthday came and went.'

Ruby smiled.

'I see you couldn't resist a return visit,' Robert whispered.

Ruby was strangely comforted by his presence. 'I intend to get my fiver's worth,' she replied, out of the corner of her mouth.

'Five?' he repeated. 'You didn't actually give them five pounds, did you?'

'Yes, I did.' Ruby felt proud of her small display of individuality.

'That was far too much,' he replied, with sarcasm. He removed his hat.

Ruby observed his thinning hair. 'Do you always wear that?' she asked cheekily.

'Always. Except, of course, when I'm forced to take it off. It's a bit warm today for hats.'

Ruby admired his lack of self-consciousness. It was an unusually hot and humid day. The room was stifling and someone was struggling to open a window. It appeared to be locked tight. Everybody groaned. It was bad enough being there without having to suffer any further discomfort.

Ruby picked up a magazine, the same one she had flipped through last time. She threw it back down. She dipped into her handbag and pulled out a small hand-held fan. She turned it on and placed it on the table. 'I came prepared.' She smiled at Robert.

'Here. Today's paper. Far more interesting than breast implants.' Robert proffered it.

The fat woman folded her arms and grunted. Ruby took the newspaper and opened it, poking Robert in the eye.

'It should be compulsory that all newspapers come in tabloid form.' She rattled the pages awkwardly. 'Heaven knows, it doesn't cost that much,' she added.

'It doesn't?' Robert said.

'No. Actually, it's relatively inexpensive. It's the retraining of staff that costs,' she replied.

'How do you know so much about newspapers?' He closed the *Irish Times*.

'I work for one,' Ruby answered. 'Unfortunately,' she added, as an afterthought.

Robert held up the *Irish Times* and dangled it in her face.

'Good God, no!' She laughed.

'How low should I go?' he enquired. He picked up another newspaper and shook it.

'Not that low!' she said.

People were making fans from the magazines. Father Ebbs put his head round the door. He glanced at Ruby's fan, whizzing round and round. 'Robert Ryan, please,' he said, in a businesslike fashion.

'Time for my acting class,' Robert whispered into her ear, and left the waiting room.

Ruby amused herself with her nails until, finally, Father Ebbs returned and summoned her. Robert was coming out of the priest's office. 'If you hang around, I can drive you back into town,' she offered. 'I don't think I'll be long.'

'Thanks,' Robert said. 'I've plenty to read.'

★ ★ ★

Ruby sat in the comfortable high-backed chair. She was a lot more relaxed now that she knew the routine. She would be in and out in no time.

Father Ebbs blew heavily into a mucus-soaked handkerchief. 'Forgive my sniffling. I've had a dose for some time now. Can't get rid of it.' He brought up a mountain of phlegm and spat into the hankie. Then he fiddled with the archaic tape-recorder until it spluttered into action. 'There we go, now, eh, Mrs *Blake*,' He emphasised her name to prove he had done his homework.

'Let us start, then. Did you manage to write out details of your wedding day?' he enquired.

Ruby handed him three pages of perfectly punctuated facts.

'This is excellent, Mrs Blake, I shall read it carefully, of course.'

The previous weeks had seen a build-up of hurt feelings. Ruby asked herself why she had omitted to tell the priest about Marjory's letter. Somehow she felt the priest would judge her if she did tell him. He would think it hardly worth mentioning. At the end of the day, it wasn't a *letter* that had torn apart their marriage.

Father Ebbs started the session. 'OK. Let's continue, shall we? It would do no harm if you were perhaps to tell me a little bit about your honeymoon. Where did you go?' he barked.

'To Inis Meáin for a week,' Ruby replied.

'Ah, yes. The Aran Islands, beautiful,' he commented.

He depressed the record button. Question: where did you go on your honeymoon? Answer: Inis Meáin. 'Would you like to tell me a little about that holiday and how it went?'

Ruby leaned back in the chair, and soon forgot that she was in the Archbishop's House. It was the first time she had had an opportunity to tell anyone how she had felt at that time.

★ ★ ★

Eamonn had always wanted to visit the west, and they had yearned for some peace and quiet, somewhere that didn't acknowledge telephones. They had agreed that the island

141

would offer the perfect retreat. They booked, ironically by telephone, a two-bedroom cottage. They boarded the Galway train at nine thirty on the morning after the wedding. They enjoyed the three-and-a-half-hour journey, with the beautiful scenery.

When they arrived in Galway's Eyre Square, they connected with a small tour bus that took them to the tiny airport. Ruby winced at the sight of the eight-seater plane. They boarded it with a little trepidation for the nine-minute flight.

The small aircraft bobbed, ditched and dived, but the pilot reassured them that turbulence was normal: winds were always heavy on approaching the island.

They landed in the middle of a field. A nosy cow came to investigate and poked its head at the window. They fetched their luggage and were brought to a makeshift shed. They had arrived in Inis Meáin.

At the gate of the field, a weatherbeaten old man greeted them with a typical Irish welcome.

'*La go deas!*' he exclaimed. He was dressed shabbily in a pair of dirty overalls and wellington boots. His worksoiled sleeves were rolled up beyond rough elbows. He tipped his cap at Ruby.

She blushed and, not remembering her

Irish well, looked to Eamonn for assistance.

'How — do — we — get — to — the — cottage?' Eamonn enquired.

'We walk,' the man replied, in perfect English.

'Is there no transport?' Eamonn said, taken aback.

The man gave a hearty Irish chuckle. 'No need,' he said. 'There's only two Land Rovers on the island. We walk just as quick.'

The endless cobblestone walls all seemed to lead to the many coves and sandy beaches. The silence was eerie, broken only by gulls squawking, the wind in the trees. Hares and stoats scurried here and there. Every now and then a relaxed 'moo' from the cows.

Ruby took a deep breath. 'This is paradise,' she said, glad they had elected to come after all.

The old man picked up their bags, hauled them over his strong shoulders, and they set out on their walk to the cottage. After twenty minutes of climbing steeply, then back down again, they caught sight of smoke, plummeting from over the hill.

Suddenly, it came into view. Standing between two hills, it looked like the Seven Dwarfs' cottage. Some stray cows and goats had gathered in the surrounding gardens to greet them. A ramshackle cobblestone wall enclosed it.

A handmade clothes line swung across the garden. The man fidgeted for the key and finally opened the door. 'I started a fire for ye.' He smiled. 'If ye need anything, I'll be yonder in the pub.' He bade them farewell and went on his merry way.

They were alone at last.

They examined the cottage and its two tiny bedrooms, kitchen and living room. Ruby tested the large double bed. It creaked loudly, and dust rose in a cloud. She sneezed twice, and hoped her asthma would not start to play up. She retrieved some musty-smelling blankets from the wardrobe and hung them out on the clothes-line to air. The bed had put her in mind of lovemaking. Now that they were alone, she could hardly wait.

Eamonn was walking around the kitchen. The old range was just like the one his grandmother had. The presses and cupboards held an assortment of old crockery and stainless steel pots and pans. Some copper utensils adorned the walls.

'Look at this, this is the real thing. You'll never taste anything like the grub that comes out of this.' Eamonn reached under the oven door. 'Might be a little bit difficult to get it going, though. There doesn't seem to be any electrical points. We'll have to gather wood, just like the old days, eh?' They looked at each other, searching for reassurance.

They went to explore the other rooms.

'No TV . . . or radio. I'm afraid we're going to have to occupy ourselves in other ways.' Eamonn pulled Ruby close. She snuggled up to him.

'C'mon, let's get the range going. There's work to be done.'

Outside they gathered as many sticks as they could find and threw them into a old coal bucket they found in the yard.

The light was fading quickly and they scoured the rooms for candles. They found them in a press by the window. 'How romantic,' Ruby commented.

They unpacked the tinned food they had purchased in Galway and set about making some soup. The driver of the bus had explained that the island got its main supply of goods from Galway so they should stock up. If the weather worsened, the locals would not be able to make the daily trip. The island had only one shop and one pub.

Ruby found an old tablecloth in the kitchen drawer. She opened it out and a number of moths flew into the candlelight. She screamed like a banshee.

'They won't harm you!' Eamonn had

snatched at one and held it in his palm.

'If you come one step closer, I swear I'll kill you!' Ruby started to run and Eamonn chased her . . .

* * *

Ruby paused.

'Have you had enough, Mrs Blake? Perhaps a little break?' the priest asked gently.

Ruby found it difficult to return to the Archbishop's House. Her mind was in Inis Meáin. Her heart was racing and her throat ached. 'Yes, please,' she managed. She excused herself and went into the smoking room.

Robert Ryan was reading. Ruby lit up and smoked three cigarettes in a row. Then she reached for her inhaler and took a few puffs. Robert eyed her above the paper.

'I think I'll be a bit longer than I thought,' she said eventually. 'If you need to go, don't let me keep you.'

Robert folded his paper. 'Hey, I'll be in Bewley's having some coffee if you care to join me afterwards?'

Ruby's thoughts were muddled. 'Perhaps,' she said doubtfully.

Back in the room, Father Ebbs was replacing the first tape. Ruby didn't wait to be asked to continue. Inis Meáin was still fresh in her mind.

* * *

They had eaten heartily that night. Eamonn had bought a nice Hungarian red wine along with some garlic bread in Galway. They devoured the soup, then Eamonn boiled an old kettle at the hearth. The fire fanned and threw assorted shapes across the ceiling. They drank the sweet tea from a real old-fashioned teapot in the peace.

'How about a little walk?' Eamonn suggested. 'Perhaps we could find the pub. There's a flashlight here, don't know if it works, though.'

They dressed warmly in woollens and went outside. Ruby put her two hands before her and couldn't see a single thing: they were engulfed in blackness. 'Maybe this isn't such a bright idea after all,' she commented.

Eamonn turned on the flashlight, which illuminated the tiny road just enough for them to see a few steps ahead. 'Don't worry,' he reassured her, 'our eyes will adjust in a few minutes.'

Ruby put her arm through his, and let him lead the way. Pretty soon they were laughing and talking.

'Wow! This is incredible. How do they survive without electricity, without cars? How do we know we're even going the right way?' Ruby laughed.

'Look over there.' Eamonn pointed to a faint light in the distance. 'There's only one pub, so that has to be it. We can't get lost anyway, all the roads meet up with each other at some point.'

* * *

Ruby stopped. Somehow the memories felt sacred. She did not want to share them with a stranger. It just didn't seem right. To speak of them felt like a violation. She wondered if Eamonn had felt as protective under Father Ebbs's probing and questioning. She closed her eyes and felt the darkness of the Inis Meáin evening envelop her.

* * *

They had stopped abruptly in the middle of the road, their arms finding each other in an urgent embrace. Eamonn had slid his hand inside her shirt. He tried to kiss her and missed her face by a mile. They had laughed ... laughing and laughing and laughing until they toppled over on to the grass verge, rolling like children in the blessed darkness.

★ ★ ★

Ruby opened her eyes and Father Ebbs was staring at her. She coughed and apologised for dreaming. She fast-forwarded the story some twenty minutes to the point where they arrived at the pub. They had heard the faint sound of music and people chattering, she told Father Ebbs, matter-of-factly.

★ ★ ★

They quickened their steps. Soon, they were outside the pub. Inside the islanders' voices rose in traditional Irish ballads. Only the barest of furniture was evident: the hard cement floor was dotted with bocket tables and chairs. The islanders sat mostly at the bar. They fell silent when Eamonn and Ruby entered. Ruby sat in the corner feeling awkward, but Eamonn struck up a conversation with the barman. Whatever he had said pleased the locals, and they began to sing again. An enormous coal fire dominated the room, and they warmed their hands beside it. A patron approached and offered Ruby a shot of whiskey. Not wanting to appear rude, she downed it, gasped and coughed.

The islanders burst into gales of laughter.

Then the chairs and tables were stacked to the side. A group of red-faced musicians had gathered at the door. An accordion, a violin, a bodhran and a flute joined together to play a lively jig. From the back came ten set dancers. The crowd yelped intermittently.

The dancers grabbed Eamonn and hurled him into the middle of the circle. Ruby joined in. They laughed until they felt sick: neither had any rhythm whatsoever. The barman told them they were a disgrace to their country and culture. Ruby was dizzy from the whiskey and all the spinning. They retired to their seats and let the professionals continue. The night went on until, somewhere in the small hours, they decided it was time to head home. They staggered back with only the flashlight to guide them, singing their heads off.

★ ★ ★

Ruby paused again.

'Do you wish to continue?' Father Ebbs asked gently.

It was the jumping-off point. Ruby knew that Father Ebbs was waiting for the meat of the marriage. She had managed up until now

150

to avoid any mention of their sex life. Now, she felt as though a boulder the size of Ireland was wedged in her throat. She could not get the words out. She could not bring herself to open her mouth. It was too precious.

'I really don't think I can go any further today,' she said quietly, smoothing down her skirt and picking a stray hair off her woollen suit.

'I understand.'

Ruby let herself out of the room and slowly made her way to Reception.

Robert Ryan was gone, and she was glad that he was not waiting for her. The memories of her honeymoon still burned. The wonder, the awe, the newness. The feeling that anything was possible. Her husband's eyes alive with love, his hands, his smoothness, his legs, warm against her own. The feelings urged her to step into the truth, but her mind knew she didn't know what it was yet. That was another day's work.

10

Ruby was an age trying to get back on to the Drumcondra Road. The traffic seemed very far away. She sprayed some air-freshener and double-checked that the windows were shut tight. She hated dust and flies getting in. She steered towards town blindly, not sure of anything any more. Not sure of what she wanted. A car whizzed past her at high speed. She didn't care: normally, she would report such unruly behaviour to the police — she hated people who broke the rules.

She had played by the rules throughout her marriage — throughout her life. She had expected her due return, the pay-off, for abiding by the rules. It hadn't been enough.

Ruby spotted Bewley's from the corner of her eye, and remembered what rotten luck it had brought her. She passed it, then abruptly brought the car to a halt. She spent an age parking, going backwards and forwards and making sure she was directly parallel to the kerb.

He'll probably be gone by now. Anyway, I could do with a coffee, she thought. She took her kit with her: some decaffeinated coffee in a old Valium jar, some Canderel tablets and a small silver spoon.

★ ★ ★

Inside the café, Robert Ryan was donning his hat and coat. He had been a fool to wear them. He berated himself for coming to Bewley's. Then, again, a man has to eat sometimes. Ruby waved from the door. Robert waved back: she had seen he was about to leave and now he couldn't figure out what to do.

'You were just about to leave,' she said, as she came up to him.

'You're here now. Let me buy you a cup of coffee. I'm not in any great hurry.'

Robert pulled out a chair and Ruby sat down. 'Just some boiled water, please.' She placed her kit on the table.

Robert made to remark on it and swiftly changed his mind. It was none of his business. He ordered coffee and scones for himself. When it arrived with the boiled water, he watched her make her coffee in some amusement.

'It's decaffeinated coffee. I can't stand other people making my coffee or my tea.' She explained.

'Thirsty work, eh? The annulment, I mean.' He smirked.

'God, I hate it. I wish I'd never started the thing.' Ruby had opened her mouth and no amount of willpower would close it again. 'I'm trying to get away from the past. Now I'm being asked to relive it, so that some idiot priest who knows nothing about anything can tell me it never happened.'

Robert remained silent, his eyes down. He watched Ruby dip the silver spoon into her cup and make perfect circles without spilling any.

'I mean, what kind of a religion is it, anyway? How can a priest possibly know about marital relations or sexual conduct? Who is he to judge? The Catholic Church is a homosexual explosion, for god's sake! They're buggering our children and telling me about *my* sexuality? *I'm* supposed to trust *them*? Even the bishops are at it. Probably bonking the housekeeper while I'm spilling the intimate details of my failed marriage. Christ! And that bloody tape-recorder, *whine, whine*!' Ruby made a hideous high-pitched squeak. She picked up a paper napkin and spooned stray pieces of scone on to it. Then she folded it into an exquisite triangular party hat.

Robert remained still, hand covering his mouth. A grin threatened to explode into laughter.

'Did you read that article in the *Irish Times* today? Did you? Another bloody priest found guilty of child abuse. He got at seventeen children before he was caught. Seventeen! It turned my stomach. Why can't *we* question *them*? Why haven't we the right to question their authority?' She slammed her cup down on the table.

'I was taught by priests in school,' Robert said. 'Some of them were brutal.'

'You see? Are they sadists or what?' Ruby asked defiantly.

'No. Just priests . . . ' Robert sighed.

An elderly woman, who had been eavesdropping from the table beside them, leaned backwards and whispered into Ruby's ear: 'Don't forget the randy nuns, dear. Just as bad, if you ask me.' Her companions nodded in agreement.

'Exactly. That's another thing.' Ruby was on a roll. 'What about the nuns eh? Some of them are worse. I know, I was taught by them. Vicious, evil bitches! Made a pass at me, one of them. What did *we* do? Slap an image of one on our five-pound notes, that's what! Turned her into an historical figure! Made her out to be a heroine!'

Ruby took a deep breath. Then another. Then another. 'Is it any wonder we turned out the way we did? What chance did our

155

marriages have of surviving, when even the bishops can't keep their dicks in their robes?'

Robert winced.

Ruby began cleaning the table like a waitress. She packed the saucers and cups neatly in a pile. Then she wiped down the Formica top with a napkin. Robert watched as she fulfilled the peculiar ritual. 'You did initiate the annulment, did you not?' he probed.

'Yes, I did,' Ruby answered.

'You have to learn to take blame out of your life,' Robert said.

'What?' Ruby puffed on her inhaler.

'You heard me,' Robert said.

'Well, whose fault is it? It has to be somebody's!' She had raised her voice just a little too much: the café became quiet and patrons whispered behind their hands.

'Nobody is to blame, Ruby. Life is life whether you accept it or not.'

'Oh, that's so easy to say. What are *your* grounds for an annulment, Mr Serenity? Let me guess. Not enough salt on your chips?'

Robert laughed, not in the least perturbed by her wrath. 'Close. Actually she's had a sex change.'

★　★　★

Ruby spat out her coffee — and was horrified by the temporary lapse in her normally impeccable manners. Robert burst out laughing. Ruby patted her chin furiously with a tissue. Then she began to see the funny side. A smile hung in her brown eyes waiting for release.

'She should charge John Paul for the inconvenience. After all, God made her. It wasn't *her* fault, right?' She played along and Robert laughed again. The woman at the other table blessed herself.

Then Ruby realised he might just be telling her the truth. What if it was true? The poor man!

She began to apologise and he put her mind at rest. 'I am joking, you know.'

Ruby heaved a sigh of relief. 'Oh, God. It's finally happened, hasn't it? I've lost my mind. I'm sitting in a coffee shop with a stranger, behaving like a mad-woman.' She covered her mouth. Her shoulders shook with laughter.

'You'll be OK,' Robert said. 'But I think we'd better leave, before we're thrown out.'

'I apologise. I've been outrageously rude. I'm really sorry. I don't know what came over me.' Ruby had calmed down now, and was feeling embarrassed.

'I've enjoyed it. In fact, I agree with you — if not on all points.' Robert led her to the door. 'Fancy a walk in St Stephen's Green?' he asked outside.

'Sure, why not?' Ruby replied.

They headed up Grafton Street on foot. Musicians dotted the street. Robert tossed a few coins into an open violin case. Ruby couldn't figure him out: her outburst in the coffee shop hadn't caused him so much as a ripple of discomfort. For the first time in a long time she had let herself slip up. It didn't feel as bad as it usually did.

Inside the park they walked until they came to a bench. Some brazen pigeons waddled up. Robert threw them some popcorn from his pocket. 'My granddaughter,' he explained. 'I always find something in my pockets when I've had her over.'

'Grandchildren?'

'Two,' he said.

'How many kids have you?' Ruby enquired.

'Three. All grown-up, married and gone, thank God. You?'

'None. No kids.' Ruby's dimples disappeared with her smile. She stared at the pond, hoping he'd change the subject. 'I'm a godmother, though,' she volunteered, wanting to have something in common with Robert. Yes, she knew a lot about children. She felt guilty then: her visits to Jessica and Ben lately had been few and far between. She couldn't

help it, though. Jessica made her feel so
. . . Why had she kept her distance? Jessica
was only a child, a beautiful little girl just
like . . .

'Why exactly have you applied for an
annulment, Ruby?' he asked.

'Honestly?' She squinted: the sun was in
her eyes. 'I really don't know. Perhaps I just
wanted to end it finally. You know. A clean
cut?'

Robert laughed. 'There's no such thing, I
fear. Clean cuts only happen in hairdressing
salons! They are rare in marriage. Especially
where there are children involved.'

Ruby sneaked a cheeky sideways glance.
This man was a little unhinged, but she liked
that. It was a fresh perspective. She liked
Robert's calm exterior, his acceptance of life
on life's terms. He was different. Perhaps a
little too different for her comfort: she prided
herself on her ability to be predictable,
disciplined. Robert wasn't anything like that.
Ruby felt a little excited. It was OK to be
around the unhinged, as long as the door
didn't fall off! Nothing seemed to bother him:
he was happy to go along with it, eagerly
anticipating what life had to offer next.

They sat in the park, forgetting their roles.
They abandoned their pigeonhole titles of Mr
or Mrs, husband or wife, son or daughter,

and became their separate selves.

'What were we thinking when we got married? What was it you expected?' Ruby asked him.

'Oh, God. I really don't know. If you had asked me that two years ago, before I started out on this crusade, I would have given a different answer. I was so young. Perhaps I was looking for a surrogate mother. The most honest answer I can give you is that I don't really know.'

'I thought I knew what I wanted. And I got it. Only to discover it wasn't what I wanted at all. I really can't fault Eamonn. He's a good man, but something deep down inside is missing. Sometimes I feel I expected my marriage to be the final 'coming home', that in that union, I would find myself. I would become whole. The searching would end. But I found it was only beginning.' Ruby delved into her bag of tricks and pulled out some lip balm.

'I agree. That's exactly what started me on this path. Mary was a wonderful woman, a wonderful mother. She did nothing wrong. I don't blame her for seeking love elsewhere.'

★ ★ ★

Ruby sat quiet. She let Robert choose to continue or end this train of thought. It was up to him. She opened her bag again and pulled out a pair of glasses.

Robert looked into the bag.

'What?' Ruby asked.

'Just wanted to see if the kitchen sink was in there.'

Ruby was embarrassed. 'I'm very fussy about some things,' she said haughtily. 'I can't help it.' She felt a little awkward about having to carry everything in her bag, just in case. In case of what? she thought. Why do I have to be like this? she asked herself, for the hundredth time. Always making sure everything is perfect, in order, under *control*.

'Yes. So, I see! Mary Poppins, eat your heart out!' Robert mused.

Ruby tried to conceal a grin.

'She had an affair.' Robert sighed. 'It ended when I challenged her about it. Things were never the same again, though. We tried counselling, but the trust was shattered. The bond had been broken. I never saw her as 'mine' again.'

'Was she *yours to own* in the first place?' Ruby hadn't meant it to sound harsh.

'No. You're right. I didn't own her. That was half the problem. Men are very territorial, you see. They frequently treat women like objects of possession, which only serves to send their partner further away

— which was what I was trying to avoid in the first place! How ironic!'

'I've never had an affair,' Ruby said honestly. The words hung in the air like a humming-bird.

The starving pigeons scurried around their feet. They made the most of Robert's generosity, pecking at each other in the hope of an extra mouthful. Somehow, they symbolised her love-starved existence. How hungry she was now . . .

11

Eamonn burst through the doors of the waiting room dragging the black sack behind him. People looked at him as if he had just been released from a psychiatric hospital. He heave-ho'ed across the room, knocking the table and spilling the magazines on to the floor. 'Excuse me. Sorry. Excuse me. I apologise.' He nodded at the spectators. He took a seat and patted the black sack lovingly. People continued staring.

Eamonn was unperturbed. He opened the *Irish Independent* magazine and began to read as if everything was perfectly normal. Father Ebbs eventually appeared to call him.

★　★　★

Eamonn dragged the black sack behind him. Father Ebbs watched him struggle. He'd thought he'd seen it all. What was in there? His mother-in-law? 'Can I help you with that?' he ventured, fearing Eamonn was close to a nervous breakdown. He had experienced that kind of thing before in his offices and it

163

had been very unpleasant.

He winked at Bill, the caretaker, in case he needed assistance. Bill nodded an acknowledgement, gave him a thumbs-up. Eamonn slammed the black sack on to the desk.

Father Ebbs tried to remain calm. He remembered his training: always maintain eye contact. This was proving an impossible task. The black sack separated them and Eamonn's words came muffled from the other side. Father Ebbs stuck his head around it.

'Is it essential that this, em, article remain in its present position?' he asked.

'Of course not.' Eamonn jumped up and pulled it off the table. He opened it and proceeded to place the items it contained, one by one, on the desk. 'As you can see, Father, I have my evidence with me today. Now, let's see. There's the video. The photographs. And — oh, yes — the invitation list. Very important!' he jested.

Father Ebbs wiped his brow in desperation. He had had enough crackpots in his day, but this one took the Marietta biscuit. 'Very interesting, Mr Blake, but that isn't necessary. If I could just explain to you perhaps you might understand better the — '

Eamonn didn't wait for him to elaborate. 'It's quite unnecessary for you to explain anything, Father Ebbs. I understand perfectly.

You have to prove my marriage didn't exist. *I* have to prove it did.' His voice was rich with confidence.

'First of all, Mr Blake. I do not have to prove anything. I am not the judge. I am the judge auditor. In layman's terms, that translates to mean that I am gathering information to pass on to the judge who will in turn decide whether your marriage should be nullified. Second, the Tribunal's job is to establish whether or not your marriage was valid *at that time*. Not whether it existed or not. Do you understand me so far?' Father Ebbs had altered his tactics. He was now down to a one-word-at-a-time approach.

'I'm afraid I don't really understand.' Eamonn rubbed his temples.

Father Ebbs sighed heavily. 'You will have every opportunity to give your side of the story, Mr Blake. I might suggest to you at this stage that you have very little to be bothered with. You will not be asked to appear in front of the judge. You can have an advocate and procurator appointed on your behalf by the bishop. Your case, of course, will also be argued favourably, by the Defender of the Bond.'

★　★　★

'The what?' Eamonn thought about his theology degree certificate, proudly displayed on the wall at home. He reminded himself to transfer it to the toilet where at least it would have some practical use.

'Mr Blake, I know this is an upsetting and confusing experience for you. I understand your anger and frustration. My job is to make a case for you. Without your complete co-operation, it will be difficult for me to do that.'

Eamonn stared at the priest, who had studied for seven years. Perhaps he had learned a thing or two along the way.

Father Ebbs pushed on. 'In order for representation to be made, a mandate must be made available from you.'

Eamonn felt like an idiot. He had not realised that the Tribunal was a legally binding court.

Father Ebbs explained that the process was serious and meticulous. 'It might also be helpful to mention to you at this stage that you have the right to call any witnesses who might help your case.' He twiddled his thumbs and smacked his lips.

'What kind of witnesses?' he Eamonn asked.

'Family, friends. Have you had any counselling?'

'Only once. I don't believe in getting outside help. It was Ruby's idea,' Eamonn replied, with a hint of arrogance.

'Anyone who knows the circumstances of your difficulties within your marriage can be called as a viable witness.' Father Ebbs fiddled with the tape-recorder. 'For the time being, it would be wise to continue with the task in hand. As I have already explained, the purpose of our interview is to gather as much information as possible to make a case for your defence.'

'All my witnesses will be the same as Ruby's.'

'What about the best man?' Father Ebbs asked.

'Stan? I'm afraid he left the country some years ago. In any case, he really wouldn't have known anything about our married life.' Eamonn chewed his fingers.

'Perhaps your father?'

'He's an old man.' Eamonn knew he could not involve his father in something like this; besides, he too knew little about the ins and outs of the marriage.

'I shouldn't be discouraged, Mr Blake. Witness accounts do not have any bearing on the court's final ruling. They are only useful if they have something to tell us that we may not already know.'

'I see,' said Eamonn.

'Shall we?' Further Ebbs's left hand hovered over the recording button.

Eamonn nodded.

'Could you take me through the honeymoon period, Mr Blake? In your own good time, of course, we have plenty of that.'

Eamonn understood his predicament now: if he didn't testify, he would be leaving himself open to an assumed verdict and losing his chance of a hearing. He had to co-operate and tell them the truth.

His recollections of the honeymoon period were more or less in line with Ruby's. He was soon unaware of his surroundings and had launched himself into the past with relative ease. He recalled the journey to the island, the night in the pub, their drunkenness on returning home. Eamonn confirmed that he had enjoyed it immensely. He had felt free. The pre-wedding dynamics had vanished into thin air. The anxiety, pressure and exhaustion had fallen by the wayside. He mentioned that it was probably the first time in weeks that Ruby and he had shared any quality time alone. The release of it all was stupendous. The big day and the preceding weeks of preparation were finally over. He had been relieved that he and Ruby could resume their normal lives and be themselves once again.

Had they not been themselves all along?

'Can you tell me what happened on your return to the house, that night?'

Eamonn's face twisted with emotion. He rubbed his chin, struggling to speak. 'It was wonderful.' He sighed. He wished he had something else to say. But it was the truth. It *had* been wonderful. 'We made love all night and all the next morning. Then we slept through the afternoon. I don't think we made any other journeys out of the house for the rest of the week. We ate, we slept, and we made love. God, it was great! I apologise, Father, for being so uncouth.'

'That's quite all right, Mr Blake. We are adults. There is no poetic way to discuss one's sexual experiences. I am not here to judge your behaviour, only to collate what information I can. Please continue.' He repeated Eamonn's words into the tape-recorder.

There seemed to be extra emphasis on the content. Eamonn wondered why. The priest continued to stare at him, waiting for more.

Eamonn stared back. 'I'm not sure what else you want me to say,' he said eventually.

'Well, this is my difficulty, Mr Blake. At this juncture, I may need to clarify some points with you.'

Eamonn waited.

'You mentioned that you and Mrs Blake

'made love' all night. Could you elaborate? When you say 'made love', can you tell me exactly what took place?'

'*Excuse me?*' Eamonn exclaimed.

'I know it seems a peculiar thing to ask, but we need to identify that sexual intercourse did in fact take place.'

'Why?' Eamonn demanded, in a high-pitched voice.

'Mr Blake, I think it would be wise to let you know that, at present, we are unsure of what grounds may constitute a case, if indeed there are any. We are still in the exploratory phase so all grounds must be covered as a possible way forward.'

'What's that got to do with our sex life?' Eamonn's face burned.

'As I said, all grounds must be looked into. That would obviously include the possibility of non-consummation.' It had been evident to Father Ebbs from the start that this would not be a clear-cut case and that Ruby might be barking up the wrong tree. Nevertheless he was obliged to follow that line of enquiry, down to the very last twig.

'Are you asking me directly, did I have sexual intercourse with my wife?' Eamonn stared at him.

'Yes.' Father Ebbs's expression was grave.

'For God's sake!' Eamonn erupted.

So this was her game! To turn their marriage into some seedy peep-show. To degrade and humiliate him in front of some gobshite priest who probably didn't know the difference between a 'blow-job' and a 'blow-dry'.

'I'm sorry, Mr Blake. I appreciate that this is embarrassing.'

'Embarrassing? What an understatement! I can't believe my ears.' Eamonn felt like a seven-year-old boy making his first confession. He took a deep breath. 'Just for the record, then. Just to clear this up, once and for all, Father. Yes. I made love to my wife. If there is any doubt as to what that means exactly, I entered my penis into her vagina, I ejaculated, over and over and over. I know because I was there. In fact — '

Father Ebbs was quick to interrupt before Eamonn got carried away. 'Mr Blake, you needn't — '

'Hold it right there! How do you think I feel sitting here telling you about my bodily functions? What right have you even to ask me such a question? What right has she got to do this to me? Jesus Christ! I fucked her! I fucked her! And it was great! Do you hear me? It was the best sex I ever had in my whole life! We got into positions that the *Kama Sutra* hadn't discovered. I was never off her. We fucked until we could fuck no more and when I couldn't get an erection I went down — '

'Mr Blake, please!' Father Ebbs shouted. He had broken into a cold sweat. He snatched open a drawer and pulled out a white handkerchief. He mopped his brow. He was a shivering wreck. 'Perhaps a short break, would be a good idea,' he choked.

Eamonn stood up abruptly and went outside. He let himself into the smoking room and wondered what he was doing in there. An elderly man held out a tin box of small cigars. 'Smoke?' he offered.

'Thank you.' Eamonn lit the cigar. He didn't normally smoke. In fact, he hated smoking. Somehow the cigar seemed appropriate. He felt like he had just given birth.

Like a proud new father, he paced the floor, assuring himself that his resentment was justified. He was furious with her. He wanted to smash her face in. He wanted to make love to her too. The latter almost overwhelmed him. How could he hate her and want her at the same time? He was disgusted by his own weakness. How could she betray him like this? To suggest their marriage had not been consummated was a joke. Surely the priest knew something? Maybe he just relished the idea of hearing about sexual encounters? Had he grilled Ruby? What had she said? What evidence could she possibly have to support such an outrageous allegation? Eamonn felt insane with desire, insane with anger. The confusion was giving him a headache.

★ ★ ★

Father Ebbs had been mulling things over. He wondered how to take the sting out of the interview and put Eamonn Blake at ease again. He called him back in and approached from a different angle. 'Mr Blake, do you understand that your wife's testimony will be given under oath?'

'No. I already explained to you, Father, that I didn't think she was being serious. Frankly, I'm amazed it has even gone this far. Can she really claim that our marriage hasn't been consummated?' Eamonn asked.

'It is *my job* to suggest possible grounds to the Tribunal. That is why I must consider every possible angle. Do not be concerned. Your wife must be able to submit substantial evidence to support her case, whatever case that might turn out to be,' Father Ebbs said, in a bid to reassure him. '*Ratum non-consummatum* is one of the most difficult grounds to prove. For instance, she will be

173

asked to undergo a medical examination. She is not obliged to take it. In any case, I feel quite certain that we needn't worry about this particular ground as you have testified quite vehemently against it.'

'Lovely,' Eamonn sneered. 'Fucking lovely. Sorry, Father.'

Father Ebbs showed no reaction to the bad language. He had heard a lot worse in his day. His experience had taught him to sort through the chaff and come up with the grain. He knew instinctively that Ruby Blake hadn't the faintest idea what she was doing and, to date, he had not uncovered one single piece of information that might support the necessity for a full-blown hearing. Sean Ebbs knew that, in all probability, it wouldn't get past the second stage. But it was within his brief to help where he could: he was loath to inform Eamonn that there were other grounds she could contest — the man had had enough for one day.

★ ★ ★

Eamonn had quietened now. He was mortified by his outburst. It was not the priest's fault, it was Ruby's. She had deliberately manipulated things. 'I apologise, Father. I realise you're only doing your job.

My anger was misdirected.'

The priest nodded an exhausted acknowledgement. He prompted Eamonn to finish his story and encouraged him to get to the end for his own peace of mind. He reminded him that when the interview was complete he would not have to repeat it.

But Eamonn was no longer listening to Father Ebbs. He was lost in his own thoughts. He was back in their honeymoon bed, back in the warmth of her smooth skin. The sweetness of their mingling sweat, the labouring of lovemaking.

★ ★ ★

It was early morning. Ruby's body was damp, her hair stuck to his cheek. Her breathing was short and urgent. She moved to her side. Eamonn traced the curve of her waist with his forefinger. He lay behind her, lifted her hair with his mouth and kissed her neck.

She arched her back. He moved downwards, slowly, teasing her with the tips of his fingers and his tongue. She turned to face him. He gripped her hands and pushed them above her head, entwining his fingers with hers. His body hovered above her. They were inches apart. She raised herself in anticipation and he moved her legs apart with his.

175

'Let me see you come,' he whispered. 'I want to see you come.'

Inside her, he moved, slowly at first. He led her to that secret place. Climbing, with her, every breath, every move, driving her rhythm, waiting, waiting, until finally, wave by wave their spirits collided . . . They lay there, breathless, satiated. He held her and dared not move . . .

★　★　★

Now, sitting in the leatherbacked chair in the Archbishop's House, Eamonn was awash with desire. He wanted to escape this hideous reality. He wanted his memories to remain untarnished, unblemished by this interfering scenario. He hated her for taking away his precious memories. They were all he had. She had turned him into a laughing stock. She had turned their marriage into a circus act. It had become a freak show. Only the bearded ladies were missing.

Eamonn began to speak from the heart. He was oblivious to his surroundings. Somehow, he felt compelled to continue, to make right what had always been right. He told Father Ebbs about the rest of that morning. How happy they had been. He recalled sleeping until midday when they were awoken by a strange sound coming from the kitchen. Ruby had left the bed and Eamonn went to investigate. She was leaning half-way out of the kitchen window, having a full-blown conversation with a cow . . .

★　★　★

'Moo!' she said.

'Who's the friend?' Eamonn asked.

'She must have wandered through the gate last night. Can you believe they would come right up to the window? Cheeky devils. Mooooo!' she shouted into the cow's face. The cow continued to chew.

'Why don't you go back to bed? I'll make us some breakfast.' Eamonn kissed her neck. She laughed and went barefoot to the bathroom. Eamonn watched her perfect naked body as she floated past.

They ate heartily and read papers from the day before. They were happy. Just being. Just being together . . .

★　★　★

Eamonn stopped, heavy with sadness. The tape had ended and whizzed round and round, making a whine that echoed through the room. Father Ebbs ejected it. They sat quietly, embracing the moment.

'What happens now?' Eamonn asked, after a few minutes.

'Well, the next step will take some time. We will endeavour to interview your wife's witnesses, if any. Often these things can be delayed. Appointments are cancelled, people don't turn up at the last minute, that kind of thing. The Tribunal will be appointing your defence in the meantime. When I have all the information I need I will submit it to the Tribunal. For your part, Mr Blake, your interview is complete. You have co-operated fully. That will be noted.'

'Is there anything else I can do to help speed things up?' Eamonn asked quietly.

'I'm afraid not, Mr Blake. Not at this point.'

Eamonn stood up and stretched. He was tired. He bade the priest farewell.

As he reached the door. Father Ebbs called him: 'Mr Blake?'

'Yes?'

'There is one other thing you can do.'

'There is?'

'Pray.'

12

Brenda Power sat at the nurses' station, struggling to keep her eyes open. It was four a.m. and she still had two more hours to go. Not for the first time she wondered why she had chosen such a taxing career. She spent most of the hours when she should have been sleeping taking care of the twenty-four residents in the Sacred Heart home. She read the horoscope and problem pages of her magazine, and yawned loudly. The head nurse, Sarah, was writing the evening's report card, checking off the duties one by one. A flashing light drew their attention.

Sarah sighed and looked at Brenda. It was number eighteen, their number-one client. 'It's Kit again ... I'll go,' she added reluctantly.

'It's OK. I can handle it.' Brenda was on her feet. She knew Kit's antics off by heart. 'For a minute there I thought we were going to get the night to ourselves without her.'

'Think about it. What would we do without her? Things just wouldn't be the same without her,' Sarah joked.

Brenda's soft shoes rubbed against the polished oak floor along the corridor to Room 18. She pushed open the door. Kit was sitting up in bed frowning. 'Now, Kit, what are you up to? It's four in the morning,' Brenda chided her.

'I can't sleep.' She pouted. 'The room is stifling hot.' She fanned herself.

Brenda rested her palm on Kit's back and gently motioned her forward. She took the three pillows and puffed them up.

'It's either too hot or too cold,' Kit complained.

'Did you take your medication, Kit?' Brenda asked, already knowing what the problem was.

'Of course I did,' Kit said defiantly.

Brenda opened her palm. Two small red tablets rested inside it. She pushed them under Kit's nose. 'Then can you explain why these are under your pillow?' She tried not to smile.

'I don't know where they came from,' Kit lied, her face red and bold like a two-year-old's.

'Kit, how many times have I told you? You must take your medication as prescribed. If you don't, you won't sleep. Why do you insist on being such a stubborn mule?' Brenda scolded. She poured a glass of water from the jug beside her bed and handed the red tablets to the old lady.

'Now, Kit, I want you to take them immediately,' Brenda urged her.

'What for?' Kit answered angrily.

'Kit, take them. Now,' Brenda said, a little stronger.

'What for?' Kit repeated, digging her heels into the blankets.

'Kit, if you don't take them now, I will have to call Nurse Sarah.'

Kit reluctantly took the tablets and put them into her mouth, grumbling and groaning as she did so. She sipped some of the water and let it fill her cheeks out.

'Swallow,' Brenda ordered. She was one step ahead.

Kit obeyed. 'The other girl doesn't make me take them.'

Brenda gave her a smile. 'She doesn't?' She played Kit's favourite game.

'No. Never,' Kit swore, her soft blue eyes wide with deceit.

'Kit, you rascal! You know quite well there is no other girl.' Brenda was as good as her. She grinned at her favourite client. Despite her grouchy behaviour, Brenda loved her best. She was convinced that Kit deliberately complained: it was her way of getting attention. Something she had been left short of, in her previous home.

Kit would never have admitted it, but she loved the Sacred Heart home. People paid attention to her, but she didn't believe they would unless she constantly demanded their presence. So every night she did the same thing, and every night Brenda came running. It was a game Brenda enjoyed playing. Her job brought her a degree of satisfaction that didn't exist in other areas of her life.

Kit laid her head on the pillow and closed her eyes. Brenda adjusted the oversheet and blanket, turning them down at Kit's waist. Kit grumbled, and Brenda bent down to kiss her silver hair. Kit smiled.

Brenda left the door ajar, and returned to the nurses' station, her night's work almost complete.

'You have the gift,' Sarah remarked.

'Why does everyone say that?' Brenda said. 'I try to be kind, that's all. I would hardly call it a gift.' She sat down and put her feet up on another chair.

'Perhaps,' Sarah responded, 'but you have immeasurable tolerance. Now, that is a gift!'

Brenda sat there moodily.

'What's the matter?' Nurse Sarah asked.

'It's nothing.'

'It's definitely something,' Sarah pushed.

'It's just stuff.' Brenda shrugged her

shoulders. She thought of her friends and how their lives had expanded. Ruby and Eamonn and their failing marriage. Judy living the life of Reilly with the gorgeous George. Marjory blessed with two children.

Brenda was turning towards her forties, no boyfriend, no children and what she considered very average looks. She was tired of her dull grey eyes, her rounded figure and her boring lifestyle. She was tired of being told she had a gift when she knew, deep down, it was a poor replacement for a relationship with another human being. She wanted that more than anything, but opportunities to mingle with the opposite sex were few and far between. That is, if you didn't count the men under her care who ranged from seventy-five to ninety-five years old. Hardly a match for Brenda, who felt that her life was slipping away. She didn't care what a wonderful job she was doing any more. She was sick of being good and kind. Just for once, she wanted a chance to explore the world, to attend to her own needs.

'Sarah, do you believe in an afterlife?' she asked suddenly.

'Why do you ask?'

'I think about it a lot,' Brenda confided.

'How morbid. Life is for living, Brenda. You shouldn't dwell on such things.' Sarah eyed her from behind her glasses.

'Maybe it's my job.' Brenda played with a chestnut curl, pulling it backwards and forwards until it bounced back into place. 'I can't help thinking about it lately. When I look at Kit, sitting there day in and day out without any of her sons and daughters visiting her, I feel so sorry for her. She's so lonely.' She shivered.

'She has us to look after her. That's what we're paid for,' Sarah said, with authority.

'What if she had no money? What if she had no family to help pay the fee?'

'The health boards would take over.' Sarah looked at her suspiciously '*Is* there something wrong, Brenda? Why all these questions?'

'It's nothing.' Brenda looked out to the wards, each bed occupied by a lonely soul. Her eyes filled with tears as the ultimate question, once again, shouted itself: *Who will look after me when I grow old?*

★　★　★

Judy Rowland passed through Stansted airport for the millionth time. She was so accustomed to the journey that she always came well prepared. In the ladies' toilets, she tried to perk up her tired eyes with some eye-shadow and mascara. Then she put on a

184

few dabs of her favourite perfume, and was ready to embark on the second part of the journey. She caught a train to London's Liverpool Street station, then hailed a taxi to the hotel.

There, she checked in, went to her room and dropped off her small overnight holdall and makeup box. She availed herself of the bathroom, then changed into her power suit. As she surveyed herself in the full-length mirror, she wished again that George had been able to accompany her. Lately he had seemed to be too busy for her, either with work commitments or his family. He made more and more excuses these days. Yet when they did meet, the passion was overwhelming. She reminded herself of that. George was worth it. Judy enjoyed every moment she spent with him and tried hard not to think about when they would meet again. After all, she had known from the beginning that he was married and it had suited her down to the ground. Anyway, it wasn't always *George* who was the unavailable one! she reminded herself. Her own busy lifestyle and hectic career wouldn't suit every man. George encouraged her independence. Yes. It was the perfect relationship except at times like this, when Judy felt the loneliness of the long distance runner.

She glanced at her watch and sighed with relief: the worst part of the day was over. The journey was always irksome and tiring — she had too much time to think when travelling. Now she would come into her own. She would turn on the charm, make the sales pitch and watch as men fell over themselves in their haste to sign cheques. She had amassed a small fortune from her makeup products, boldly courting the largest chain supermarkets and chemists. She frequently paid unannounced visits to the local stores to check that the range was properly displayed.

She had watched the profits soar through the roof, especially at Christmas time. Money was no problem. Getting time alone with George was. Judy chastised herself. Hadn't *she* chosen to make money her God? Everything else had had to take a back seat. She had paid handsomely for her success in lack of romantic relationships. Thinking of George made her feel all warm inside. Lately her ambitious streak had been on an extended holiday . . .

She made her way to the conference room, trying to ignore the stares of reception staff. She walked with an authorative air, head held high. Purposeful. Powerful. Successful.

Inside the conference room, the meeting was well under way. Judy took her place, trying to ignore the stares of men who were not used to doing business with ambitious females. She launched into her spiel with gusto. Much later the deal was signed, sealed and delivered. Another success for Judy. Another financial feather to put in her cap.

She retired to the bar and ordered a brandy with ginger ale, then sat in a corner to drink it, hoping that perhaps, this time, her business associates might care to join her. She watched the men in a circle in the next snug. Their laughter rose intermittently, and Judy looked at her watch. She decided she would try George's mobile again before she went to bed. She might even leave a message. Yes, that would surprise him. On second thoughts, perhaps she'd better not: someone else might hear it.

At ten she retired to her room. She examined the antique furniture, the ornate chandelier, the splendid country-house-style curtains. Such things had once brought her pleasure; now they were just objects. Cold, impersonal objects. She looked out of the window: in the busy London street below, couples linked each other. Happy couples, going out for the night. Judy was ready for bed, her makeup routine completed and nightdress on.

She dialled George's number four times,

then gave up. Each time, the playback voice asked her to leave a message after the tone. She decided against it: the last thing she wanted was to make him angry and jeopardise the chance of a sooner rendezvous. She just had to wait until he contacted her. She hated being powerless over his movements. She had tried to contact him all day. If she hadn't known better she would have assumed that he was deliberately avoiding her. He used to ring three or four times a day. How exciting it was! The mere thought of it made her all goosepimply and starry-eyed.

She laid her head on the pillow and listened to the chattering mob passing beneath her window and the loneliness crept in again. Where is he? Why hasn't he even left a message for me? Then she remembered that tomorrow she would be back in Dublin. Perhaps George had forgotten she was away. Yes. That was it. He was sure to call her tomorrow. There was no point in worrying about it any more. It would all be sorted out tomorrow . . .

13

Ruby exchanged telephone numbers with Robert Ryan. She had found a good friend, and she didn't want to discuss her private life with the girls: they were too close, too emotional. She knew they would support her, no matter what. Somehow she needed a second point of view, an outsider's opinion. Robert Ryan had proved interesting, knowledgeable and entertaining.

Throughout the summer, their phone calls continued. They began to meet regularly. Robert's annulment case was coming to a close. Ruby's hung precariously in a strangely silent interlude. The waiting was torturous. Robert helped her through it, marking out the stages, so that Ruby knew what to expect.

She doubled her workload, and decided to redecorate her apartment. When the marriage had broken down, they had decided to sell the house. Ruby had been certain that she couldn't stay there and Eamonn had felt the same. With her share of the sale, she had moved into a small apartment block, not far from her parents' house.

She had a beautiful view of Howth and easy access to the city centre, where she still worked. She buried herself in household chores, thinking up more jobs as she went along. The light switches benefited from some Jif spray. The carpets had a second shampooing. She descaled the kettle and the washing-machine. She attacked the iron with a Brillo pad and cleaned the windows with vinegar and newspaper. She treated the silverware to some Silver Dip until it looked like it had just been purchased. Still yearning for more, she climbed into the attic. Great! At least another couple of days' cleaning!

She hounded her solicitor to push harder for a court date. Eamonn repeatedly returned the unsigned document, finding fault with the tiniest detail. She filled her hours and minutes with activity, and more activity. The busier she kept, the better she coped. Her days were crammed with chores, appointments, phone calls. She exhausted herself mentally and physically. It should have been enough to keep the demons away. There was only so much running around she could do. Time passed. In February, the familiar marking on the Archbishop's House envelope landed on her hall carpet.

Dublin Regional Marriage Tribunal,
Diocesan Offices,
Archbishop's House,
Dublin 9

Nullity of Marriage: Reece — Blake
J.2 254/95.

Personal and Confidential
12 February 1996
Dear Mrs Blake,

I am writing to you concerning the present position of the above case for nullity.

Ms Marjory Hand, the witness nominated by you, has not attended for interview.

Perhaps you could have a word with her, so that this case can progress to the next stage.

With kind wishes,
Yours sincerely,

Aidan Mason
Tribunal Secretary

Ruby sat at her kitchen table. The weather had taken a turn, and the cold seeped through her bones, making her shiver. She turned up the heat and sipped her coffee. The letter from the Archbishop's House lay open in front of her. It had been months since she had heard anything. She contemplated phoning Robert, but knew that she really needed to talk to Marjory. The thought of phoning her made her uneasy. She tried to be logical. Maybe there had been some clerical error. Perhaps she hadn't received the notification from the Tribunal. Perhaps the letter had got lost in the Christmas post. Perhaps she had forgotten. But she still found it hard to ignore the knot in her stomach, and the tiny voice telling her the truth: Majory had probably decided not to attend. After much deliberation, Ruby decided she had to tell someone. She lifted the phone.

Judy answered almost immediately.

'Judy, it's me, Ruby.'

'Hello,' Judy answered.

'How are you? It feels like years since I talked to you.'

'Ditto.' Judy yawned.

'I've just had a letter from the Archbishop's House.' Ruby paused, giving Judy the opportunity to take up the cue if she knew something already, but Judy remained silent.

'You know about the annulment, don't you?' Ruby pushed.

'Yes,' Judy replied flatly.

'They say Marjory hasn't turned up as witness and they suggested I contact her. What do you think?'

'What do I think about what?' Judy answered, with no emotion.

'Should I contact her? Have you spoken with her? Do you know why she hasn't gone?' Ruby chanced.

'I'm sorry, Ruby, it's best I don't get involved,'

'Why not?'

'I just can't.'

'Judy? What's going on? Do you know something I don't?'

'Look, please don't keep asking me. I told you, I don't want to get dragged into this.'

'Can you please explain to me why you've suddenly decided you don't want to be involved?' Ruby was flummoxed.

'You won't like it.'

'Try me.'

'OK, you asked for it. I understand you're applying for an annulment on the grounds of non-consummation,' Judy said, with a hint of disgust.

'What? Who told you that?' There was a long silence at both ends.

'Look, I suppose I shouldn't know, but I do. How could you stoop so low?' she asked.

'For goodness' sake! You don't understand. The Church has to look at all possible grounds, I just . . . '

Ruby tried to defend herself but Judy interrupted: 'Oh, c'mon, Ruby, we all know you had a sex life! For Christ's sake, what do you take us for?'

'Who's 'us'? Marjory's been in touch with you, hasn't she?' Ruby's stomach turned over.

'Oh, enough of this bullshit! So what if she has? Do you think we were all born yesterday? Ruby, for once in your life get real. What do you think this is — a game of chess? Don't you have any conscience whatsoever? What about Eamonn? Don't you think he's suffered enough? It's not his fault!' she pontificated.

'It's my fault, then. Isn't that what you're implying? It's my fault! Who's side are you on, anyway? You've never even asked me how I feel,' Ruby said, plainly hurt.

'Hey! Since when did I get *permission* to ask you? Ruby, you never tell us anything, do you? I hardly ever hear from you and when I do it's usually because you want something, like now!' Judy said angrily.

'That's not true,' Ruby said, wishing she sounded more convincing.

'Things didn't go exactly according to plan, so you changed course. Just like that!

You just do your own thing, regardless of the consequences. You make a decision, then insist it happens. Life isn't like that. You can't make life do what you want it to do. Tell the truth, Ruby! You know damn well what this is *really* all about.'

'I don't know what you're talking about!' Ruby was hysterical, her words tumbling out in an avalanche of fear.

'When are you going to stop making him pay for something he didn't do?'

Ruby gripped the phone. Suddenly, the penny dropped. It landed with a clank so loud it reverberated and echoed through every brain cell. 'I see,' she said, holding her dignity. The recent recollection of Marjory's letter had made her suspicious again. Paranoia, coupled with anger, made her jump to outrageous conclusions.

'I see quite clearly now,' Ruby repeated, quickly putting two and two together. 'How easy it is for you lot to pronounce judgement. I appreciate your supposed good counsel, but I wasn't born yesterday either. This is all coming from Marjory, isn't it?' Her voice had become soft.

'What? What the hell are you on about?' Ruby could tell that Judy was feigning ignorance.

'Marj and Eamonn!' Ruby still hoped there

was a chance she was wrong. 'Ever since that bloody letter on our wedding night. She always wanted him for herself.' Ruby remembered the flowers. It was crystal clear.

'You're paranoid!' Judy screamed at her. 'It's all about the baby! This is all about the fucking baby, Ruby!'

Ruby slammed the phone down ignoring Judy's words, all she could think of was Marjory. She berated herself for having thought that Marjory would take her side. Marjory's attraction to Eamonn had always been evident, but it had been unrequited until now. She tried hard not to dwell on her obsessive thoughts. Eamonn and Marjory? The mere thought of it made her feel sick. She didn't know whom to turn to any more. Perhaps they were all taking Eamonn's side.

She dressed hurriedly and called Robert Ryan. He agreed to meet her in their favourite coffee shop in Phibsboro. They were certain of privacy there.

By the time Ruby arrived she was shaking with fear. Robert was calm and attentive. She explained what had happened on the telephone with Judy.

Her hands moved swiftly. She lined up the pepper, tomato ketchup and vinegar to form a perfect triangle. She drew circles in the sugar bowl with the Valium bottle, stamping the surface every couple of seconds — some grains spilt on to the table, giving her extra work. She dotted her finger on them in until they had all been collected.

'Please don't tell me I'm imagining things. I've always had my doubts about Marjory. That I can handle, but I'm surprised at Judy. She knew what was going on. Now I'm wondering does Brenda know too? Why haven't they called to get my side of the story? And Eamonn? I'm shocked at Eamonn. Oh, why are men so easily led?' she asked, her concern for Eamonn's conduct indecently exposed.

'I can see what's happening. The way to keep the door closed is to pile people up against it . . . ' Robert paused 'besides, you have no evidence whatsoever to assume they are having an affair,' he said calmly.

'Oh, please! She's been seeing him. She even knew what grounds I had made the application on. The humiliation!' she seethed.

'Look, calm down,' he said quietly, and reached across the table. She slipped her fingers into his palm. It was warm and comforting.

'What are the grounds?' he said suddenly.

Ruby bit her lip.

'*What are the grounds?*' he repeated, holding her eyes with his.

Ruby bent her head. 'I believe I have a case based on non-consummation,' she answered, with great sadness.

'I see,' Robert said, rubbing the back of her hand with his thumb. 'Very difficult.'

She nodded. Her right hand was free to roam. She began to gather up the crumbs that lay scattered on the table.

'Do you want to talk about it? You will have to eventually.'

'Why?' Her head jolted up.

'Because you have committed yourself.' He squeezed her hand tightly.

'I can't,' she said.

Robert shrugged his shoulders and let out a deep sigh. 'It's sink, or swim,' he said, staring deeply into her eyes. 'How's your swimming?' he added, with a sly smile.

Ruby burst out laughing, her dimples dancing up and down. Robert lifted her hand to his lips and kissed it. Ruby watched with curiosity: her hand had disobediently succumbed. Then she pulled back, appalled at her lack of self-discipline. 'How long has yours gone on for?' She tried to regain her composure. She filled the ashtray with foreign objects.

'Four years.'

'Was it worth it?' she asked.

'Yes, every single minute of it,' he said

quietly. 'Ruby, you're full of little plots and plans.'

'I don't understand you. What's so funny?' she asked.

'You have a way of dealing with life, which, frankly, I think you should consider reviewing,' he said gently.

'I've done my best!' she defended herself. 'I did all the right things. I tried to be a good wife. I was a good homemaker, good at my job too,' she said, with certainty. Robert just kept grinning. 'What?' she said.

'Just because we do all the right things doesn't guarantee that life will run smoothly. You seem to think that if you keep in line with the rules of the world everything should come your way, there should be no difficulties. You have paid your debt and you should receive your just rewards.'

'Exactly. That's what I think. I'm glad you agree.'

'I never said I agreed.' He cocked his head sideways.

Ruby opened her mouth and shut it again.

'It's quite natural for people to disagree, Ruby. Life would be very boring if it was as simple as you think it should be.' He laughed.

'I don't understand you, but I would like to be able to think the way you think. I confess,

I have had great expectations from life,' she confided.

'Expectations only lead to disappointment. If you hadn't expected anything you wouldn't feel so cheated,' Robert commented.

Ruby squirmed. She couldn't argue with him because she felt there was truth in his words, which made her feel most uncomfortable. 'Well, why bother playing by the rules?' she asked him. 'Surely there is some merit in trying to get things right?'

'Of course there is, but what is the motive underneath? Do you want to be right or do you want to be happy?' Robert challenged her.

Ruby instinctively thought of Eamonn. She began to apply Robert's theory to their marriage.

She opened her mouth and, wave after wave, her life with Eamonn spilled out. She couldn't control her tongue. She tried to bite it, but it just did its own thing. The table was cluttered with empty coffee cups. Robert kept buying more. Ruby stuck to her boiled water and decaff.

'And another thing.

'And another thing.

'And another thing.'

Ruby let it come. The words rolled off her tongue, and soon Marjory was not the centre of the conversation any more. Ruby was. She talked about herself for the first time ever. She really talked. She hardly recognised her own voice.

Way back in 1988, when they had married, it had all seemed so simple. At least, that was what Ruby had been led to believe. You find the one you love, you marry them and you live happily ever after. Listening to herself now, she could not identify with one single solitary facet of that old Ruby. The one that was stuck in a box. A box of her own making. The box had been labelled: 'I am whatever you want me to be.' A human chameleon.

She had done it for so long she had lost touch with what she was, who she was and what she really wanted to be: free, loved, wanted, accepted, content, Ruby Reece.

The first two years of marriage had been good. Weren't they always? She raised an eyebrow at Robert who sat, head cupped in hands, listening with a wise ear.

★ ★ ★

Ruby's memories were subtle, and observant. Robert was loving it. It was his first chance to hear a female point of view. He could connect Ruby's feelings to his ex-wife's and understand her pain. This was helping him too

— helping him to complete the circle of his own healing.

Ruby and Eamonn had bought a nice house near to their offices in the city centre. It was an old, three-bedroomed semi-detached on the North Strand, large enough for an extending family. It was solid, roomy and accessible. The property climate had been good — recession was rife — and they picked it up for a steal. Ruby insisted on redecorating. She had wanted her own home all her life and had to make her mark.

True to her own fashion, she peeled away each layer of wallpaper, dismantled every kitchen unit, stripped off every paint stroke, dug up the garden and raided the outhouse. It was hers. She was going to make it an altar. A place that marked her identity. A sacred domain. A place that you knew instantly was Ruby's home.

Eamonn showed little interest in the redecorating; he was busy with work commitments, as usual. Ruby didn't mind: it gave her more control. Each day Eamonn returned to a new house. Sometimes he failed to notice even a major reconstruction. The house was constantly in disarray.

Bulldozers permanently occupied the front garden, which was strewn with gravel and bricks. Sweaty workmen traipsed in and out of the kitchen. Lorries and trucks arrived. The bedroom was green on a Monday, pink on Friday. Eamonn showed no concern for the endless expenditure. As long as she was happy, he rolled out his signature at the bottom of any piece of paper she handed him.

They tripped over cement bags, slid through narrow gaps between parked vans and cavorted with stepladders.

The only room that had any sense of harmony was the bedroom. There, they left the workaday life behind. Barriers fell, inhibitions melted, passion spilled. Their well of love seemed as if it would never dry up. They never tired of each other's company. The way Eamonn left the lid off the toothpaste amused Ruby. The crumpled underwear on the landing thrilled Eamonn. Ruby took a dive into the curious world of culinary takeouts: Indian, Chinese, Greek, lots of Italian. Eamonn loved it.

She patted his paunch proudly. After all, she had played a part in its birth. She had helped to round it into a finely sculpted pot-belly. Like a pregnant mother, Eamonn stuck out his masterpiece, proud and dignified.

Robert burst out laughing at this image of Eamonn.

Ruby stopped. The word 'pregnant' hung in the air like a dying wasp, waiting to implant its final sting.

She stared at Robert, willing more words to come, but they were wedged tight, locked in a voiceless throat.

Robert pulled a green blade from among the stems in the flower vase. He opened her hand and placed it in the palm. Then he concocted a story.

Ruby listened gratefully, knowing he was taking her back to the coffee shop, back to reality, the real world.

'Do you see this?' he started. 'Now, this blade of greenery comes from the land of the humpy-back rabbits.'

Ruby smiled.

'Great kings and queens have wandered over the hills and lands looking for it. It has great powers, you see. Horses have ridden on it, dogs have shat on it and lovers have . . . well, you know what lovers have done.'

Ruby threw back her head and laughed. 'You're mad. They'll annul your marriage, no question. It's a clear-cut case of insanity.' Then she placed her gift carefully in a white tissue, opened her bag and lodged it in one of the inside pockets. 'To add to my collection,' she joked. 'You're a natural storyteller. Where did you get it from?' She leaned over the table, her lips inches from his.

'It's something I picked up as a grandfather. My grandchildren love stories,' he replied.

'No one will ever know,' she whispered.

'Know what?' he whispered back.

'That you're a crackpot!'

'And *I* promise not to tell . . . ' Robert paused.

'Not to tell?' she repeated, sweeping the table with her open palm.

' . . . That you're an obsessive-compulsive cleaning addict.'

'What?' She feigned ignorance, embarrassed again by her quirks. But somehow Robert hadn't offended her. This was odd: the same remark from someone else would have put her in mind never to speak to him or her again. She decided to pretend not to know what he was talking about.

She leaned forward and pinched his cheek. Her nail scraped his skin.

Robert glanced at his watch and Ruby followed suit. She saw that they had talked for over three hours. Her limbs were tired, as if she had just run a marathon. 'Ever thought of being a counsellor?' she asked, in the middle of a big yawn.

'What?' He smirked.

'You'd make a good counsellor. Ever thought about it?' she repeated.

'You think I'm the crazy one? What kind of an idea is that? Look at me, I can hardly button my coat, for Christ's sake.'

Ruby went to his aid.

Robert stood awkwardly until she had finished. 'Thanks, *Mammy*.'

'No problem, *Daddy*.'

Robert's face turned to stone. Ruby wondered why.

They said goodbye, and Ruby kissed his cheek, like a dutiful daughter. Robert patted her back, then went across the street, tipping his hat. He waved without turning.

14

Eamonn was falling in love again. The object of his affection had long blonde hair woven into two plaits, a rather noticeable brace and knobbly knees. Jessica had always been the apple of Eamonn's eye. He frequently took Jessica on outings to the zoo, the pictures and McDonald's. He enjoyed being a godfather and took the responsibility seriously.

Today was Jessica's eighth birthday and Marjory had organised a fancy-dress party at home. Twenty-one boisterous kids had stormed the house. The parents had been taken hostage. Jessica, acting as commander, had led the coup. Volunteer helpers, verging on a nervous breakdown, were already absconding when Eamonn arrived.

He smiled as he remembered Jessica in Ruby's wedding dress. He had explained to Marjory that it had been in the back of the car. When Marjory asked what it was doing there he was lost for words. He had made up his mind there and then: if Jessica wanted it, and Ruby didn't, he was happy to give it to her. He knew Jessica would love dressing up in it. He carried it with six beautifully wrapped presents, in his arms — like a miniature Leaning Tower of Pisa — and had made it to the door, when they began to topple.

★ ★ ★

Marjory had been watching from the bedroom window. Her heart thumped as Eamonn walked towards the door. She took the stairs two at a time but still managed to look calm as she greeted him. Eamonn laughed as Jessica spun round in circles holding the dress up to her envious friends. She was already kitted out as a princess. Eamonn scanned the hallway. They were all princesses, all twenty-one of them.

'Can I really have it? I mean, is it for keeps?' She jumped up and down like a jack-in-the-box.

'Yes.'

Marjory folded her arms, in an effort to appear unaffected.

She shook whenever Eamonn stood near her. His larger-than-life presence always made her feel like a mushy pea.

Jessica was tearing into the presents. Other children gathered around her to join in the excitement. A small boy, in a Batman suit, got quite upset when he realised the gifts were not for him. He grabbed one, stuck it up his jumper and legged it. His mother chased after him, pleading with him to return it.

'Let him keep it!' Marjory shouted over the rapidly rising din. 'You bought her far too many presents, Eamonn. You spoil her!' She slipped her arm through his and pulled him towards the kitchen.

'I wouldn't worry if I were you. It's a Barbie doll,' Eamonn said.

At the mere mention of Barbie the posse of children moved like a swarm of bees after the little boy. He dropped the doll like a hot coal, turned his mouth down, took a deep breath and let out a piercing wail.

The mammy came to the rescue. She placated him with television: she turned it on, plonked him in front of it, and the drama was over as quickly as it had started.

In the kitchen, Judy and Brenda were helping out with the table. Eamonn's large frame left little room for manoeuvring.

'You're a sucker for punishment.' Brenda elbowed him.

'She's my godchild,' he said proudly. 'I take it this is supposed to be jelly?' He held up a bowl with a green watery substance inside.

'My fault. Too much water,' Brenda confessed.

'I just stood on a coconut cream!' Judy yelled in disgust.

'Be quiet, Judy! It's not the end of the world.' Marjory bent down to examine the gooey lino. Something else crunched beneath her foot.

'Chocolate marshmallow,' Eamonn confirmed. 'I made contact myself in the hall.' He lifted his foot to demonstrate.

'My head is lifting,' Judy complained. 'Has anyone any Valium?'

'I've taken all mine and Marjory's. I've had to borrow some of Brenda's sleepers,' Eamonn joked.

'I don't believe in sleeping pills,' Brenda contradicted him.

'No, but you would if you had two kids who made more noise than a battle scene from *Braveheart*,' Judy told her.

'Quit whining, Judy. How would you like one of those sweet little things for keeps?' Marjory appeared from under the table, her knees covered in a sticky white mush.

'Then you'd really have something to complain about,' Brenda added.

'No, thanks. All I have to do is look at how much you've aged since you had those two. How do they manage to make such noise? And the brat in the Batman gear. If he was mine, I'd hurl him out the window.'

'Ssh! His mum's outside. Here, take some of these.' Brenda offered Judy some strange-looking capsules. 'A herbal remedy,' she added confidently. She pulled a tray of butterfly buns from the fridge and circled them on a large plate.

'What the hell *are* these?' Judy swallowed them like a drug addict.

Eamonn picked up the bottle and pretended to read the ingredients: 'Snail intestine, frog's breath and bats' testicles.'

Judy spewed out the tablets. 'A good strong drink is what I want,' she spluttered. As she leaned forward, her hair spilled into a bowl of cream. 'Oh, Christ! They've even ruined my hair!' she whimpered. She pushed the bowl into the middle of the table.

'We can't use that now! Judy, tie your hair up, for God's sake. It's obvious you're not used to the domestic side of life but you could at least pretend.' Eamonn sounded like a father of fifteen.

'The way it is with kids,' Brenda started, 'you have to let them know who is the boss right from the start. Right, Marj?'

'Too right.' Marjory stood with her hands on her hips, her face and hair covered in flour and a silly party hat perched precariously on her crown.

'Mam, can I open all the presents?' Jessica

bounded into the kitchen, wand and golden slippers in tow.

'Yes, love, if you want.'

'Oh, yeah, you're the boss, Marjory.' Brenda winked at Eamonn. 'I read a very interesting article about kids the other day. Did you know, for instance, that kids — '

'Ruin your clothes, your sex life, mess up your house *and* they smell,' Judy finished for her.

'Only babies smell. You're thinking of babies,' Eamonn said, with authority.

The girls were loath to make any comment. The word 'baby' had been banned from all conversations. It had the same effect as an atomic bomb.

'Babies make me cringe! The way they puke all over you and — '

Judy was assaulted by two sets of accusing eyes. They advised her to shut up *right now*.

Eamonn was busying himself with a stack of plastic tumblers. 'Is she coming?' he asked suddenly.

'Who?' Judy asked innocently, convincing everyone once and for all that she had absolutely no acting ability.

'Judy, that was pathetic.' Eamonn confirmed it.

'She's not coming,' Marjory said.

'You did invite her, Marjory, didn't you?'

he asked, a little annoyed.

'Of course she did!' Brenda answered. 'Did you see that cute little pair of dungarees from Marks and Spencer's she sent over?'

Judy made a mighty swing of her left foot, kicking Brenda under the table. '*Shut up,*' she mouthed.

'You girls are so obvious.' Eamonn arranged the plastic cups on a tray with creative flair, 'with your little tell-tale signs. You think us guys are stupid, eh? That we don't know when you're talking behind our backs?' He sounded amused.

'We don't know what you're talking about.' Marjory stuck out her tongue at him.

'Sure you don't. That's why you just made an ugly face behind my back. Remember what Mother used to say: if you make a face and the wind changes you'll stay like that.' He turned round with a triumphant grin.

'I thought it was a considerable improvement,' Judy sneered.

'Hey, Miss Free-and-Easy, what's new in your love-life? Are you still seeing Georgy-Porgy?' He changed the subject.

'Free perhaps. Easy? I don't think so.'

'Most definitely easy,' Marjory butted in.

'Speak for yourself!' Judy laughed.

'Well?' Eamonn pressed.

'Nothing worth reporting.' Judy shook back

her hair. She sat awkwardly on the edge of a chair, her long legs complicating everything.

'Come, now. I don't believe you. What's happened to the lustful Arabian nights?' he egged her on.

'I never said anything about lustful Arabian nights. You're confusing me with Marjory,' she joked, winking at Brenda. They had both seen the sudden flush in Marjory's cheeks when Eamonn arrived. While loyal to their friend, neither felt that they wanted to see that particular union come to fruition, at least not until poor Ruby had laid her ghosts to rest.

'Me? I don't think so. I don't know any Arabic men, never mind lustful ones,' Marjory mused.

'Don't you ever get tired of married men, Judy?' Eamonn went on.

'Why should I?' she answered flatly.

'Why don't you pick some ordinary bloke for a change?' Marjory asked.

'Yeah. Like, someone who wants a relationship with you,' Brenda put in.

'Someone who might even be available from time to time,' Eamonn added.

'Hey, knock it off! I love George! We have a great relationship. It's fun. It's exciting. It's full of surprises! I like it this way!' Judy said. 'I don't want any commitments. Foot-loose and fancy-free, that's me!' She dried the ends of her hair with a tea-towel. 'Why are you all so interested in my love life? Why don't you quiz Brenda? She's practically a nun. Why, I can even see her in a sexy little habit,' she jeered.

'I'm *Waiting for Godot*,' Brenda joked.

'A dark mysterious stranger,' Marjory and Judy said, in spooky voices.

'Did I miss something?' Eamonn looked at Brenda.

'You always miss something,' Judy answered for her. She gazed in Marjory's direction.

Marjory was in a dream-like state, frequently staring at Eamonn and unashamedly flashing a smile at him at every available opportunity.

Brenda and Judy had discussed the scenario on countless occasions. Both were convinced that Eamonn's heart was still locked somewhere inside Ruby's soul. No matter what Marjory might think, they were unable to envisage her friendship with Eamonn ever crossing the line into a full-blown romantic encounter.

The conversation stopped just long enough for all participants to notice that things seemed quieter than usual.

'Hey, there's an eerie silence. It can only mean one thing. Trouble. Judy, it's your turn to go and check,' Marjory ordered. She wanted a few moments to relish Eamonn's presence in her kitchen, to indulge in her favourite fantasy.

'Brenda, I think you could pick up the birthday cake now. I don't really want to leave Jessica alone with the other kids.' She laid on the hints with a trowel.

'Why didn't you collect it yourself? Thunders is only down the road,' Brenda asked, a little miffed.

'I hadn't the time, I swear,' Marjory replied.

'You can do the lotto for me while you're there,' Eamonn joined in.

Brenda obliged them both by agreeing to go.

At last, Marjory had him to herself. She knew he was too shy to drop deliberate hints but he wanted to be alone with her too, she was sure. She watched his hands as they glided over the table, his fingers working fluidly as he placed the drinks in a straight line. Just for fun, he added some cocktail umbrellas.

'You know, I always wanted a party. We never had parties when we were kids. I'm really enjoying this!' Eamonn said.

'I have noticed,' Marjory winked at him.

'You're looking very well, Marjory.'

'Thanks! And thanks for coming. I really appreciate it. Jessica is so thrilled with the dress. Are you sure you want to give it to her? You know it will be ruined,' she purred.

'Yes. Isn't it wonderful? Let them all traipse up and down until the ends are frayed! Nothing would give me greater pleasure,' he said, a hint of sarcasm creeping into his voice.

'You don't mean that, Eamonn,' Marjory sidled up to him and rested an ambitious arm on his back.

'I meant it. Not a hint of ambiguity,' he sang. She waited for the retraction, which came instantly. 'I don't mean that. You're right.' He sighed.

'She isn't talking to me, you know,' Marjory said.

'She's not talking to anybody.' He turned to face her.

Marjory looked up, her eyes misty and round like two big water-lilies. 'You still haven't told me whom the flowers were for?' She moved closer.

'Someone very special,' Eamonn tapped the side of his nose.

She was inches away from his mouth. *Kiss me*, she thought. *Kiss me now.*

Brenda had returned with the birthday cake. 'Quickly! You have to see this for yourself!' She stormed in through the door, put it on the table and beckoned to them to follow her. 'Ssh.' She put her finger across her lips, and motioned towards the living-room door, which was ajar. Through it they could just see Judy, her hair crudely put up in one of Jessica's banana combs. They peered in. She was trying to exude the authorative air of an experienced parent, but the kids behaved as if she was invisible. She eventually broke through the circle they had formed. The object of interest sat in the middle. It was the television.

★   ★   ★

Judy was stunned when she realised what they were watching. The six o'clock news for the deaf.

'Why is that guy waving his hands like that?' a little girl asked.

'Because he has no brains,' Batman replied assuredly.

'Oh,' the little girl said, accepting his explanation as gospel fact.

Judy scratched her head in disbelief. 'What's wrong with you lot? Why aren't you smashing up the place? Shouldn't you at least be watching *Terminator* or something?' The kids looked at her with bewilderment. 'Come on, now. Who wants to desecrate the fireplace?' she challenged them.

'Is she the magician?' one whispered.

'Looks more like a witch,' another warbled.

'I don't like witches,' another piped up.

'I want my mam.' The three-year-old began to blubber, setting the pace for the mother of all crying concertos. One of the princesses began to wail, another joined in, and a third harmonised with perfect pitch. Pretty soon they were all at it, reaching octaves that Maria Callas only dreamed of.

★　★　★

Marjory and Brenda listened outside. With their ears pressed against the door, they smothered their laughter.

Judy marched out of the room, purple in the face. 'Go ahead. Laugh. You have to live with them. I can leave whenever I feel like it!' she cried triumphantly.

Marjory put her arms around her.

Brenda chuckled.

Marjory's eyes wandered to Eamonn. 'Did you ever see anything like it in your life?' She tried to attract his attention.

Judy and Brenda were still rolling in the aisles.

'Eamonn? Did you hear me?' Marjory tried again.

Eamonn was oblivious to the whole scenario.

Marjory followed his eyes. They were focused on Jessica and there was a haunted look in them. It was a parental look, slightly worried, slightly in awe. There was also an indefinable sadness. It draped around him like a perilous, unyielding mist. Would he ever find his way out of it, Marjory wondered.

15

Dublin Regional Marriage Tribunal,
Diocesan Offices,
Archbishop's House,
Dublin 9

Nullity of Marriage: Reece — Blake
J.2.254/95.

Personal and Confidential

10 March 1996

Dear Mrs Blake,

I wish to advise you that we have now
arranged an appointment for you with one
of our psychologists on Friday, 15 March,
at 9.30 a.m. It will take approximately
three hours. Please complete and return
the enclosed Biographical Data Sheet
immediately and forward it to us.

The fee for psychological assessment is
£95. We would appreciate it if you would
kindly let us have this amount in advance
of you keeping your appointment. We shall

pay the sum to the psychologist on your behalf. If this request should cause you a problem please let us know and we shall be happy to do what we can to help.

It is very important to note that if you are unable to keep your appointment, you must telephone the Tribunal Secretary at least one day in advance in order to cancel it. Otherwise, the psychologist will be in attendance for your appointment, and a fee of £95 will be incurred.

Your kind co-operation in this matter will enable us to make progress with the case and will be much appreciated.

With kind wishes,
Yours sincerely,

Aidan Mason
Tribunal Administrator

Ruby arrived early for her appointment. The waiting room had returned to its former *Ice Cold in Alex* glory. She shivered with a mixture of fatigue and dead feet. Presently a kind-faced young woman called her. They walked down several corridors to a small room.

It was comfortable and warm. Thank God, she thought. She did not relish three hours in freezing temperatures with a quack. The atmosphere was surprisingly intimate: the room was darkened just a shade, an enormous family-sized box of Kleenex, a jar of water, and an ashtray lay on the table. Ruby fiddled nervously with the box of tissues, and moulded one into a fan.

There was no desk, just two comfortable armchairs facing each other. The walls were painted a cool mint green, one of her favourite colours. It was a homely environment.

The woman was soft-spoken and gentle. 'I'm Rosanna.' She took Ruby's hand and shook it with both of hers. 'It's very nice to meet you, Mrs Blake.'

Ruby was impressed that she knew her name and did not have to consult her files to find it. 'How was the traffic this morning? The Drumcondra Road is always so busy.'

'I'm getting used to it,' Ruby replied, stifling a yawn.

'Tired?' Rosanna asked.

'Yes. I apologise. I had a late night. Silly, really. I knew where I was coming this morning and I just couldn't sleep,' she finished.

'Don't worry. Perhaps a cup of tea and a biscuit before we start?' Rosanna picked up the telephone and ordered some tea to be sent to the room.

'Just boiled water,' Ruby instructed her, as she laid out the Valium jar, the silver spoon and the Canderel.

'As you wish.' The counsellor paid no heed to the ritual. 'Did you remember to bring your autobiographical sheet with you?' she asked.

'Yes. I have it here.' Ruby rummaged in her bag and handed it to her.

Rosanna read through the paper, adjusting her glasses as her eyes roamed downwards. 'Perfect!'

The tea arrived. Ruby added her coffee to the boiled water. She lifted her silver spoon and popped in two Canderel sweeteners. Rosanna ignored this and went through the sheet of paper, checking date of marriage, date of birth, etc. Then she chuckled.

'What's so funny?' Ruby asked.

'Your answer to the last question,' Rosanna answered.

'You know . . . how do you feel about this visit?'

Ruby smiled.

'You have answered: 'What's wrong with me?' '

Ruby blushed.

'I can understand your fears,' Rosanna said. 'Do you mean, why are you being assessed psychologically?'

'Yes,' Ruby said flatly.

'Well, I am not here to judge your academic intelligence. This is not a test of any sort. It is simply a process of getting to know you better. The assessment will help me understand you, and I will forward my view to the Tribunal. You are not under scrutiny, nor is there anything wrong with you, Mrs Blake. We are not looking for poor intelligence or flaws of character.'

Ruby nodded. Somehow, she trusted Rosanna and was not adverse to having the assessment.

'Now, Mrs Blake, given what I have already told you, just relax, take it easy. We will first do what's known as a CPI test,'

'What's that?' Ruby asked, trying not to sound stupid.

'The California Psychological Inventory,' Rosanna said. 'Just listen to the following statements that I am going to make. All I want you to do is tick on your page where you might think you belong in regard to that statement. For instance, if the statement would be true of your character, tick 5, if not tick 1, if you're not sure 3. Can you do that for me?'

Ruby nodded, feeling like a schoolchild. She reminded herself that it was not an intelligence test.

"I have a natural talent for influencing people." Rosanna read out the first statement.

Ruby ticked 5, thinking about her job. She thought about other situations with Eamonn. Should she change it to 3?

"I am lacking in self-confidence."

Ruby wavered between 4 and 5. Her pencil hovered with uncertainty.

The statements kept coming. Ruby ticked the sheet as honestly as she could. Before long, they were finished. Rosanna collected the paper and placed it in a folder.

'How am I doing so far?' Ruby enquired.

'Just fine,' Rosanna reassured her.

'The next test we are going to do is called a TAT. The Thematic Apperception Test,' she said.

Ruby shrugged her shoulders, trying to remain dignified.

'I am going to show you a selection of picture cards. I want you to look closely at the picture then tell me what you think might have happened prior to the event, what is going on in the event, and what may be the outcome of the event.'

Ruby's head spun. She had never been a storyteller. She picked up the first card and tried to concentrate. Her mind was blank. She was struggling to imagine anything other than the complete eejit she must seem, holding this bloody card.

'Ruby? Can I call you Ruby?' Rosanna intervened.

Ruby peered over the card like a bold two-year-old. She was consumed with embarrassment.

'Just look at the picture, study it, let your mind ramble,' Rosanna encouraged her.

The picture showed a boy sitting at a piano. Ruby sighed and pushed her blonde hair behind her ears with a perfect circling motion. 'I think the boy would like to play the piano. Perhaps his mother came in earlier and gave out to him for something. I hope he reaches his hands out and plays it afterwards.' Ruby peered at Rosanna over the card, looking for affirmation.

'Interesting,' Rosanna said, making notes in her file. She handed Ruby another card.

Ruby studied it. The picture was of a woman sitting on the edge of a sofa, looking back over her shoulder at an older man with a pipe in his mouth. He seemed to be addressing her.

She took her time, trying not to smile. Robert Ryan jumped right on to the card. Ruby tried to will him away. Emotions played with her composure.

'Well,' Ruby murmured, 'this woman has her back turned. Maybe she doesn't really want to have a conversation with him. Perhaps she was deep in thought before he interrupted her. She's sitting on the edge of the seat. She's ready to run. Perhaps he's her father. He's some kind of authority figure. He's older, sterner-looking. I wish she'd turn round to face him and pay attention to what he's saying. It could be important.' She lowered the card.

★ ★ ★

Rosanna was fascinated. She sensed that in Ruby's life the picture on this card held a deeper meaning. The test was working its magic without any help from her. Each card drew more of Ruby's character to the surface. She struggled with specific issues immensely — issues of denial, of being bullied, perhaps? A strong streak of perfectionism, a need to be always correct?

Rosanna scribbled across the page, barely able to keep up. Ruby was doing all the work. It was all happening perfectly. Eventually her pen stalled.

★ ★ ★

'Excellent. Now I am going to show you some patterns. I want you to tell me what you see in them. People often see objects, words or pictures in them.' Rosanna handed her a brightly coloured collage of shapes and lines.

Ruby found this much more difficult. She was being asked to use her imagination.

'You don't have to look at it one way only. You can turn it upside down, sideways. Explore, Ruby.'

Ruby turned the card upside down. 'Oh, I see clouds, there in the corner ... a mushroom-type thingy — no, maybe it's a butterfly, I don't know?' She looked to Rosanna for help.

'That's it, just keep looking, describe to me what you see, no matter how silly it seems.'

Ruby was thoughtful. She took her time, turning it up, sideways, over and back again. She held it an angle. She placed it on the table before her and leaned over it.

She looked deeply into myriad patterns. She drew an imaginary line down the middle, across to the right and ended in the corner. She was becoming agitated, restless, shuffling in her seat. She scratched her head, fiddled with her hair, clenched her fist, and bit her lip. Then she began to wheeze.

She raised her head. A lone tear was making a solitary journey along her jawline. No sound came from her mouth.

Rosanna took her hand. 'Look again,' she

said. 'It's OK, Ruby. What were you pointing at? What is it?' She moved out of her chair, stood behind Ruby and rested her hands on her shoulders.

Ruby began to heave. Almighty shudders rocked her body. Her finger wavered unsteadily, and then drew an outline on the strange patterns.

'It's a baby?' Rosanna guessed.

Ruby's throat expelled a mournful wail. 'It's my baby!' she cried, tears splashing downwards. They poured on to the table, on to the card. 'My dead baby!' She wept. Rosanna held her tightly, rocking her.

Ruby swiped at the tissue box and began mopping her eyes, then she attacked the table, making wide sweeps across it with her tissue, polishing the already perfectly polished table. She performed the act as if she was in a state of suspended consciousness, as Rosanna watched.

'Good, Ruby,' she whispered. 'It's OK now. Everything is going to be OK now. I promise. Just let the sounds out. Good girl. Let the sounds out.'

Ruby sobbed, each wave of grief more intense than the last.

Rosanna placed her hand on Ruby's arm, gently guiding it away from the table. She took the tissue from her clenched fist.

The sadness engulfed Ruby, physically penetrated her. Her body was being attacked by long-withheld emotions, which withdrew momentarily, only to gather more troops and assault her again. She felt their swords stab at her heart.

Rosanna buzzed Reception and called for Father Ebbs. Ruby, unaware of anything except the pain of the moment, tried desperately to retrieve her composure. The tears came without permission. She was powerless to stop them. Rosanna kept repeating, 'Let them go. That's good. Let it go, let it out.'

The door opened.

'I hope I didn't disturb you.'

★ ★ ★

Father Ebbs was surprised to see Ruby Blake, knees fastened inside her arms, rocking backwards and forwards in her chair. She looked like an orphan beggar. Her makeup was destroyed, mascara smeared down her cheeks. Her clothes were in disarray, her bra strap exposed for all to see. Rosanna adjusted Ruby's blouse.

Unsure of what to do, Father Ebbs laid a consoling hand on her shoulder. Ruby had stopped weeping now but was still sniffling into a much-used tissue. She didn't seem conscious of her state.

Rosanna took Father Ebbs outside for a moment to fill him in. He knew the ropes. He had seen this happen before. Petitioners frequently broke down and he was called to complete the journey from fiction to truth. Ruby was ready for that now. It was time to close the case.

'I think you should take things from here, Father Ebbs. I feel this would be a good time to talk. Perhaps Ruby can put some things to rest now. You know, strike while the iron is hot?' She had opened Ruby's heart: now the contents would be revealed.

Father Ebbs returned to the room, prepared to meet objections. He sat quietly at first, awaiting the aftermath, the denial. The inevitable 'exit stage left'.

To his amazement Ruby did not take flight, but remained seated, slowly moving herself into a more comfortable position.

★ ★ ★

Ruby felt sore and tired, as if she had done a strenuous workout. But she had started the journey and she would complete it. Battered and bruised she took the bull by the horns. 'I don't know where to start,' she said meekly.

'The beginning would be a good place. Would you like a cup of tea first?' he asked, and settled himself for the duration. Ruby nodded, then lit a cigarette. She took some long drags, then reached for her inhaler and did the same with that.

'You know, it was the lack of understanding,' she began. 'It was the loneliness. I was married, yet inexplicably lonely.' She eyed the priest, wondering how he could understand a woman's isolation. 'I could have dealt with everything with a little support, you know? Just a little support, that's all I needed. Nobody talked about it, nobody acknowledged it, when I lost the baby. Just because I was only three months pregnant. People assumed it wasn't a real baby, not a real death. Oh, but it was to me.' Ruby burst into a fresh bout of tears, her previously steely reserve shattered to the core.

'Mrs Blake,' Father Ebbs removed his glasses and crossed his arms, 'I understand you're distressed but I really need to clarify a point so that I can begin the process of elimination regarding what grounds we can make application on.'

'What do you mean?' she asked, through loud snuffles.

'If you conceived, Mrs Blake, then you had

obviously engaged in sexual intercourse,' he said.

'Of course I had sex with my husband, you imbecile! How else would I have conceived? Through Immaculate Conception? They don't happen very often on the North Strand.' She was humiliated beyond belief.

Father Ebbs scratched his head. 'Mrs Blake, I understand how embarrassing and intrusive such a question may seem but there is no right time for such a query. It is my duty to draw my own conclusions and pass them on to the Tribunal. At this juncture, I feel we must make headway and leave what is not useful behind us. Do you understand?' He leaned forward, directing his question at point-blank range.

'Yes,' she responded.

There was a long, awkward silence.

'You have stated in earlier sessions that you feel you have a case for non-consummation. I must clarify this,' he said.

'What difference does it make whether we had sex or not?' Ruby asked angrily.

'I'm afraid I don't understand you.'

'What is sex? Is it not a God-given gift? The gift of procreation? Is that not what God intended when he created man and woman and their sexual orientation? That they make children? What use is it to me? What use is it to Eamonn? The very thing it was meant to do did not materialise. The act of sex failed to deliver us a child. Is a child not our God-given right? Father? How can God say my marriage was consummated in the true sense without that blessed baby to show for it? Where is the proof of our sexual union? Where is our one truly wholesome *reason* for being men and women?' she asked, and stabbed out her cigarette.

Father Ebbs grabbed at the packet and lit one himself. This distracted Ruby briefly. His nerves were shattered, she thought. After all, she had challenged his theological certainties. Then she wished the ground would swallow her whole. Her cheeks were red with embarrassment. How could she acknowledge her sex life when it had rendered her barren and childless? It seemed a cruel hand to have been dealt. A mocking lie on God's behalf. She took another cigarette and lit up. They sat opposite each other, hoping to smoke away the stupidity and embarrassment.

'Mrs Blake, I do take your point. It is a point worth debating within the structure of annulment applications. I dare say the clergy could spend many interesting hours discussing your theory. I must admit, I never thought of it that way. I'm sorry.' Father Ebbs looked bewildered.

'No, Father. I'm sorry,' Ruby said. 'I should have spoken before now. I thought it would sound better, you see, if I said nothing at all. Anything would have sounded better than the truth. The truth is I found it hard to acknowledge a sex life without there being a child. They go hand in hand, don't they? It didn't lead me to that long-awaited baby and somehow sex became unimportant. It failed to live up to my expectations. On that basis I felt sure I had grounds for non-consummation. I know it sounds silly.' She shuddered.

'Mrs Blake, I am deeply moved by your observations. I can indeed understand why you might think that. You have put forward a very persuasive argument. Unfortunately, though, having sex constitutes consummation of marriage, and there is no way around that.'

'This means I have no case, right?' She looked up at him.

'No. There are other grounds we can explore,' he said wearily.

'You must think I'm the greatest idiot you ever laid eyes on,' Ruby said, ashamed.

'On the contrary, I have found you to be a very smart lady. These technical terms have been misinterpreted in the past. I assure you, you are not the first to do it and certainly won't be the last. I had to train for many

236

years to understand fully the meaning of an annulment and its deciding factors. Please do not feel stupid. I am perplexed, though, Mrs Blake. I am not at all convinced that you understand exactly what this is all about,' Father Ebbs warned her.

Here was a woman who knew everything about sex. Here was a man who knew nothing about it. Yet neither understood anything without the help of the other.

'To continue, I must be assured that what you are telling me is the truth. Do you understand, Mrs Blake?' he said forlornly.

'I give you my word.' Ruby sniffled. 'I just felt I would be judged if I told the whole truth.'

'Mrs Blake, nobody is here to pronounce judgement on you. That includes your own judgement of the situation. There are two sides to the story.'

Ruby nodded, ready to cry again. Any show of compassion would render her inconsolable.

'Good.' The priest nodded. 'Would you like to tell me the real story, Mrs Blake?' he asked.

Ruby was about to walk the tightrope. Father Ebbs would provide the safety-net. In the meantime, the bearded ladies prepared to make their début appearance.

16

When Eamonn and Ruby had been living in their new house for a year, they decided to try for a baby.

Ruby had secretly longed for a child. She rarely confided this notion to Eamonn, always aware of his work commitments, and wanting to give them both time to settle into married life. Time to frolic and have fun without responsibilities.

The plan to have a child came about without much discussion beforehand. Eamonn returned one evening from work to find Ruby knee-deep in pink paint in the boxroom. That was that. They had taken the necessary leap from frivolous lovers to would-be parents. Eamonn mucked in, changing his suit for an old sweater and pants. Ruby painted the walls, Eamonn tackled the ceiling. Ruby noticed that spots of paint came frequently in her direction. She kept painting. Then a massive glob landed on her back. He did that deliberately, she thought. She carried on playing his game.

Eamonn whistled to himself happily. A slap of pink emulsion landed on his backside. He reached behind and dipped his free hand into the bucket that balanced precariously on the stepladder. He flung a handful over Ruby's head and it landed on the wall. It made its way down to land with a squelchy plop on the bare floorboards.

Ruby turned, brush in hand, and smacked Eamonn with it. He picked up the tin and poured the paint over her head. A battle ensued. The room looked like a pink bomb had imploded. They splashed and swam in it, fighting tooth and nail. Ruby could hardly breathe. Paint ran down her face, but the noxious fumes only made her laugh harder. 'Stop! You're going to cause an asthma attack!' she pleaded.

Eamonn was having a ball, diving at her feet like a baseball professional. The curtain-less window exposed their antics to passers-by on the street below. Eamonn opened it and threatened to drown a neighbour. Ruby joined him, her hair matted in emulsion. 'I apologise for my husband's behaviour,' she shouted. 'He can't help it.' They stood breathless in the centre of the room, paint dripping everywhere.

'Now look what you've done,' Eamonn said, in boyish innocence. 'You've gone and ruined the baby's bedroom.'

Ruby eyed him through streaky pink hair,

then wrapped her arms around him, bursting with joy. He kissed her soggy face and they rubbed sticky cheeks.

'Baby?' she said, hopeful she had not misinterpreted.

'Why not?' He licked paint off her neck.

'Eamonn!' she objected.

'How do you know it will be a girl?' he purred in her ear.

'I don't!' she replied.

'Pink for a girl, right?' he said.

'Somehow I think we may have to redecorate the room,' she said. 'We can go blue if you like?' she added, hands on hips looking around.

'Maybe we should settle for green,' he said.

'Environmentally friendly eh?' Ruby laughed.

'I suggest we start straight away.' Eamonn threw her on to the floor, dismantled her clothes and they made love without inhibition. The window remained open, but they didn't care two hoots who heard: they were busy making babies.

Three months later Ruby bought a home pregnancy-testing kit. Her heart soared when the result was positive. They were going to have a family. Their parents would be thrilled. Ruby was excited and scared all at the same time. She imagined the tiny thing growing inside her. All perfect and wonderful and awesome. She didn't have to do a thing! It was so easy! She estimated her delivery date: 14 November 1989, or thereabouts. She couldn't wait to tell Eamonn. She surveyed her slim figure in the mirror. She longed to be fat with life. She relished the idea of bursting at the seams with creative force.

She yearned for backache, piles, and swollen ankles, the more afflictions the better! She ached for breathing exercises, maternity clothes and visits to Mothercare. It was a journey she hoped that Eamonn would join in with just as much enthusiasm. She was in the estuary of possibilities. They had patented a new human being. It was already growing inside her. She couldn't feel anything, except for unusual tiredness. Her breasts were larger than normal. They felt a little swollen and tender to the touch. Nature was preparing them for battle. I love it! I love it all! she thought, dancing around the room in a pair of pants.

Ruby recalled Eamonn's reaction with crystal-clear clarity. He had returned home that evening, tired and weary. The bank was planning a major takeover. Eamonn had been called to negotiate at the head of the table. His communication skills were renowned and sought after. He longed for an end to be in sight. These days, the end in sight had become returning to Ruby. The thought had kept him going through boring luncheons, irritating breakfast meetings and long-drawn-out boardroom quarrels.

That night when he came in, music was blaring and Ruby greeted him at the kitchen door. 'Hi,' she said quietly.

'Hi, pet.' He kissed her.

Ruby could see the exhaustion on his face. She had made preparations in anticipation of this. She led him into the bathroom. The tub had been filled. She had poured in some nice oil and laid out fresh towels. A bottle perched on the locker, two champagne glasses ready for employment.

'What's this?' he said.

'I knew you'd be tired. Have a nice bath and I'll have dinner ready when you're finished.'

'Hey, thanks.' Eamonn kissed her, evidently grateful for her thoughtfulness. The bath would be a welcome treat, Ruby thought, when he must be feeling tired and dirty.

'I see you were shopping again,' he remarked, as he slipped into the warm, scented water.

'I went a bit crazy,' Ruby admitted, thinking of the many bags on the bedroom floor. She poured some wine for him, leaving her glass empty. She handed it to him.

Will I tell him now, in the bath? No. He might drown. She went to the kitchen to check on dinner. The table was perfectly laid out. She heard Eamonn swishing around and singing along with the music.

He appeared at the kitchen door with nothing on except a small towel around his waist. Droplets of water splashed on to the tiles. His large frame threw shadows across the room. 'In Veritas again?' He eyed the familiar logo on the paper bag. 'Anything interesting?'

Ruby leaned down slowly and took a book from out of the bag. She opened it. Eamonn was drying himself vigorously, whistling as he was prone to do. She flicked through the pages, then cleared her throat.

'What is it?' he asked.

'A name-your-baby book,' she said. 'Let's see . . . Ruby. 'The ruby gem,' it says.'

'Nice.' Eamonn lifted a saucepan lid and had a sniff.

''Eamonn: the hidden. No man shall see the face of God,' it says here.'

'Fascinating,' he replied drily.

''Genevieve: white wave'.'

'We don't know any white waves, do we?' Eamonn asked cynically.

'Not yet,' Ruby replied, her face against his.

He peered into her beautiful brown eyes.

They were bright, dancing with glee.

When his eyes were locked with hers, she moved hers down to her tummy. Eamonn's followed. She reached for his hand and rested it at the base of her abdomen. He froze.

'Feel any waves?' Ruby smiled.

'Genevieve?' he barely whispered.

'Yes. I'm going to have a baby,' she whispered back.

Eamonn looked at her tummy, still flat. 'You're . . . Oh, God . . . I can't bring myself to say it.' Eamonn's eyes were filled with tears of magical joy.

'Yes. I'm pregnant!' she cried, overcome with emotion.

'Christ,' he said, holding her tiny body against his.

They ate and drank together, but exchanged little conversation. Each tried to take in the enormity, the sacredness of their shared news.

Ruby felt that Eamonn was seeing her with new eyes, as if she were transformed, a different person. He behaved differently — as if he didn't know how to behave, how to react. He held her hand as they watched a movie, neither taking it in. Later that evening, they lay in bed looking at each other as if for the first time. Her hair spilled over the pillow and he touched it lovingly, playing with a handful.

She had nodded off happily encased in Eamonn's arms and the glow that only an expectant mother could feel.

* * *

Father Ebbs was intrigued. Ruby was speaking from the heart and he was loath to interrupt her. Just when he was tinkering with the idea, Ruby disclosed another snippet of important information.

* * *

Three weeks after the announcement of her pregnancy, a celebratory get-together was held in the house. Ruby hadn't been enamoured of the idea. Already morning sickness had made itself a permanent resident. The nausea brought her to her knees. The only respite was in the evenings when she just about managed to keep down her dinner. Eamonn organised the party, and invitations were sent out to both their families and some friends.

Eamonn gushed with pride at his impending fatherhood. He told anybody who would stop to listen, the neighbours, the milkman, even the newspaper vendor on the street corner.

When the evening arrived, Ruby made a concentrated effort not to complain. She got herself ready and tried to help Eamonn in the kitchen. He had laid out a beautiful buffet, but the aroma of food made her feel ill again.

The girls, Judy, Brenda and Marjory, arrived together bearing cute little gifts for the baby. Ruby's parents presented her with an envelope containing a Mothercare gift voucher. She was delighted to receive such a practical present. But Ruby was short-tempered and agitated and didn't know why. The prospective grandparents had not rendezvoused since the wedding day, and Ruby was apprehensive about them meeting again. Apart from short visits to Arlene and Anthony's house, she had kept Arlene at arm's length. However, Doreen and Richard Reece had known Ruby's friends since school. They laughed and talked while Eamonn fetched drinks.

Brenda's gift was a particular topic of conversation.

'What the hell is that?' Judy asked.

'They're worry-beads,' Brenda said, fiddling them.

'What, in God's name, does the baby want *them* for?' Judy said.

'They're not for the baby,' Doreen put in. 'I'd imagine they're for Mum.'

'I heard some women use them in labour,' Brenda said.

'A fat lot of good they're going to be! Fucking worry-beads? A nice shot of heroin would be more appropriate.' Judy had them all laughing.

'What's it *really* like? Doreen? Marjory? C'mon, tell us,' Brenda asked.

Marjory declined. She looked to Doreen for help.

After much thought Doreen gave an honest answer. 'It's like doing a big shite,' she said loudly.

The room burst into spontaneous laughter.

'I was extremely worried that Ruby would inherit her father's nose,' she added.

Arlene and Anthony Blake stood awkwardly at the door. Nobody had heard them enter. Ruby's face fell like an unopened parachute.

'Hello there.' Anthony shuffled from foot to foot, a bottle of wine under his arm.

'Hi — em, sorry, we didn't hear you come in. Here, take a seat.' Eamonn saved the day. He took his parents' coats — to a background of coughing and shuffling — and gave them to his wife.

Ruby took them into the hall where she was greeted by a virtual car-boot sale. The floor was littered with baby items. Second-hand baby items. She stepped carefully between the objects. Moses basket. Christening robe. Cot. Car seat. Pram. What the hell is this? She picked up a strange-looking article: it looked like a tooth extractor.

'I hope you like them.' Arlene appeared from behind her. 'I kept them all. I knew a grandchild would be coming some day. That's a breast pump,' she said, nodding at the contraption in Ruby's hand.

'I see,' Ruby said. The Moses basket was blue. The christening robe was horrible. Ruby decided just to appear grateful. 'Thanks, Arlene, you shouldn't have gone to so much trouble. I had planned to purchase these items in the near future,' she said.

'Well, now, you won't have to!' Arlene chuckled with delight.

'The basket is blue,' Ruby said, irritation creeping in to her voice.

'Blue for a boy,' Arlene said, smiling. Ruby grimaced. Sometimes Arlene seemed to be deliberately trying to rile her. Or was it just that Ruby felt unwell?

'It's a hard life, dear, and you'd need two lives to live it!' Arlene sighed.

Ruby didn't want the Moses basket: she wanted a new one, a clean one, her own one. She didn't want the christening robe either. The pram was archaic, fossilised: the Moore Street traders wouldn't have insulted their fruit with such a contraption. Ruby tripped over a steriliser. It was as old as the hills. She peered into the black sacks that contained maternity wear from the turn of the eighteenth century.

She looked through a crack in the living-room door. Eamonn was happily ensconced in a conversation with Marjory. She tried to get his attention but failed.

Ruby turned back and picked up an old toothbrush. 'You'll have to start brushing soon,' Arlene said.

'Sorry? I always brush my teeth.' Ruby was getting increasingly irritated.

'No, no, dear! Not your teeth! Your nipples!' Arlene said, as if Ruby was a complete and utter fool.

'Huh?' Ruby stared at her.

'Well, if you're going to breastfeed, you have to start preparing now.' Arlene took her voice down to a whisper: 'An old trick I learned from my mother. You brush your nipples with a toothbrush. It hardens them up. Do it every morning and night from now on,' she instructed.

'I haven't decided if I'm going to breastfeed yet,' Ruby said sternly.

A fresh explosion of laughter from Eamonn and Marjory echoed in the living room. 'Excuse me,' she said to Arlene.

She marched in and fixed a glare on Eamonn. He looked at her, apparently mystified. And what had he done wrong? Ruby asked herself. She knew Arlene didn't mean any harm, but she wasn't in the mood for humouring her. She was angry that Eamonn had not been there to rescue her from his mother: he had been too preoccupied with Marjory's jokes. Her resentment against Marjory rose. She poured herself a glass of wine and tried to pull herself together.

However, the evening kept deteriorating, with Arlene's incessant chattering: she gave lengthy, gruesome accounts of labour with Eamonn, how big his head was and how many stitches she had had, her agonising piles, the sleepless nights, the colic, the teething — she went on and on and on. On a good day Ruby would have enjoyed her tales of woe, but tonight she just couldn't control her annoyance.

'What about you, Ma?' Ruby said to her mother, when Arlene paused for breath.

'Pregnancy made me as randy as hell. Your father was worn out by it,' she answered.

They all laughed a bit too hard.

'What hospital have you decided to go to?' Marjory asked Eamonn.

'We haven't decided yet,' Ruby said

abruptly. The wine had made her a little tipsy: she hadn't touched a drop since she found out she was pregnant.

'I hope you go to Holles Street. It *is* the National Maternity Hospital, you know,' Marjory said to Arlene, looking for her support.

'I never went to a hospital,' Arlene said. 'I had mine at home.'

Then there was the question of the baby's name.

'It has to be Eamonn. You have to name the child after its father. It's custom!' Marjory said, as if they were too lacking in brain cells to suggest anything else.

'I'm calling *her* Genevieve,' Ruby almost shouted.

Eamonn went to her side. The atmosphere was explosive.

'Special name, special person,' Brenda put in, trying to calm things.

'I'm only making suggestions,' Marjory said coolly.

'Well, I think it's up to Eamonn and Ruby to decide,' Judy said loudly. Her words fell heavily on the damp atmosphere.

Eamonn refilled glasses in a desperate attempt to get things back to normal.

Ruby's eyes were alight with rage as he passed her with the wine. 'Judy, do you still know that guy who makes Moses baskets?' she asked boldly.

'Sure. Beautiful handcrafted wicker ones. Let it be my gift to the two of you.' Judy's talent for causing ructions was in gainful employment. Marjory and Arlene must have been getting on her wick too, Ruby thought.

'You know, I sense a lot of tension between all of you. It's not surprising really. The moon is opposite Saturn today, and that never helps,' Brenda threw in innocently. Her timing was perfect — perfectly awful. 'I have a great astrology book about in-laws and families. You should all get together and try to put your differences aside.'

'Shut up, Brenda,' Judy snapped.

Ruby stormed out into the kitchen. Arlene put on her coat and stood up to go, Anthony following suit. Arlene stalked out into the hall, gathered up the baby things and returned them to the car.

'What a disaster! Even then, the future was destined to be fraught with difficulties. We couldn't even throw a party without something going wrong! I misinterpreted everything. My behaviour was disgraceful and I still don't know why. I can only assume it was the pregnancy making me so tetchy. His parents were only trying to help.' Ruby wept. She could see it all more clearly now:

Eamonn's parents had not been the problem. It occurred to her starkly just how obvious Marjory's indifference had been. Why had she chosen to ignore it all? It angered her to think of all the times she had put up with her because she was her friend. Examining Marjory's actions and words now, she couldn't comprehend how she had clung to the benefit-of-the-doubt theory for so long. She wondered, yet again, had Marjory *ever* been a friend?

★　★　★

Father Ebbs reached for another cigarette, but the packet was empty. He had smoked them all. He had a cramp in his left leg and he wanted to go to the toilet. His empathy with the Blakes was growing daily. Listening to Ruby now made him angry. The Tribunal interviews appeared to be causing more rifts, making them more and more stressed. Digging in the dirt aroused ancient hurts. At that moment he could not see how this rehashing of Ruby's life was being of any benefit. The woman looked like she was having a nervous breakdown. He felt in some part responsible. He tried to persuade himself that emotional pain came first and serenity later, but he wanted to heal the couple right now: Ruby's poignant recollections made him sad.

He wanted to tell the pair to terminate their application before it was too late. They were headed for the same results as other couples: their marriage would be upheld. The Tribunal would maintain that it was valid because they had taken their vows in earnest. A fat lot of good that would do them. He dreaded the day when he would have to inform them of the court's ruling.

There was only one way to avoid having to impart the fatal news. Now, more than ever, that option seemed attractive.

17

The showdown at the party had done its damage. Eamonn and Ruby had their first really big fight. Ruby blamed Eamonn. Eamonn blamed Ruby.

'Why didn't you say something?' Ruby attacked him as soon as everyone had gone.

'Say what? Dad brought the stuff down, he was only trying to help! Why didn't you just take the bloody things? You didn't have to use them, you know. How would she have known whether you did or not?'

'That's not the point, and you know it! I'm sick of people interfering! Might I remind you that you are married to me now, not your family!' Ruby screamed.

Eamonn drew himself up to his full height. It was time for both to don the short pants.

'I know quite well who I'm married to and I've never allowed anyone to interfere with our marriage! While we're on the subject of families, you'll treat mine with respect, God damn it! Don't you dare talk about them like that again.'

'Like what? I've never spoken ill of your family! Not once! I just want people to understand this is *my* child! Do you hear? *My* child! I will call it whatever I want and it will sleep in a hay barn if I so choose!' Ruby put her foot down.

'It's *our* child!' Eamonn reminded her. '*Our* child! You have to learn to share, Ruby! You can't control everything! What's wrong with you anyway? Ever since you got pregnant you're like a bag of cats. I don't know what's got into you!'

'You ignorant thick!' Ruby snarled. 'I'm having a baby. If that confuses you, go and ask Marjory about it. She seems to know what's best for us!'

'What the . . . ?' Eamonn was flummoxed.

On and on it went, into the night, each firing hideous, hurtful remarks at the other. The core of the argument remaining undetected, shrouded in their constant bickering.

Ruby told Father Ebbs that she felt she had lost the battle there and then. No matter how hard she tried to convince Eamonn that other people were becoming a problem in their relationship it failed to register with him what she *really* meant.

In fairness to Eamonn, Ruby now recognised that the 'other people' were in fact only one person, and that one person was Marjory. She rued not having talked about her specifically.

She acknowledged now that fear had kept her from saying what really bothered her. It was fear that had held her back from asking him about the letter Marjory had given him on their wedding day. It was fear that had kept her peace of mind at bay, fear that stopped her taking courage and asking him straight out what his feelings for Marjory were — if he had any at all. What if he *did* have feelings for her? She would never have handled it. Sadly, she realised, had she done that, she might have learned the truth: that Eamonn loved Ruby and nobody else. However, her invective had only resulted in making him defend himself. The more he did that, the wider the distance between them grew.

Communications broke down slowly but surely. Apologies weren't aired. Nothing was resolved. Both parties mooned around the house like wounded animals. Neither would give in. Ruby was shocked at Eamonn's stubbornness and questioned his love for her. She was vulnerable and scared. He couldn't seem to see past his own pride. Eamonn thought she was being unreasonable and blamed her hormones.

There was a big elephant on the table, but they ignored its presence, tiptoeing around it. They hoped it would eventually find its own way back to the jungle.

Around the end of her second month of pregnancy, Ruby's morning sickness got worse. Her tiredness increased; she lacked the energy to do the simplest things. Eamonn was moody and resentful, his image of fatherhood shattered. He was angry with the child now. It was the child's fault. He hadn't expected it to be like this. He felt he had lost Ruby to some alien world.

Returning from work one evening, he noticed straight away that that the kitchen was filled with smoke. An empty pot burned on the hot ring. He called out for Ruby but got no answer. Panicked, he took the stairs two at a time, only to find her bent over on the floor.

'Jesus! What's wrong?' he shouted.

Ruby held her stomach. She was hunched over on all fours. Her face was a ghastly white and she whined like a dog. Eamonn bent down beside her.

'Ruby, what's wrong? Ruby, you're frightening me!'

'My stomach,' she muttered. 'Pains in my stomach.'

Eamonn grabbed the telephone by the bed and dialled 999. He demanded an ambulance and gave them the address. He tried to get Ruby to lie on her side but the pain was too intense for her to move into any other position. She rocked herself backwards and forwards, one hand on the floor the other on her abdomen.

'Where is the pain?' Eamonn demanded.

Ruby pointed to her left side. 'Help me!' she whimpered, tears pouring down her face.

The ambulance arrived. They were calm and efficient, moving Eamonn out of the way. One man spoke to Ruby as the other tried to calm Eamonn. They gently lifted her to her knees. Eamonn could see the pain in her face, and tried to stop them. 'We have to move her, and fast.' The man reassured him that they were doing the right thing.

They scrambled into the ambulance. Eamonn feared the worst: was she losing the baby? He asked the ambulance men. They declined to answer, feigning ignorance. They raced through the evening traffic, sirens wailing. Eamonn stared out of the window, watching strangers bless themselves as the ambulance sped past.

At the casualty department, they whisked Ruby away on the stretcher. Eamonn watched as his wife and future child were taken out of his control. He stood at the coffee machine crying. One of the ambulance men put some coins into it and handed him a plastic cup of scalding coffee.

'Everything's going to be fine, mate,' he said.

'Yeah,' Eamonn replied, searching the man's eyes, desperate for affirmation. He nodded to himself. 'Everything's going to be OK. Yes. Everything's going to be OK.'

Then he made the mother of all catastrophic mistakes. He dialled Brenda's number at least twelve times before he realised she was on duty at the Sacred Heart home. Then he phoned Marjory. In minutes she was at the hospital demanding to talk to a doctor.

They refused to answer her questions and ordered her to return to the waiting area. An hour later Eamonn was called. Marjory got up to accompany him. The nurse blocked her path. 'Husband only,' she said coldly.

Marjory resumed her seat.

Ruby was dozing, her eyelids fluttering every now and then, tubes attached to her arms and patches stuck to her chest. Her breasts were exposed for all to see. He covered them. She looked like a baby. Her hair was wet with perspiration. The machines and equipment frightened him. What was going on?

'Mr Blake?' A doctor appeared from behind the curtain.

'Yes. Is she OK? What's going on? Is the

baby OK?' He asked a million questions one after the other.

'I'm Dr White.' He extended a sweaty hand. Eamonn took it and shook it limply. 'Your wife is going to be fine, Mr Blake.' He smiled confidently.

Eamonn expelled an enormous sigh of relief. 'Thank Christ!' he muttered.

'Unfortunately, the baby will not,' the doctor added, choosing his words with care.

Eamonn looked at him and then at Ruby. 'What do you mean?' he whispered.

'I'm afraid we must terminate the pregnancy immediately. Your wife has a condition known as an ectopic pregnancy. The fertilised ovum has become implanted in a Fallopian tube. It can't survive. We will have to abort as soon as possible. I need your consent, Mr Blake. I understand that this is difficult to take in.'

Eamonn stared at the doctor. 'What happens if we don't ab — ' He couldn't finish the sentence.

'We don't have a choice, Mr Blake. The foetus will self-abort anyway. To prevent any further risk to your wife's health we must operate now. It is the safest thing to do.'

Eamonn looked at Ruby's face. Then he looked into the doctor's eyes. The doctor was firm, unemotional. He scribbled away on a chart as he talked. 'I am very sorry, Mr Blake, but your wife's health is seriously at risk. If we leave this situation any longer she may die.'

'Then do it,' he said, quietly, resigning himself to the worst.

★   ★   ★

Outside, Marjory listened as Eamonn relayed the doctor's story. 'Oh, God.' She sighed. 'This is very sad indeed.'

Eamonn went to the vending-machine and stared at it. He jingled some coins in his hand, then realised he didn't know what he was doing there. His mind had taken flight. A perilous flight to the consequences of this tragedy in both their lives. He pictured the nursery that they had lovingly prepared. The tiny clothes that lay folded neatly in the wardrobe. The handmade Moses basket. The white baby bath, complete with towels and nappies, placed underneath. The minuscule Babygros. Booties that well-meaning friends had knitted. How he and Ruby had laughed when they had spread them out: they were so, so small. This was a disaster. He knew somehow that things would never be the same again.

★   ★   ★

Ruby vaguely recalled sleeping on and off after the doctor and Eamonn had spoken. Each time she awoke it took some minutes for her to remember. Had she been dreaming? Had she really heard the doctor and Eamonn speaking? She was frightened of the hospital sounds and smells. Something had gone wrong, but she couldn't remember what.

She felt woozy and tried to sit up, but her head spun, like she had a hangover. She felt light-headed and drugged. She let her body fall back into the comfort of the thick pillows. A nurse appeared at her side. 'What's going on?' She grabbed at her, unable to pull herself upwards.

'Now, calm down, Mrs Blake. Dr White will be with you shortly.' The nurse paged him. It was true. She had not been hallucinating. Another nurse sat on the edge of the bed holding her hand, rubbing it, mothering her. Ruby feared the worst. She had lost the baby — she could feel it. She could feel the empty space where it had been. She could see it in the nurse's compassionate eyes. The life force was gone, had been sucked out. She cried for Eamonn.

'Please, Mrs Blake, don't upset yourself, there's a good girl.' The kind nurse patted her arm until Dr White appeared and crouched at the side of the bed.

'Where am I? What happened?' she cried, terrified of the answer but knowing she had to hear it.

'You're in the National Maternity Hospital, Ruby,' the doctor said softly.

'Who are you?' she asked childlike.

'I'm Dr White. Ruby. There's been some complications.' Then he explained what an ectopic pregnancy was. He told her that he had had to terminate the pregnancy.

Ruby's eyes closed tight as she tried to take it in. She hadn't been dreaming, after all. Then she asked, 'Was it a girl?'

The doctor looked downwards and played with his glasses.

'I need to know,' she urged him.

The doctor looked at the nurse, who shook her head.

'We don't know,' he whispered.

Ruby turned her head sideways and sobbed into the pillow. It didn't really matter what he said. She knew it had been a girl. She was sure of it. The doctor patted her head, and waited for her to regain her composure, but Ruby had left them. Dr White made his exit, and the nurse set about fixing the bedclothes.

Ruby drifted in and out of sleep again. Her mind travelled a grief-filled journey. She attended a private funeral in her mind. She lifted the tiny white coffin and carried it up the church aisle. Jesus was seated at the altar, enshrined in a splendid aura of pristine white. He opened his arms and took the offering of the dead child. Then he placed his hands on his chest. Ruby saw her daughter embedded in his heart, laughing, playing and waving goodbye.

Jesus was happy. 'Suffer the little children, to come on to me.' Genevieve had gone home. Ruby waved goodbye and blew a kiss. The image began to fade. Goodbye, darling. Goodbye, darling . . .

When she woke again, Ruby was attached to a drip. The nurse explained she needed it. Nothing was wrong. The operation had been successful. Ruby noted the word 'operation'. Nobody was referring to the baby any more. The baby had become an operation.

The nurse administered some more pain-killers, and Ruby relaxed into temporary relief and slept again.

★   ★   ★

Eamonn had been patient enough. He paced the waiting area like a demented animal. He was tired, dirty and hungry, and Marjory was irritating him beyond belief. He was sorry now that he had called anyone.

'Why don't you go to the cafeteria?' she asked.

'I'll stay here until the doctor comes. I can handle it, you know,' he snapped. 'Look, it's me they want to talk to, stay out of it.'

'I'm only trying to help,' she said sulkily.

At last, the doctor arrived. 'You can see her now.' He showed them towards the room. Marjory marched ahead. The doctor caught up with her and stood in her way. 'I'm sorry, family only.'

'I am family!'

The doctor reluctantly agreed. Perhaps he thought that Ruby might welcome the company of another woman.

Eamonn went straight to Ruby's side, took her hand and kissed it.

Marjory positioned herself at the end of the bed.

Ruby woke up. 'How are you feeling, love?' Eamonn said, trying to disguise his own anguish.

'You look tired.' Her voice was croaky, barely distinguishable.

Eamonn was awash with guilt. He felt guilty about all his sulking in the previous months. How could she think of *him* at such a moment?

Marjory came forward. 'Now, Ruby, don't you go getting yourself upset over this unfortunate little incident.'

Unfortunate little incident. 'Get out,' Ruby croaked.

'You can always try again . . . '

Eamonn turned to Marjory quickly — he had not seen her follow him in.

'Get out!' Ruby said again, this time attempting to get out of the bed.

Marjory turned on her heel, shocked by Ruby's response.

Eamonn tried to say something.

'Get out,' Ruby repeated, throwing his hand as far away as possible. Eamonn made a second attempt, tears in his eyes.

'I said get out!' she screamed at him, and lashed her hand across his face.

Eamonn brought his hand to his cheek in disbelief. In a confused daze, he made for the door, not looking back or wanting to.

★　★　★

Ruby was crying again now.

'It was the beginning of the end for me. I could have excused everything else that had happened before, but the last person I wanted to see at that moment was Marjory. In all my grief and heartbreak, to have to see *her* beside him at that very private exchange! How could he have been so insensitive?' Ruby reached for the box of tissues and drew out a fresh one. Her exhaustion was evident to Father Ebbs. They had been together for two hours. He stretched; his feet had gone to sleep. He stamped them on the floor, trying to wake them up.

'You're tired, Mrs Blake,' he commented. 'We are both tired,' he amended. 'I think we should call it a day. Too much too soon can have devastating effects. I want you to do some simple things for me. I want you to drive home slowly. I want you to order some nice takeout food. No cooking today, do you understand me? You have been through a lot. You need to rest. Recharge your batteries.' He reached for the telephone and called for the psychologist to return.

Rosanna breezed through the door. Father Ebbs explained that the interview should be terminated for now. Rosanna agreed. They had made the break, which was important. The rest would come in good time.

'I want you to do as Father Ebbs has suggested, Ruby,' Rosanna said quietly: 'Can you spend the evening with someone? Sometimes, after such an emotional outpouring, we are overwhelmed by our feelings. I would be happier if I knew you had someone to keep you company this evening. I don't want you to exert yourself any further. You are going to sleep like a log tonight — I promise you the best night's sleep in years!'

★　★　★

Ruby smiled at them both. She felt peculiar: vulnerable, soft, and so, so tired. She could have crawled into bed there and then and slept soundly for days. Her minders were looking at her with worried expressions. 'Look, I'm OK,' Ruby said, staggering a little as she got to her feet. 'I'm just tired, like you said. I'll be fine. In fact, I'm beginning to feel better already. God, I never knew all that stuff was in me.'

'More will be revealed,' Rosanna said softly.

Ruby was too tired to panic about that. Her whole body felt like it had been dragged through a rocky terrain, then back. 'There is someone I can call,' she said, thinking of Robert, then wondered whether that was such a sensible idea. In this state of emotional turmoil she was liable to do anything.

'Is it someone you trust?' Rosanna quizzed her.

Ruby paused. 'Yes. Actually, yes. It is.' Ruby decided she had no choice but to trust her intuition.

★　★　★

Father Ebbs said goodbye, then set about organising his notes. He had written in shorthand and made do without the tape-recorder. Now he could hardly read his own scrawl. He took the main points of the interview and recorded them at length, checking for new grounds as he did so. It was not over yet. Several grounds now came to mind: lack of due discretion and lack of judgement, to name but two. Ruby still had a case for an annulment, however slight: he was obliged to follow it up.

With the details in check and his file taking shape, he allowed intuition to decide his next move. He picked up the telephone. There was no time for letters.

'Mr Blake? Father Ebbs here.'

He explained to Eamonn that there had been an unusual turn of events and that he would like to proceed without delay. Was he available to come to his office?

★   ★   ★

Eamonn was delighted to hear this and was possessed of new hope. He agreed to go in the following morning. He had been hoping for good news and this was it. He put down the phone and rubbed his hands together. He'd known she'd crack sooner or later. Now they would dismiss the case and things would return to normal. Everything was going to be OK, he told himself. For the first time in a long time, the urge to call and see her became unbearable.

He had to slow down, take it easy. She might still be on the defensive. Better not to move too soon. But Eamonn's usually razor-sharp logic couldn't fight his feelings. Logic was sleeping peacefully. His compulsion to see Ruby was something against which he had no defence. It gnawed at him like a rat throughout the night. He couldn't see it, but he knew sure as hell the bastard was there.

18

Ruby didn't hesitate when she arrived home, and Robert answered the telephone almost immediately. She explained what had happened at the Archbishop's House. He insisted on coming over for the evening.

She stood in the shower, too tired to wash. She let it run over her head and body like a refreshing waterfall. Afterwards, she smoothed her skin with some expensive body lotion. She noticed her nails were chipped and her nail polish had faded at the tips. She went to repaint them, then stopped midway. What difference would it make? Had Robert befriended her because of her beautiful nails? She thought about all the wasted time she had spent on getting everything 'perfect'. Who was she doing it for and why? Suddenly, her own behaviour appeared to her to be *very odd indeed*. She had never thought that before. It had seemed humorous, comical, even. The lining up of objects, the obsession with straight lines, perfect hair and makeup, silly habits that added nothing to her life but extra work and stress.

She felt different. Still reeling from the

emotional outpouring, Ruby let her thoughts do as they pleased. They meandered and raced, then slowly paced up and down. She surrendered to them.

She gave way to the vacant hole that had been left behind. She had emptied her soul and was too tired to refill it. Everything felt new and strange.

★   ★   ★

Robert stood at the door, a little shocked. A different Ruby greeted him. He wasn't sure if it was curiosity or concern that rushed through his mind. Her face was pale and he thought she was ill, but then he realised that she was wearing no makeup. He had never seen her without makeup before. She had a fresh natural beauty. The paleness was evidence of the emotional trauma of the previous events of that day. Gone were the staunch suits, the high heels, the immaculate hair. She wore a simple pair of tracksuit bottoms, a T-shirt and her hair, still wet, was roughly curled behind her ears. He could have been visiting his aunt. Something enormous must have happened to cause such a display of trust and vulnerability. He was touched. Ruby was letting him in. The Great Wall of China had begun to crumble, just when he had become skilled in the art of climbing.

Now he was facing Croagh Patrick, a place where one went barefoot and negotiated the terrain by touch, feeling, through the soul. He was on sacred ground. A holy place. A stone's throw away from the summit.

Ruby invited him in, without excessive pleasantries. She made him a cup of tea and sat beside him on the couch. Robert sipped the tea in perfect silence. He grappled with a box, now embarrassed at his own impulsiveness.

'Have you come bearing gifts, Oh wise one?' she teased him.

Robert raised an eyebrow and placed the box on the coffee table.

'C'mon, what is it?' she said, without a hint of compassion. He had always been the brazen, outspoken, honest one, now Ruby was giving him a taste of his own medicine.

He slid the box over to her. 'I'd prefer it if you opened it later,' he said.

'OK.' Ruby gave in; apparently she didn't want to play the game to an early death.

'It was rough then?' he asked, not wanting to seem nosy.

'Very.' She began puffing up the cushions.

Robert understood: she had done enough talking. He remembered his own psychological assessment and how tired he had been afterwards. He began to tell her his own story.

'You marry someone, have kids with them, sleep with them, and eat with them. Then, all of a sudden, you don't know what you're doing. If you didn't know, then how did it all happen and why? Surely there is a reason for everything. Everything is relevant. Isn't it? I mean, I wouldn't have arrived here had I not gone through the process. I guess the best thing I can say is that I learned a lot about myself through the various stages. I wasn't what I thought I was. I wasn't anyone or anything special, just an ordinary bloke who didn't know his arse from his elbow, you know?'

Ruby nodded.

'I don't know anything more about marriage. I still don't know what constitutes a good one or a bad one. I only know what I am and what I'm capable of. My limits are becoming narrower, as I grow older. I'm not sure I could marry again. I'm too set in my own ways now. Some years ago I was wondering how I'd survive without my wife. Today I'm wondering how I survived with her.'

'Maybe, you've just got used to being alone, Robert. I want to be free *in a relationship*! Do you think that's possible? To be able to talk honestly and not fear the outcome?' Ruby asked.

'Of course. We have a relationship, don't we? We are free with each other. I hope.' Robert was wondering where all this was going.

★ ★ ★

Ruby scratched her breastbone, thinking of Eamonn and of how they had been virtual prisoners of a misunderstanding. She realised just how important communicating was, how it might have saved their marriage and all the consequent pain. She found herself also wishing that he might still feel something for her. Perhaps through the annulment process he might learn about his own mistakes. Perhaps they could heal the past. She chastised herself for thinking such stupid things.

★ ★ ★

Robert was struggling. He tried hard not to stare at her finger as it exposed just a flash of white that the sun had not been allowed to play with. He watched her hands, their long fingers, curling in gesture. Frail wrists, adorned with gold. Slim neckline, sleek skin. He imagined her shoulders, creamy, curved, the dip in her throat.

'Are you listening to me?' she asked, apparently midway through a sentence.

'No,' he answered truthfully.

'I can't say I blame you.' She poked him with her clenched fist. In a spontaneous rush, he grabbed it and held it. He waited for her to resist, pull back. She loosened her fist, spreading her hand out like a fan: he opened her fingers and slipped his through them. Their fingers entwined in perfect synchrony. They slotted in without a wrestle; they fitted, just like a glove.

★　★　★

Ruby didn't know how she felt. He had held her hand in the coffee shop, a friendship gesture. She had felt childish. Her box of romantic tricks had rusted with age.

She cocked her head sideways, devoid of words. She leaned her head on his shoulder, trying to fight a losing battle. She wanted to surrender the fear of letting someone know her. She had always believed that sex would do this. Now she realised how close she was to Robert — and they had only ever held hands.

Robert took her head and kissed her on the lips. A small kiss, light, soft. She kissed him back, a little harder, afraid of taking her lips away, afraid of leaving them there, for too long. Her stomach twisted in knots. She was uncertain of her own feelings.

He hesitated, only slightly, then pulled her head under his and opened his mouth. She responded, letting him open her lips with his tongue. His hands held her neck. She fell into his control, allowing the souls to meet, to find their own rhythm. He bit her lip gently, then more passionately, and his hand fell gently on to her breast. He was uncertain whether to go any further.

Just when he had decided he would, Ruby pushed him away violently. 'No!' she cried. 'I can't do this! I can't.'

★   ★   ★

Eamonn's face danced before her. As much as she willed it to go away, it hung stubbornly before her eyes, refusing to move an inch. Angrily, she argued with him in her head: Go away! Go away!

'Oh, God, I'm sorry,' Robert put his head in his hands. 'I'm sorry, Ruby, forgive me,' he whispered.

'It's OK, Robert, it's not your fault. I swear it's not your fault. You haven't done anything wrong. It's just that . . . well . . . I can't seem to . . . ' Words failed her. She felt foolish for leading him on. She wanted to sleep with Robert, but something was stopping her. Or did she *really* want to sleep with Robert? Why did she feel so close to Eamonn? It was absurd. The marriage was over. It was over! She couldn't make sense of it, no matter how hard she tried. She was certainly not going to air her thoughts to Robert. They would have been hurtful and insensitive. She straightened her clothing and fixed her hair behind her ears.

'It's my fault,' Robert insisted. 'You went through an emotional storm today. You needed a shoulder to cry on and I got carried away. I'm so sorry. I'm disgusted with myself.' He hung his head in shame.

'Oh, Robert.' Ruby pulled him towards her and cradled his head. 'It's nothing to do with you! It's me! Can't you see? Right now, I feel like my whole life has been thrown to the sharks and I'm swimming around in there trying to avoid them! I can't trust myself. I can't let go of anything. I've always been like this. Controlling. Everything has to be perfect. I don't know how to behave in any other way,' she concluded, surprised at her own honesty.

'I don't care what you say. What I did was offensive. I should have known better,' Robert insisted.

'Now, who's trying to be perfect?' Ruby smiled at him.

'Can we still be friends?'

'Of course!' Ruby said, surprised. 'Robert, I find you very attractive. It's just not the right time. I'm sorry I can't explain it any better. I feel like I'm still suspended in the past. I don't want our friendship spoiled because of that.'

She took Robert's arm and put it round her shoulders. 'Robert?' She stared out, her brown eyes glazing over with sadness.

'Yes?' he asked.

'Will you stay with me a while? I mean until I fall asleep.' Her voice quivered.

'Of course,' he said, pulling her into an affectionate embrace. He led her to the bedroom and she followed, trance-like.

'I'm scared of what this annulment is doing to me,' she confided.

'I know. I know it hurts, but right now you're beginning to come to terms with some major issues in your life. I know it doesn't feel like that but I think it's helping you, Ruby,' he said. They lay on the unmade bed.

★ ★ ★

Robert looked around her room. Newspapers and magazines lay strewn here and there. One or two dirty cups had gathered on the floor. Ruby hadn't cleaned up. She hadn't washed the dishes, Hoovered the floor or even bothered to hang up her clothes. He reckoned she hadn't cleaned for at least two days. It was a good start. 'Yes,' he said, nodding. 'I really think things are going to get better for you. Don't worry yourself any more.' He kissed the top of her head. She didn't respond. Robert looked down at her face. Ruby's eyes were closed, her mouth ajar. She was fast asleep. Robert pulled the duvet up and over them both. He closed his eyes, felt her warmth beside him, and held her. Like a child curled up on his shoulder she slept soundly.

★ ★ ★

Outside the apartment, Eamonn sat silently in his car. He watched the bedroom window without blinking. The dim light disappeared with the flick of a switch.

He had been unable to sleep again. His mind was racing with endless thoughts about Ruby, and he had found himself planning a dawn raid. What he intended to do, he did not know. What the hell am I doing here anyway? he asked himself. This is insane! But it was a small comfort to sit outside her apartment. Just knowing she was in there eased his tortured soul. He waited, and waited, and waited a little longer. At six a.m. the front door opened. It was still pitch dark.

Eamonn could only make out the shadowy figure of a man. The bedroom window opened and Ruby hung out of it like a regular Juliet. 'Robert? Robert Ryan?' she shouted unashamedly. The man stopped and looked back to her. He waved. Eamonn sat hunched in the car near the kerb, shrouded by the trees that lined the road. He watched the figure disappear into the dim morning light.

He took off the handbrake and let the car roll gently until he reached the corner. He started the engine and drove slowly to Ballsbridge. His mind was strangely calm, not at all in the turmoil he had expected.

The best he could hope for was that it had been an evening of illicit sex. He could forgive her for having sex. But this was not just sex: they had obviously fallen asleep together. Ruby hated sleeping with anyone. Yes. It was the sleeping-over that really got him. This had been no ordinary date. This was someone important.

Her words from the window echoed in his head. Numbness set in. He couldn't feel anything. He wasn't angry now, or even jealous. He knew her well enough to grasp that this had been much more than a fleeting romantic encounter. A mixture of sadness and confusion engulfed him. He had agreed to come to the Archbishop's House that morning. Now he wondered whether Father Ebbs knew of Ruby's mysterious relationship. Was that why he had called him in?

He turned into the tarmacadam driveway.

In the waiting room, he perused the newspapers. The *Catholic Herald*. The *Messenger*. *Reality*. Riveting stuff. He stared out of the window. Green fields rolled beneath it, a lone man sauntered around in circles, pausing now and then to stare at his feet. Eamonn gazed at the man staring at his feet. He empathised. He was devoid of any emotion, feeling as if the life had been sucked out of him. If Ruby was in love with another man, it was over. He had never envisaged that situation. He had never even entertained the idea that she might meet someone else. But it was years since she had told him she loved him. How long had this been going on? Had she been in love with this man before they broke up?

The questions came. The answers evaded him. Like torpedoes, unseen but sensed, he waited in terror for the next, and the next, and the next. Sadly, Eamonn's anger had only been on sabbatical: it would return within the next few minutes, as wild as a typhoon, as destructive as a tornado. It would sneak up on him without warning and wipe out everything in sight.

The room was quite empty that morning: a woman sat with a calculator, tapping away lightly, oblivious to her neighbours. A man with a crooked wig tapped his toes delicately to some hidden tune in his brain. Another man with a hat took up half the room with a morning newspaper.

Father Ebbs peered around the door. 'Mr Ryan, please? Robert Ryan?'

The man stood up, taking care to fold his newspaper correctly. He nudged Eamonn in the eye with a corner of his elbow. 'Excuse me,' he smiled, 'sorry about that.'

19

Father Ebbs had requested an audience with the Archbishop. He had hoped it would not be held this morning as he had called in Eamonn Blake on spec and did not want to keep him waiting. However, the Archbishop had responded swiftly and Father Ebbs was loath to change the appointment. Now he waited silently in the library for His Grace. He paced back and forth with his arms behind his back, his unruly black curls swept at an unkempt angle. Robert Ryan's file lay on the table. He watched it with protective eyes, wondering how on earth it had come to this.

Presently, the housekeeper saw him into the Archbishop's quarters. The room was splendorous, but dark. Large oil paintings hung on the walls, but there was insufficient light for their full potential to be apparent. Father Ebbs crossed the luxurious Persian rugs, and stood before the Archbishop. 'Your Grace.' He dipped his head.

'Good afternoon, Father Ebbs. You are most welcome. Please take a seat.' The Archbishop motioned to the tall Queen

Anne-style chair. Father Ebbs sat, one foot tapping nervously on the floor. He placed the file on the table, and cleared his throat.

'Father Ebbs, before you start, let me tell you that I am already aware of the circumstances that have brought you here today.' He picked up the file and flicked through the pages. 'It has been brought to my attention that you are experiencing some unhappiness in your present position as auditor. I appreciate the difficulties involved in such work. I understand the pressures it can bring to bear on one's faith. In the course of my career, I too have had my faith tested within the boundaries of such challenging work.' He paused. 'I have taken the liberty of arranging a year's sabbatical for you. You have been most gracious and tolerant in your attitude towards the work involved in annulment cases. It has been noted. We will, of course, be sorry to see you move on, when it is evident to all how gifted you are in the mediation process. It is a pity. However, I am certain that your talents can be put to good use elsewhere.'

'Your Grace, I humbly acknowledge your kind offer, and do not deny that I have been somewhat troubled over the last few months. However, I would like to draw to your attention the reason why I requested today's meeting.' He reached for Robert Ryan's file and thumbed his way towards the final page. 'I am somewhat mystified, Your Grace, over the final decision reached in this case.' He paused, kicking for touch.

'Proceed.' The Archbishop locked his hands in prayer fashion.

'The ruling from Rome was to uphold this marriage. Having personally counselled Mr and Mrs Ryan over the years and interviewed them at length, I simply cannot fathom why this ruling was made. It was very clear to me, right from the outset, that this couple's marriage should *not* be upheld.' He swallowed hard.

'Are you suggesting, Father Ebbs, that the court in Rome is incompetent?' The Archbishop raised his eyebrows over his glasses.

'Not exactly, Your Grace.' Father Ebbs laughed nervously.

'Not *exactly*?'

'If you can bear with me, Your Grace, I shall try to elaborate. The case in question was clear-cut. Mrs Ryan admitted her infidelity. Mr Ryan was an innocent party. Now he finds himself in a position where he is no longer involved with Mrs Ryan. She has set up home with her new partner. Yet, in the actions of this ruling, he is to be married to *someone else's* wife for the rest of his life. We have, by this very action, ruled out any chance of a second marriage for Mr Ryan. I cannot abide by this decision. I think it is grossly unfair.'

'I understand your misgivings, Father Ebbs, but it is not for us to decide such matters. Infidelity does not constitute grounds for an annulment. I am troubled as to why you should pretend not to know that. I am satisfied that the court in Rome has handled this case with professional and objective competence. You know quite well that a marriage has to be proved to be invalid at the time a couple exchanged their vows. In this case, those vows were taken in earnest. The question of infidelity does not arise, as it is an event that took place years later,' the Archbishop argued.

'I understand that, Your Grace. However, it seems ludicrous to expect Robert Ryan to accept this outcome. I suppose what I am trying to say is that while I of all people understand the grounds for and against an annulment I just don't . . . *agree* in some cases.'

'Don't agree, Father Ebbs?'

'There are other cases, for instance,' Father Ebbs responded swiftly.

An uncomfortable lull ensued.

'Father Ebbs, please . . . ' the Archbishop tried to intervene.

He was too late: Father Ebbs had already

taken the first steps across the bridge. He continued to run towards the other side, appreciating its weak structure. It was likely to collapse in the middle. He moved swiftly, not wasting another second. 'An example, Your Grace. A young woman, in her late twenties, her husband habitually beats and sexually assaults her. She, too, had her case dismissed. We have sentenced her to a life of misery. She is an innocent victim of what should have been an honourable union. She has turned to the Church for help. Instead we have sent her away. Are we not in some way responsible to this woman? We have the power to free her from a union that no human being should be asked to endure. I cannot and will not align myself with such obvious punishment!' Father Ebbs's face burned with anger.

'Father, I refuse to enter into any debate regarding annulment cases. They are not ours to negotiate. I have full confidence in Rome's decisions and accept them without rancour. I suggest you do the same. I suggest it with great passion!' The Archbishop rose up.

'I'm afraid, Your Grace, that I cannot. It is simply unthinkable. Inhuman!' Father Ebbs replied.

'I see.' The tone of the Archbishop's voice had simmered down. 'Perhaps the year's sabbatical will help you to review your misgivings on such matters?' he tried.

'Forgive me, Your Grace, but I am thinking in terms of a much lengthier sabbatical.' Father Ebbs lowered his head.

The Archbishop raised his head and looked Father Ebbs directly in the eyes. 'Am I to understand that you are leaving us, Father? I am most vexed!' he said.

'If what you say is correct, Your Grace, then it is I who must look inward. If I am led to believe that it is not the court in Rome that needs questioning, then the onus must fall on me! Perhaps it is I who doubts, Your Grace! Perhaps it is my vocation in the priesthood that needs to be rigorously examined.' Father Ebbs struggled with his emotions.

'Perhaps. This is a very serious matter indeed! Father Ebbs, do you realise what you are saying?' The Archbishop was saddened.

'Unfortunately, yes.' He wiped his brow.

'I am still advocating that you seek help with this temporary crisis you find yourself in. It is God's will that our faith be tested from time to time. I strongly advise that you finish whatever cases are pending and take a short holiday. I would be most distressed to see you throw in the towel over annulment cases. Surely you agree that that would be a hasty decision?' the Archbishop said.

'I can assure you, Your Grace, I have been very thorough in my inventory. My doubts stem from way back. It is not just the annulment cases. Perhaps they have served as the catalyst. However, I still have many unanswered questions.'

'You would be a great loss, Father Ebbs. I am most distressed, and would be greatly calmed if you would speak to one of the chaplains. I have someone in mind who might be of assistance to you.'

'I thank you for your kindness, Your Grace.' Father Ebbs rose to his feet. 'I will consider all options. I am grateful for your good counsel and shall make my decision only after great deliberation, as advised.'

The Archbishop rose also, extending his hand in good faith to the pot-bellied priest. 'May God bless you and keep you,' he said.

Father Ebbs dipped his head. 'Thank you, Your Grace,' he said.

As he walked slowly to the door he let out a great big sigh of relief. He felt lifted, exonerated. It was the first time in a long, long time that he had felt content. He knew for certain, in his heart of hearts, that he had taken the first steps towards freedom. It felt so good. *It felt so, so good!*

★ ★ ★

Robert followed Father Ebbs into the interview room, where he was handed a brown-paper envelope containing his personal papers. He had insisted that he would collect them himself. They included his birth certificate, marriage certificate and a variety of other documents. He did not want them lost in the post, as had happened before when he had applied for a passport. He had also come to settle his account. He scribbled the required fee on a cheque and handed it to Father Ebbs. They shook hands.

'I am most grieved by this outcome, Robert,' Father Ebbs said. 'My condolences are genuine.'

'Thank you, Father. I am grateful to you.' Robert acknowledged the priest's empathy and compassion.

He took one last look at the room, and then, his business finally concluded, he departed the Archbishop's House for the last time. He hoped that he would never have reason to be there again — even if he was chosen to be the next bishop. After four years of baring his soul, he walked away empty-handed, wondering what it had all been about.

★ ★ ★

In the waiting room, Eamonn's feet had begun to tap vigorously. He could have done the River Dance without any choreography. There was nowhere to run, nowhere to hide. His throat ached with the desire to scream. Did that bastard not know who he was? Of course he didn't! The smarmy fucker! Shagging my wife while attending the Archbishop's House for an annulment? What kind of a conscience had he?

Never mind him! What about Ruby? He couldn't believe she would stoop so low. Could she not have waited until the whole thing was over? Maybe Father Ebbs was having a go at her too.

Eamonn stared out of the window and watched Robert Ryan amble down the avenue. He seemed to be smiling to himself. The bastard! Eamonn watched him kick a pebble carelessly across the Tarmac. He prayed for Father Ebbs to arrive soon. He would no longer be going to court for just an annulment if he didn't hurry up. He wanted to climb down the drainpipe and wipe that fucking smile off Ryan's face.

'Mr Blake? Mr Blake?' Father Ebbs shouted at him. Eamonn turned round, shocked. He didn't know how long the priest had been there. 'Follow me,' Father Ebbs said agitatedly.

While helping him in one way, his visit to the Archbishop had drained Father Ebbs in another. Now he had little interest in the day's obligations. The doubts he had harboured were suddenly unleashed: they overflowed and spilled forth. The flimsy twig of faith, to which he had clung, sank in the flash flood. It was Saturday. Gardening day. He hated anything that interfered with his gardening day. He had scheduled to plant the annuals this morning, one of his favourite pastimes. He was angry that he had had to forfeit his plans yet again. He basked in the reassuring knowledge that these days of saintly restraint were coming to an end.

He dwelt on this for a moment until a voice that had been distant became suddenly very close. It was a loud voice, a very loud voice, a familiar voice. Father Ebbs pulled himself together, remembering with shame that he was still interviewing Eamonn Blake.

'I demand an explanation!' Blake was yelling. 'What kind of a sham is this? You knew all along my wife was seeing that old fart, didn't you? I had a right to know! You are morally obliged to inform me of such a thing! You should have told me about Robert Ryan!'

Father Ebbs raised an eyebrow at the mention of Robert Ryan's name. He had liked the man from the start. He was an honest, forthright character, who had co-operated fully with the Tribunal's requests. He felt responsible for letting him down. He was a representative of the Church, of God's ability to forgive, of His Son Jesus's merciful love. But he could no longer continue in that role, could no longer align himself with such hypocrisy. He looked at Blake: had the man lost his mind. What on earth was he going on about?

'It's one thing to have the hand of God ruin my marriage! But to have him dip back in and humiliate me further! How much more of this fucking shit do I have to go through? It's a goddamn circus act, this thing you call an annulment. What about *her* grounds, eh? I want an answer now! Answer me!' Blake slammed his fist on the table as he screeched the last words right into the priest's face.

Father Ebbs's cup of tea wobbled — it was touch and go whether it would keel over. It did. A river of tea ran across the bureau, over the side and downwards to form a lake on the floor.

'Mr Blake! Now look what you've done! I must request that you refrain from taking your temper to such extremes! Please do not abuse the furniture again!' he snapped. He pulled open the drawer and began meticulously to mop up the liquid.

'You haven't heard a single word I've said, have you? This is all a game to you lot! Get them in and out as fast as you can! What kind of a God would allow this sort of thing to happen? I want some answers and I want them now!'

Without warning Father Ebbs leaped into the air and slammed his own fist down on the bureau. The windows rattled and his chair fell backwards. 'You want answers, Mr Blake? Let me give you the answer then, shall I? I DON'T BLOODY WELL KNOW THE ANSWER, OK?'

The two men's faces were inches apart now. Father Ebbs breathed through his nostrils like a bull ready to charge.

If one of them didn't back off a murder was imminent. They waited in silence, their heavy breathing the only sound in the room. It was almost as if they expected a booming voice to come from behind the wallpaper and explain it all to them.

No voice came. The two men sat down again. Father Ebbs cleared his throat. His hands shook. He could not believe what he had just done. 'Mr Blake,' he croaked.

'Oh, stop calling me Mr Blake! Speak to

me like a person, for Christ's sake? Can't you at least do that? My name is Eamonn. Eamonn, OK?' He wriggled in the seat, his frustration at bursting point.

'Eamonn,' Father Ebbs started again, 'you seem to think I have magical powers, that I know everything. I hate to disappoint you by telling you that when I chose to become a priest I was not automatically blessed with ESP! I do not have a hotline to Jesus whenever I have an unanswered question, do you understand me? I am a man! Only a man! I am just like you! I still have all my emotions. I am only a human being!' He was still quaking in the wake of his own temper.

★   ★   ★

Eamonn looked the priest in the eyes. Indeed, an ordinary man was reflected back. He realised the irony of the whole situation. Father Ebbs was, indeed, just another human being trying to make sense of the mystery of life. He knew no more than Eamonn did. Eamonn was shocked back into reality. He realised his temper had got the better of him. He felt a fool.

Father Ebbs continued, 'I am not interested in your wife's present relationships, or yours. I am simply doing my job. My job is to gather information about your marriage so that I can forward the case to Rome. I understand your anger and frustration, much, much more than you know! However, I am an innocent party and I ask you to co-operate, Eamonn, so you, too, can be free of this unfortunate situation. I called you here today because I believe I may be nearing the end of our interviews. It will interest you to know that your wife has given us some information that, frankly, has changed the whole situation.'

'She has?' Eamonn waited.

'She has told us about the baby.'

'She did?' Eamonn said. *Ruby had talked about the baby?* It's a miracle, he thought. Either that, or she's having a breakdown.

Father Ebbs nodded in confirmation.

'It's over, then, isn't it? Surely she has no case now?' Eamonn looked pleadingly at the priest.

'I'm afraid that's not so. There are other grounds. Lack of due discretion and lack of judgement are still possibilities. For the moment, I would urge you to finish your contribution, for your own sake.'

'You mean for your sake?' Eamonn tried.

Father Ebbs threw him a look that would have withered a rose.

Eamonn shrugged his shoulders.

'Would you like to walk, Eamonn?' Father

Ebbs asked suddenly.

'Walk?' Eamonn was still reeling at the thought of poor Ruby talking about those painful memories.

'We can talk while we walk.' Father Ebbs smiled. 'The grounds are beautiful at this time of year. There are some nice little footpaths around the area,' he said.

Eamonn followed Father Ebbs outside.

The fields rolled downwards into a valley. A rough man-made track was visible. Father Ebbs stepped on to it and began to walk briskly. Out of the Archbishop's House, he seemed to relax. 'Ah, there's nothing like the smell of a lady's smock!' he commented.

'Excuse me?' Eamonn stared at him.

'Lady's smock. Can't you smell it? That plant over there, the lilac-coloured one?' He pointed to the flower.

'A plant!' Eamonn breathed a sigh of relief. 'What's that yellow bush there?'

'That's forsythia. It grows easily.'

'You know a lot about plants,' Eamonn observed, wondering why he was making such stupid remarks when he was still seething about Robert Ryan.

'It's my hobby.' Father Ebbs walked on.

'Ruby is having an affair,' Eamonn said flatly. 'I am certain of it.' He waited for the priest to respond.

No matter how hard Eamonn tried he simply could not get rid of the stubborn image of Ruby and Robert locked in a romantic embrace. His anger rose and fell, like waves on the shore. He had no idea what to do with his anger. He needed Father Ebbs to explain away the hurt.

Father Ebbs put his hands behind his back and tucked his head into his chest. He walked purposefully. 'I'm afraid I cannot discuss that with you, Eamonn. I am not in a position to do so. I am under oath too. I am not at liberty to discuss anyone's personal details,' he said sharply.

Eamonn kicked the ground beneath him. Of course you aren't. Just what the hell am I supposed to do with these feelings?

'However, I am interested in your use of the word 'affair', Eamonn.'

'What do you mean?' Eamonn asked.

'You are separated some years, are you not?' Father Ebbs said.

Eamonn smiled to himself, reading between the lines.

Yes, he was separated from Ruby, physically at least, he thought. But that didn't assuage the awful gnawing sensation he felt in his stomach every time he thought about Robert and Ruby. 'I ought to go over there and smash his head against a wall,' Eamonn muttered.

'Very unwise. Remember, if you are looking for revenge, you will have to dig two graves,' Ebbs warned. 'If there is only one army marching, there can't be a war . . . so stop marching . . . '

'Yeah, I know, it's none of my business.' Eamonn sighed, wishing he really meant it.

'The hell it isn't,' Father Ebbs said, under his breath.

They both smiled, without looking at each other.

20

Eamonn told Father Ebbs about the months after the baby's death. He recollected that it was around this time that Ruby had begun to obsess. She cleaned compulsively day and night. At first he paid no attention to it. In fact, he was pleased. For months, the house had looked like a bomb had hit it: now, Ruby spent all her free time cleaning, polishing and dusting. If she wasn't fiddling and moving things around, she spent long hours in the shower, scrubbing, scouring, mopping.

Eamonn recalled that she often changed into her nightdress as soon as she returned from work, then wandered about the house looking for dirt, or traipsed around the garden weeding or snipping the hedges.

Eamonn related what he had aptly named 'the beginning of the end': the slow and steady decline in their relationship after the tragic loss of Genevieve. He had experienced two losses: the loss of his child, and the loss of Ruby. She had remained in the physical sense, but emotionally she had disappeared into some black hole.

Her sorrow was quickly replaced by a

'mission': to get pregnant again, as soon as possible. Eamonn was initially pleased when Ruby's sexual appetite increased tenfold. At first he mistook it for unbridled passion, a peculiar mixture of sorrow and pent-up rage. Ruby seemed interested in only one thing: making love as often as possible. Eamonn described the sex as mechanical, robotic.

One evening, around six months after the loss of the baby, he returned to the smell of cooking. Ruby was dressed, the table was set, and he hoped that something good was about to happen. Ruby was at the cooker with a book in her hand. Eamonn took that as a good sign. He remembered the name-your-baby book. He crossed his fingers behind his back.

'Hi,' she said, smiling at him.

'Do I smell dinner?'

'Sit down, I made something nice for you,' she replied.

Eamonn sat immediately.

'Eamonn, we really need to talk,' she said seriously.

'Yes. We do.' He was delighted. He was tired of the long silences, yet he had known Ruby was grieving and hadn't wanted to push her. This time she had come to him and he was thrilled. He sat down. Should he eat or shut up? He didn't want to offend her.

Hesitantly, he began to put the food into his mouth. Ruby sat opposite, watching him. He could feel her willing him to finish it quickly. He rammed it down his throat as fast as he could.

'I went to the doctor today,' she said.

He held his fork, a cube of potato spiked on it, in mid-air. He was sure she was going to tell him she was pregnant again.

'You know, it's been six months,' she continued. 'At first, I didn't think about it, really. Why should I have? I mean, it was a cinch the first time round, wasn't it? We didn't have to try long before I got pregnant, so why shouldn't I conceive again just as quickly? Anyway, I got this book, you see, in the library. So I went to the doctor and I asked him, 'Why haven't I conceived again?' He said, 'I don't know, but perhaps you would like to explore it a bit further. Maybe we could run some tests on your hormone levels?' I hadn't even thought about that, you know, so I agreed. Anyway, it takes six months for an accurate reading.' She paused. 'Careful, darling.' She gestured towards the poised potato.

'Ruby,' Eamonn tried to interrupt.

'I was delighted. I was really beginning to think there was something wrong with me.' She laughed.

'There is something wrong with you. Something very, very wrong with you,' Eamonn said softly.

'It's a simple blood test, taken every month to find out my prolactine levels. Oestrogen and progesterone, you know. They peak prior to ovulation. Did you know there are only four days in every month when you can actually conceive? In days of old women used to wear a pair of knickers on their head to increase their chances of fertility, the doctor told me. I never heard anything so funny. I couldn't stop laughing. Imagine!'

'Ruby, I thought we were going to have a talk about us,' Eamonn said.

'I *am* talking about us. Haven't you heard a single word I've said? Listen to me! He told me a lot of things I didn't know. For instance, too much caffeine or processed foods can cause infertility — oh, and by the way, so does alcohol so you'll have to give it up,' she said, matter-of-factly. She whisked the plate of dinner from under Eamonn's nose and began scraping the remains into the bin.

'I wasn't finished,' Eamonn muttered, the cube of potato still suspended on the end of his fork.

'I have to start taking B vitamins. Magnesium, zinc and calcium are good too, and iron supplements. Can you buy them for me in the chemist? No, wait, I'll get them myself.' She raced on. 'There's this girl at work, right? She went to an acupuncturist. She also went to reflexology and she took some Chinese herbal medicine. She swears by it. I found out where I can buy them. I can pick them up on the way home from work.' She drew a breath.

'Do I have any say in this, Ruby?' Eamonn asked.

'What are you on about?' She waved a pair of rubber gloves at him.

'I thought you said we needed to talk? There are some things I would like to talk about.'

'What things?' Ruby asked.

'Oh, just things, like the fact that we don't talk any more. That you usually have your head in a bottle of bleach or down the toilet. Or how about the fact that we never go out? That you wear your nightdress all the time? That we haven't made love in years?'

'That's a joke! We never stop.'

'We have a lot of sex, Ruby. We don't make love. There's a big difference.'

Ruby winced as the metaphorical knife twisted in her back.

'And shouldn't we discuss the loss of our baby before we start planning another? I lost the baby too, Ruby. I have feelings too. I'm hurting.'

'There's no time to talk about that now, Eamonn. The past is the past. My biological clock is ticking. I'm running out of time.' She browsed through the pages of her book. 'I have to go to the dentist. Amalgam fillings can cause infertility. Did you ever hear such a thing? Give me that fork before you ruin the carpet,' she hissed. The potato was still dangling dangerously.

Eamonn held his ammunition close to his chest. There was no way he was parting with it. 'I want to talk about Genevieve,' he demanded, waving his fork menacingly.

'No,' Ruby said. She tried to take the fork from him.

'Talk to me, Ruby,' he shouted.

'No! I said no!' Ruby made another grab for the fork but missed by a mile. Eamonn retaliated. He eyeballed the fork between the prongs, until he had his target exactly right. He drew it back, like he was playing a regular game of darts. He let go and the cube of potato whizzed through the air. Ruby watched in horror as it pasted itself to the wall. It looked stationary, but seconds later it began to slide, like a snail, until it plopped on to the carpet. Eamonn smiled triumphantly. He stood up, strode over to the blob on the carpet, put his hands on his hips and studied it. Then he lifted his shoe and stamped it down good and hard.

Ruby was horrified. 'You bastard! You did that deliberately!'

'Quite,' he replied, breathless with victory. 'If you hand me the fruit bowl, I can get started on the purée,' he threatened.

'You wouldn't,' she pleaded.

They made a dive at the same time, and Eamonn grabbed a kiwi fruit, crushed it in his hand, then joyfully dropped it. His enormous foot hovered over it.

'Don't you dare!' she warned him. 'I mean it, Eamonn! You're not being funny!'

'You're no bag of laughs yourself, Ruby! Look at the state of you! It's a fucking carpet! You're more concerned about that damn thing than our marriage!' he screamed at her. Without further ado, he slammed his foot on to the kiwi.

'Now, it's a dirty, messy, slimy carpet, and I love it. Do you hear me? I want it that way. If you touch it, or come within two feet of it with that goddamn bleach I'll get the Black and Decker. You won't have a kitchen to clean at all by the time I'm finished. Understand?' he yelled.

Ruby stared at him as if he was an axe-murderer on the loose. The house had been turned into an open-air asylum. She turned on her heel and stormed out of the kitchen. Eamonn listened to her footsteps as they raced upstairs. He heard the bedroom door slam.

He found her on her hunkers beside the window, a pillow tucked between her arms and her chest.

'I'm sorry,' he muttered. 'The sex thing. That was below the belt.' He could see her face was filled with pain. He tugged at the pillow. 'Ruby, for Christ's sake, we can clean the carpet.' She let him take the pillow. He moved his arm round her shoulder.

'It's all my fault,' she choked. 'The baby. I did something wrong, I'm sure of it. Some germs got into my body. An infection. It was my fault.'

'No, darling, you're wrong. There was no infection. It wasn't your fault.'

Eamonn laid his head on her shoulder, but Ruby was somewhere else. He couldn't reach her.

Eamonn could not read her mind and knew he never would.

As he relayed this to Father Ebbs many things became apparent to him. He realised that he and Ruby had both been grieving, but in different ways. They were both coping too, but separately. They were both broken, but dealing with it differently. The gap was immense. A Grand Canyon of fear stood between them. They had sat quietly together, unable to help each other. Eventually Eamonn had stood up and gone out, leaving Ruby to deal alone with her grief.

Now he was appalled by his lack of understanding and compassion.

It had been their one and only conversation about Genevieve: Eamonn had resolved never to mention her again. It was too much for either of them to bear. Now he turned to Father Ebbs with tears in his eyes. 'I didn't understand, Father. Was that such a crime?' he asked.

Father Ebbs put a hand on his shoulder.

'I was a coward. I bailed out just when she needed me.' Eamonn's tears of shame and remorse came steadily.

'You did the very thing that all men do,' Father Ebbs commented. 'You walked away when you couldn't control something. You walked away because you did not understand the differences between men and women. You cannot be judged for being true to your conditioning! But in light of what you now know, if those circumstances were to present themselves again, what would you do differently?'

'I would probably react the same. It still feels like I am stumbling around in the dark breaking things and most of them are hers . . . ' Eamonn said remorsefully.

They walked further towards the Drumcondra Road, past the archway and towards the priest's living quarters.

Eamonn told the last bit of the story with emotion. After that incident, he had drifted into a state of depression, not caring about anything. He had vowed to keep his grieving to himself. He no longer wanted confrontation. He accepted that Ruby was no longer available emotionally. Whatever she asked, he did without argument or discussion. He spent as much time as possible out of the house.

Ruby became even more obsessed, buying endless cleaning products at the supermarket. She hoarded them under the kitchen sink and behind the toilet in the bathroom. Eamonn even found them in the drinks cabinet. She was convinced that germs were everywhere. She even ate her dinner wearing rubber gloves. Nothing would convince her that the house was perfectly clean. And if she wasn't indulging her favorite phobia, she was reading about infertility. She only left the house to visit the library or talk to other women with the same problem.

His concern for Ruby grew. He even suggested a visit to a psychiatrist. Ruby told him there was nothing wrong with her mind, she was perfectly sane. She suggested that *he* might benefit from it more than she.

Eamonn had lost all interest in the idea of a baby. It seemed to him that a baby had come between them, rather than bringing them closer. Ruby was no longer his wife: she had turned into a demanding mistress. Eamonn was now requested to return home at specific times of the day to perform the conjugal rites. He raced home at lunchtime, undressed, had sex and went back to work. He recalled one of these midday sessions. As soon as he had ejaculated, Ruby had sat up, stood on her head and spread her legs outwards like a scissors.

'What the hell are you doing?' he asked her chin.

'Trying to help the sperm,' she replied, through clenched teeth.

'Ruby, I'm hungry. I need food,' he said.

'Go away,' she snapped.

Eamonn went to the kitchen. He was hard-pressed to find a plate and a knife. He opened the fridge. Everything was wrapped in cling-film and dated. The knife smelt of bleach. He ate two slices of dry bread.

Ruby appeared at the kitchen door. 'We can't go on like this,' she said.

'You're damn right we can't.' Eamonn spat some of the bread on to the table.

'You'll have to be tested, Eamonn,' she said.

'What?'

'It's all arranged. You have to take tomorrow afternoon off work. There's a guy in St James's Hospital who can do it for you. He's a friend of Dr Byrne,' she finished.

'You mean you want me to have a test done to see if there's anything wrong with my sperm?' he said sharply.

'Yes. Why assume I have the problem? It could be you.' She raised her voice a little.

'OK,' he said resignedly.

'You'll do it?' Ruby said.

'Of course.'

'Oh, Eamonn!' Ruby squealed. She ran over to him and, for the first time in months, planted a sincere and passionate kiss on his lips. For a moment Eamonn had thought the old Ruby had returned. He put his arms round her to kiss her back, but she had already gone off on another tangent.

'I've decided I'm going to attend the HARI unit too,' she said excitedly.

'Hari? As in Hari Krishna? Now, look, I'm all for alternative methods but I don't want some robe-clad, bald bastard examining my privates.' He had to draw the line somewhere.

'No! The HARI unit in the Rotunda Hospital. It stands for Human Assisted Reproduction Ireland. It deals specifically with infertility problems. The professor of

313

gynaecology gives a talk there once a week. Will you come, Eamonn?' she begged.

'I don't know.' He wished she would stop.

'Brenda would come,' she said defiantly.

'Well, ask her, then. Better still, why not just put an ad in your newspaper and let everyone know our personal business? You get discount still, don't you?' he said smartly.

Eamonn stopped walking: he was out of breath. His words had frightened and sickened him: he knew now that he had thrown in the towel. He had resigned his posts of husband and father. It had become too much of an effort to argue with her. Besides, no matter what he said, he could not make her change her mind. She had been programmed, as if a computer chip had been inserted in her brain with one mission to accomplish. It ignored any other instructions. In some ways, Eamonn was secretly glad of it. He was free of the responsibility. He had had a lucky escape.

'You see?' he said to Father Ebbs. 'I let her down. I left her. I abandoned her.' He hung his head in shame as he realised, with overwhelming sorrow, that perhaps Ruby had a case for an annulment after all.

21

Ruby awoke to the sound of the first aeroplanes of the morning leaving Dublin airport. She recalled that it had rained on St Patrick's Day as far back as she could remember. She pulled back the curtains and the sun surprised her. It was only eight thirty. She wanted to call Robert. She searched the apartment for a note, then felt silly for expecting to find one. Her stomach churned with a mixture of fear and excitement. She drew a bath, slipped into the warm, scented water, laid her head back and began to think.

She had awoken feeling calm, but it had been short-lived: a new set of feelings had invaded her. She tried to replace them with Robert but they ignored her. She was angry. She resented the Archbishop's House for bringing her secrets to bear fruit. She was furious that the morning after had not delivered its promise of a romantic aftermath.

She had not crossed the line with Robert but it was the first time she had allowed another man to touch her in years. She felt warm thinking of how she had fallen asleep beside him, but the warmth fled as its rival, fear, gained considerable pace behind. There had been no lull, no drifting on clouds, no floating sensation, so common after intimacy. Instead, a barrage of painful memories clouded her heart. Ruby tried distraction. She went and sat at the window to watch the street.

Two green-white-and-orange-faced children ran past the apartment, waving their Irish flags. A third child staggered after them, a little girl. She wore a green dress and green tights to match. Her hair was held back with a tricolour headband. She fell over, and tore her tights. The frantic mother arrived and scolded her for running off.

The little girl looked up, to Ruby's window. Their eyes locked for a moment. Ruby winked at her while the mother continued to lecture. The little girl smiled up at her. Ruby observed that Genevieve would have been about her age, had she lived. She put her hand instinctively to her left shoulder. Genevieve was present. She could feel her. *I'm here, Mammy. I'm here . . .*

Ruby closed her eyes and saw her freckle-faced daughter leaping and bounding from tree to tree. This was how she imagined her. Free, happy, laughing. She imagined Eamonn pushing her on the swings, holding her hand, playing chase. Poor Eamonn!

She hung her head. She thought of how cold she had been towards him. How the pain had consumed her to the point at which she could not communicate with another living soul. How she had wanted to! Oh, how she wanted to tell him now! She had racked her brains for a reason for Genevieve's death. Had it been a glass of wine too many? Had it been sex in early pregnancy? Had it been her own fear that had murdered her child? Did he blame himself too? *What had he felt?* Did he wake now, night upon night, sweating, hearing Genevieve cry in the howling wind? Had he excused himself from people's company whenever a child was present? Had he held back the tears when he saw a pink outfit for a baby girl? Had he locked himself in the toilet at work when other staff discussed their child's bad behaviour? Had he longed to be able to participate? *Listen to me? Wait until I tell you what Genevieve did this morning! She sat up for the first time! She crawled! She said Daddy!* Did he miss all the firsts? Birthday cakes, Barbie dolls, Wendy houses, ballet classes, nativity plays? Did he feel sick when a pretty little Communion girl paraded up the road?

Oh, Eamonn, why didn't I ask you, darling? How alone you must have felt. I'm sorry. I'm so sorry I left you alone with all that hurt. If

317

only they had had another child. Perhaps that would have taken the edge off their pain. It was too late to say.

The intercom buzzed. Ruby knew who it was. She knew he had been to the Archbishop's House that morning. She greeted him in her bathrobe.

'Milady.' He extended his closed fist.

'Good morning, Robert.'

She opened his palm. She started to laugh.

'One wooden peg,' Robert mused.

'Where did you get it?' she chuckled.

'I can't reveal that information, ma'am.'

'I hope you didn't break the law.'

'Not if you don't count climbing over your neighbour's wall and borrowing a thing or two.'

'You didn't!' she said. 'You climbed over your neighbour's wall?'

'I didn't say whose neighbour's wall it was, did I?' He winked. 'I took the liberty of inviting myself over for breakfast.' He held out a brown-paper bag. Ruby peeked inside. The smell of fresh croissants reminded her that she hadn't eaten for at least fourteen hours.

* * *

'I can't remember a bright St Patrick's Day, not ever,' she remarked, as they ate and drank.

'I can't either. It nearly always rains.' Robert kissed her forehead.

Ruby didn't respond.

'Is everything OK?' he queried.

'Sure,' she lied. She wished she had told him everything the night before, but her exhaustion had rendered her incapable of uttering another word.

'Look, about last night . . . ' Robert started.

Ruby dismissed him with a wave of her hand.

Her eyes scanned the room. She spotted the untidy mound of clothes on the floor, the dirty delph heaped in the sink. It took every ounce of strength to stop herself getting up and doing something about it.

'You look a bit peaky, Ruby. Why aren't you dressed? Don't you know what day it is today?' he said, stuffing in the last mouthful of croissant.

'Of course I know what day it is. Didn't I just say it's St Patrick's Day?'

'It's also Mother's Day.'

'It is?' Ruby froze.

'Didn't you open my present?' he asked.

'No. I didn't,' she said hesitantly. She hadn't done anything. She hadn't been able to.

'Where is it?' he said, getting up to search.

'It's right there, where you left it.'

Ruby picked up the box.

'Go on. Open it,' he urged.

Ruby pulled out the box's contents. She stared in horror at the beautiful porcelain doll, not knowing what to say.

'Well? Don't you like her?' he asked.

'It's a doll,' she said quietly.

'It's for Mother's Day. I just thought, well, you know, I thought a doll would be a nice thing to give you because . . . '

'Because I'm childless, Robert? Is that what you're trying to say? You bought me a doll to remind me I'm not a mother?'

'Huh?' he exclaimed.

'Why would I want to acknowledge Mother's Day?' she asked.

'I didn't mean it like that. It was a silly notion I had. I thought a doll might cheer you up. Jesus, I didn't mean to offend you. I thought it was a good idea at the time. I'm sorry.' He went to put his arms around her.

'Have you any idea how much I don't need this right now?'

'No. I said I'm sorry. Look, you haven't spoken about it. I didn't know if you wanted to. Do you want to talk to me about it?'

'I wanted to tell you last night, Robert, but I was too wiped out from the session at the Archbishop's House. I should have told you many things before now.' She placed the doll on the kitchen table and marched out of the room. Robert followed her, and Ruby told him all about Genevieve, all that had happened with the psychologist at the Archbishop's House and her exchange afterwards with Father Ebbs.

'Ruby, I didn't know you couldn't have children. You only told me that you hadn't any. There's a big difference. Please forgive me.' He took two steps towards her.

Ruby folded her arms. 'So, now you do know, Robert. I'm sorry. It's not your fault. This annulment thing is doing me more harm than good. I wish I'd never started the damn thing.' She began gathering up the dirty clothes and put them into a washing basket. 'I was doing OK, you know. I was dealing with it. Admittedly, I could have dealt with it better, but I didn't. Am I going to have to pay for it for the rest of my life? I was robbed of my marriage! I was robbed of children! I was robbed of my peace of mind! I was robbed of my privacy! But it never ends, does it? Once you're married, you really are married for life! Even if you don't have children! We have been left stranded in a kind of no man's land, a personal Purgatory. We're superglued together with a big neon sign that says, 'Hey, we failed! Look at us! No marriage! No kids! No future! And no fucking answers either!' '

Her face had gone an ashen white. 'I just want my life back!' she cried.

She stood in the middle of the room, her fists clenched.

'Are you finished?' Robert whispered.

'You know what all this means, don't you?' Her voice quivered. 'Has it ever occurred to you that this whole annulment thing is a farce?'

'It wasn't a farce for me.'

'Don't you get it? How can my marriage be null and void, Robert? I am living with the consequences of it on a daily basis! I will always live with it! It is valid. I know it's valid, right here!' She pointed to her stomach. 'We can't eradicate Genevieve! We can't eradicate our grief! We can't eradicate each other, no matter what anyone says. My marriage and all that happened in it still goes on! It's the only thing I'm certain of in this life! I am living that marriage! Eamonn is living that marriage!'

Robert stared at her with his mouth open.

'I know women lose babies a lot in the first three months. I know it's common. Everyone has this attitude about it, though, almost like it didn't count. Not a real full-term baby. She was to me. She was my baby. I never got over it. I felt it was my fault. That I must have done something wrong . . . Poor Eamonn. He lost us both. Wife and child.'

* * *

Robert went back to the kitchen, picked up the doll and put it away. *You stupid fool*, he chastised himself.

22

Father Ebbs and Eamonn returned to the interview room. Eamonn continued to talk, as if it were a matter of life and death, and the priest was reluctant to interrupt: he was determined to have the case wrapped up by the end of the week. As soon as he had completed his work, he could concentrate on himself. Anyway, this case had a special meaning for him: it marked the beginning of the end for him too.

★   ★   ★

Eamonn recalled how, to his amazement, he had found himself taking an afternoon off work and attending St James's Hospital for a sperm test. On the one hand, his pride had told him there was nothing wrong with his sperm, but on the other, the adult side of him told him he still had to rule out the possibility. He resented the notion of having to attend the clinic. Yes, indeed! He abhorred the idea of having to perform the act. He detested the thought of relinquishing control to the hospital authorities. He was furious that Ruby had put him in this position. He had come from a long line of sons: there was nothing wrong with *his* biological makeup! It was preposterous to think there might be, he told himself. In the end, if only to prove Ruby wrong, the dirty deed had to be done.

On arrival, Eamonn approached the reception desk. 'I'm looking for Alan Kearney, please.' He smiled at the nurse behind it. She made a call and Alan Kearney ambled in. Eamonn was apprehensive — in fact, his paranoia was rampant: he imagined every soul in the hospital was in on the conspiracy. He had hoped the sight of Alan Kearney would put him at ease, but the man only unnerved him further.

'Eamonn?' he whispered. He wore a pair of glasses that had seen better days.

'Yes,' Eamonn whispered back.

'I'm so glad you could come at such short notice.' He giggled behind his cupped hand. The nurse behind the reception desk sniggered. Or did she? She looked at another nurse, who was fiddling with files, and grinned at her. Eamonn thought he would die of embarrassment.

Alan Kearney was beside himself with glee. 'Just a little joke.' He thumped Eamonn's arm playfully.

'Hilarious,' Eamonn replied drily. 'Are you a doctor?'

'Me? Goodness, no!' Alan Kearney laughed. 'I'm a laboratory technician,' he said, and cleared his throat.

Eamonn took a mental note of the bloodstains on the technician's white coat. Instinctively he moved to protect his genital area. His hand hovered over it, like that of a terrified rugby amateur about to encounter his first scrum.

'You could see a doctor, but the waiting list is endless. It's really a simple procedure, Eamonn.' He thrust a brown-paper bag under Eamonn's arm.

It ought to be a simple procedure, Eamonn surmised. This here brown-paper bag had the power to start a new life. How simple could you get? I can handle this, he said to himself. I'm being ridiculous! It's a simple test, nothing like what Ruby has to do. All I have to do is follow the simple instructions and it will all be over soon. I *can* handle this, he repeated. Stop behaving like a bloody mouse! he scolded himself. Are you a man or what? He looked inside the brown-paper bag. It contained a strange-looking plastic bottle in the shape of a bowl. 'What if I said I'd come prepared — like, here's one I made earlier?' he asked Kearney.

'Wouldn't do I'm afraid. Has to be a fresh specimen and it has to be in a sterilised container to procure accurate results.' Alan Kearney smiled a superior smile, uplifted by this momentary power trip.

'How would you know if it's fresh? Don't tell me you have to witness the job, hands on?' Eamonn whispered, feeling somewhat stupid and inadequate.

'That won't be necessary. I trust you.' The technician winked.

Eamonn looked at the bloodstains again. He could always go on the waiting list. No. It was now or never. Just do it, you bloody coward. Do it now! 'Where do I go?' he said, agitated. Better to get it over and done with — he didn't want to have to come back.

'I'm afraid you will have to use the public convenience, that door on the left.' Kearney pointed.

'You're joking, right?' Eamonn stared at him.

'Sorry, there's nowhere else. Besides, we don't want you causing a scene. There could be a run on the contraceptive cabinets.' He chuckled.

'Quite.' Eamonn's face had gone a ghastly white. 'Hey. Wait a minute. Don't I get a helping hand?' he asked. If you can't beat them, join them, he thought.

'Like?' The lab technician missed the boat.

'Like a magazine, a video, something on the lines of, say, *Busty Blonde Tart?*' Eamonn said, at the top of his, voice.

'Sssh! Where do you think you are? Harley Street? Just think of your ancestors, keeping the line going, that should do the trick.'

Eamonn thought of his rotting ancestors, and his penis felt like a wet dishcloth.

Alan Kearney directed him to his desk. Eamonn should meet him there when he had completed the task. Then he bade him farewell and wished him good luck.

Eamonn was left standing in the corridor with his plastic bottle. He eyed the girls behind the desk, then slowly made his way to the toilet. He stopped short at the door and gingerly pulled at his cuffs. He looked left, then right, and charged inside like a bolt of electricity.

He surveyed his surroundings. A small cubicle two feet by two feet. The stench of urine was hardly supportive to his waning libido.

He retrieved the bottle from the brown-paper bag, and examined it curiously. It was small and round. He looked at his crotch, then again at the bottle. How on earth was he supposed to come in that thing? He crouched precariously, propping one leg on the edge of the toilet, and jamming the other knee against the door. That didn't work.

He turned sideways and elbowed himself in the jaw. That didn't work. He knelt on the toilet, bent forward with one leg wrapped around the pan. This worked, if you didn't count the fact that his arse was stuck in the cistern.

'OK,' he said. He had the position. Now all he had to do was get the adrenaline going. He thought of Madonna, but Mother Teresa came instead. He thought of Marilyn Monroe, but Mary Harney drowned her out. After her, he knew the situation was hopeless. His eyes were level with the key-hole and he peered out at one of the nurses on the reception desk. His humiliation had come full circle: now he was a dirty, lecherous peeping Tom. He concentrated hard.

Don't let me down now, I'm depending on you! You can do it!

He pumped and pumped — and hey presto! He was surprised that it had happened so quickly. He put it down to the fear of being caught. He cleaned himself up and exited the toilet.

The bloody shame of it! This has to be the Guinness Book of Records *in rock bottoms!*

He passed the woman at the desk. She nodded at him. He nodded back. Close up, he realised, she looked nothing like 'Divine Brown'. He was consumed with guilt.

As soon as he had turned the corner he legged it down the corridor to the laboratory.

Three cheers for Eamonn's sperm! Hip-hip hooray! 'My sample!' He slammed the bottle down on Alan Kearney's desk, still out of breath. 'Thanks to a certain redhead on the reception desk.'

'Hey, what did you do? Masturbate behind the photocopier?' Kearney looked at his watch. 'Jesus, five minutes! I think that's a record.'

Eamonn had already left the room. He departed from St James's Hospital, his manhood intact, and returned to work feeling proud of his achievement. He imagined his sperm wriggling about under the microscope, waiting to be unleashed in egg heaven. Give them hell, he said, waving his fist in the air.

★   ★   ★

Father Ebbs tried to hide a smile. He choked back a guffaw. Eamonn let out a stifled chuckle. Father Ebbs sniggered.

Then Eamonn burst into uncontrollable laughter. Father Ebbs let rip. They rolled around for some five minutes.

The caretaker, Bill, passed the door. He

330

stopped outside and heard the rumpus. He made a mental note to stop ordering that expensive wine for the sacristy.

★ ★ ★

Eamonn hated Sundays, and especially the one after the worst Saturday in his life. They were long, tedious and famous for family outings, his number-one pet hate. This Sunday, although it was a festive one, he hadn't the energy to play the game. After the previous day's events with Father Ebbs at the Archbishop's House he was worn out from fighting his thoughts. No matter how hard he tried, he simply couldn't get Robert Ryan's face out of his mind. If it wasn't his presence assaulting his consciousness, it was Ruby's words thrown from the window-ledge. *Robert Ryan.* The offending name echoed in his brain, tormenting him until he could stand it no longer.

He sat at his CD player and put the headphones over his ears. He turned up the volume, pressed play and settled down to listen. He read the cover sleeve. Schubert's Symphony No. 8 in B Minor, D.759, 'Unfinished'. 'Unfinished,' he said aloud. Then he laughed at the irony. Indeed, his very existence seemed unfinished. He had been in

Purgatory for too long. Just when did a marriage end? he asked himself.

He got up and walked round his apartment, surveying its impeccable cleanliness. Everything was in its place. His black leather shoes shone under the bedside locker. The furniture gleamed with polish. The carpets were stain-free. His wardrobe held the finest designer suits, but they were just that: suits, pieces of clothing. His humble abode lacked warmth. It was a place to live, not a home. No love, no life, no energy intruded into the chilly atmosphere of perfect bachelordom.

He had been a slave to the god of ambition, prestige and ladder-climbing. He had done well in his career. Yet he was the personification of loneliness and misery.

The apartment was turning on him; it transformed itself into eerie shapes and forms to haunt him.

Now he yearned to smell Anaïs in the bedroom. He craved the days before Ruby had acquired her phobias. He ached to see the laundry baskets overflowing, dirty underwear strewn across the landing. He longed to see tights lined up along the shower rail, and hair clogging the wash-basin. He wanted dinner-plates caked with curry sauce from yesterday's takeaway, the familiarity of the

Tampax box wedged behind the toilet.

He wished. He wanted. He hoped.

What is a man? What should a man be? How should he behave? he wondered. He had failed as a man. The questions remained unanswered. How could he fix what was wrong when he didn't know what it was? He had been a good husband, had he not? He had never been unfaithful, had never gambled, missed anniversaries or been lazy around the house.

He went over to the telephone, picked up the address book and flicked through the pages. Business contacts: he hadn't a friend in the world. He leafed through it again, and stopped at the letter H. He bit his lip. He scratched his head. He lifted the receiver and dialled the number. 'Hello, Marjory, it's Eamonn.'

★　★　★

Marjory was flattered: Eamonn's visits and phone calls were increasing in frequency. She was certain that the day would come when he would reach out to her. She had to play her cards right. One mistake, though, and she would lose him for ever. She had to appear neutral. There was no point in damning Ruby: that would only alienate him. She listened to Eamonn's voice as the old dilemma returned ten-fold. She was uncertain as to where her loyalties should be. She had refused to attend the Archbishop's House as Ruby's witness. However, she had also decided to refuse to attend for Eamonn. She was sure he would deem it unfair of her to take sides. After all, they had both been excellent friends to her.

'Marjory, I'm sorry to put you on the spot,' Eamonn started.

'It's OK. I'm glad you called. It's just . . . it's not easy, Eamonn. I'm in the middle, do you understand?' she asked softly.

'Of course,' he said. 'I'm just having it rough at the moment.' His voice trailed off.

Marjory heard the struggle in his voice. 'Sundays are the worst,' she commented.

'You're damn right about that. Look, where are the kids?' Eamonn chanced.

'Ben went to the parade with his dad. Jessica is here. She's watching it on television.'

'Why don't you come over for lunch, bring Jessica with you. That's if you haven't got anything else planned?'

He sounded brighter — Jessica always gave him a life, Marjory thought. 'Hey, that's a great idea. I'd love to come over. We can have a good talk then.' She hung up.

★ ★ ★

An hour later, Marjory and Jessica arrived. Eamonn bundled Jessica into his arms and carried her inside. 'Who's a princess?' he asked her. He had almost forgotten Marjory was there too.

'A humble offering.' She shoved a bottle of red wine under his nose.

'Bulgarian — nice,' he commented. He led her into the main room, where the dining-table was set for three. 'Lunch is almost ready.' He took her coat, and she went to stand with her back to the open fire.

'It's goddamn freezing out there!' She shivered.

'Throw a few more briquettes on, if you like.' He brought Jessica into the kitchen to help him.

'Something smells good,' Marjory shouted to him.

'Moussaka,' he called back, 'and trifle for her ladyship.' He smiled as Jessica made a mess of the salad bowl. 'How's Ben? Has he been behaving?' He put his head round the corner.

'He's a lot better. He's gone out with Sam for the day. The third time this week.'

'He seems to be with him now more than ever? Ironic, eh?' he said, entering the room with two plates. Jessica stayed in the kitchen having fun with the salad bowl: Eamonn had halved the tomatoes and cut them into crown shapes.

They sat down to eat.

'Do you want to know something, Eamonn? I stand at the window every Saturday until his car pulls up. I can't wait to see him turn the corner because I know I'm going to get some time to myself? Selfish, eh?' she said.

'I don't think it's selfish at all. Running a home, raising two kids alone, and trying to do a job. Jesus, I couldn't do it! I admire you. Any time you need a babysitter for Jessica, all you have to do is ask.'

'There's nothing to admire, Eamonn. I have to do it. I have no choice.' She sighed.

'But you *did* have a choice, and as far as I am concerned you made the right one.' He smiled at her. 'Jessica? Hurry up. Your lunch is getting cold.'

'I'm thinking of going to night school.' Marjory hesitated.

'Great idea.' He looked at her. 'What's the matter?'

'Just thinking about it exhausts me. How am I supposed to do all this and go to school? I'm barely managing as it is,' she said.

'Where there's a will there's a way. Can I

ask you a personal question, Marjory?' He spoke quietly. Jessica wasn't too far out of earshot.

'Of course, Eamonn. You can ask me anything,' she purred.

'Do you and Sam . . . I mean, are you and Sam friends? Like, do you talk to each other?'

'Well, I keep the conversation strictly business. We only discuss the kids. I used to be nice to him when we first broke up. I guess I felt sorry for him, even a bit guilty, but he always got the wrong message. He assumed I was trying to get us back together. Now I keep my distance. It's easier that way. You should adopt this approach with Ruby. Keep your distance,' she advised. 'Why do you ask?' she said.

'I can't talk to Ruby any more. It was always difficult, as you know. Now I know about the affair she's having, I can't bring myself to face her at all. I mean, the fucking hypocrisy! Applying for an annulment and screwing someone at the same time.' He choked on a piece of aubergine. He was furiously jealous. He reached for his wine and gulped it down as he saw Marjory's jaw hit the floor. Evidently she knew nothing about an affair.

'Eamonn, if Ruby's seeing someone, it can hardly be termed an 'affair', now, can it?

337

You're separated a long time. The annulment has nothing to do with any other relationship she might be having. But I have to admit I'm a bit taken aback. I had no idea.'

'C'mon, Marj, you must have known. Don't play dumb with me. I know Ruby tells you everything.' Eamonn eyed her suspiciously.

'Eamonn! Ruby hasn't spoken to me once since I refused to go to the Archbishop's House. The nerve of her blaming me and you!' She laughed.

'What?' Eamonn thought he had misheard.

'Didn't you know? She thinks we are having an affair! She never forgave me for giving you that letter on your wedding day. I know from Judy that's she's positively convinced you and I are an item!' Marjory blushed.

'What letter?' Eamonn stared at her as if she was from Mars.

'Don't you remember?' she asked.

'No!' he gasped.

'Exactly!' She seemed annoyed, he thought. 'Remind me,' he said to placate her, and then, 'Jessica? What are you doing? Come in here now!'

'I gave you a letter on your wedding day. It upset Ruby. Judy told me she thought it was a bit odd of me. I didn't mean any harm by it,' she said.

'I vaguely remember something now. Yes, you did give me a letter. What was the big deal?'

'Well . . . I think Ruby thought it was out of place.'

'I can't remember what was written in it — or half of the night for that matter. Christ, I was really drunk.'

'Did you show her the letter?' Marjory asked.

'No. If I remember correctly, I told her it was a card. How would she have known it was a letter anyway? I just can't believe she said that. The bloody cheek of her! She's the one who's having a fling. God, you should see this guy! He's old! I mean, *ancient*. It's a bloody insult to me. What can she possibly see in this old geezer? Sometimes I wonder who Ruby is, you know. She's like a stranger. Christ, when I start to think about that bastard, all I want to do is get his head and use it for a football.'

'There's only one course of action you can take,' Marjory said slowly. 'If you keep taking other people's bullets, you could be left with a smoking gun. You must challenge her, face to face.'

23

Dublin Regional Marriage Tribunal,
Diocesan Offices,
Archbishop's House,
Dublin 9

Personal and Confidential

19 March 1996

Nullity of Marriage: Reece — Blake
J.2-254.94.

Dear Ms Power,

We invite you to attend the Archbishop's House for interview on Friday 22 March at 9.30 a.m as witness in relation to the above case. Should you have any reservations or queries regarding this interview, please feel free to telephone us at your convenience.

Should this appointment be unsuitable, please let us know as soon as possible and we shall let you know an alternative time.

With kind wishes,
Yours sincerely,

Aidan Mason
Tribunal Secretary

Brenda Power arrived at the Archbishop's House twenty minutes early. The waiting room was empty. She wondered if she had misread the letter. Had she got the date wrong? She had no idea what to expect, or why she had been called for an interview. She wondered what information she held that might be of interest to the Tribunal.

While she had been close to Eamonn and Ruby during the turbulent latter years of their marriage, things had changed recently. When they met the atmosphere was strained, and Brenda felt like a sneak, a nosy-parker and a busybody. She tried to remind herself that she was there at Ruby's request.

She stroked the amethyst crystal that hung round her neck and admired the grounds from the window.

'Ms Power?' A priest was peering from behind the door. 'I had no idea anybody was here yet. Forgive me for leaving you to wait,' he said politely, and offered a friendly handshake.

'It's Brenda, Father.' He had a solid

handshake, she thought. A good, down-to-earth strong one.

'I'm Father Ebbs. Thank you for attending, Brenda. I appreciate it, as I'm sure Mrs Blake does.'

Brenda felt important. It was nice to be needed, to have something to offer the world. For too long now she had felt an emptiness that consumed her every waking moment. The only thing that kept her going was her post at the Sacred Heart home. Now even that offered little comfort or consolation: her favourite patient, Kit, had been taken ill in the last few days and this had affected Brenda deeply. She had been warned of the consequences of getting emotionally involved with the patients, but she had felt she had no choice. She had tried to contact Kit's relations, but no one had turned up. She found that inexcusable.

There had to be someone who knew her. How lonely Kit must be, she thought. She couldn't bear the idea of the old lady dying alone. Brenda tried to throw off the sadness but it crept back in, reminding her of her own isolation in the world.

She tried to concentrate on the job in hand: the priest was explaining the purpose of their meeting.

'You have been called here to testify on

behalf of Ruby Blake, who as you are aware has applied to the Catholic Marriage Tribunal for an annulment. Let me put your mind at ease by telling you what this *does not* mean — rather than what it means!' He had a nice smile, Brenda thought.

'Think of it as a day in court,' he continued. 'I will ask you some questions pertaining to the marriage. You will answer them to the best of your ability. You will note that I will record these questions and answers on this tape-recorder. You may find it distracting to start with, but you will get used to it. I'm not interested in your personal opinions of the marriage, only the facts. Do you understand me so far?'

Brenda nodded. She noted his mop of black curls, how they had a mind of their own, just like hers. She could smell a hint of Brylcreem. She knew it well. Hadn't she used it herself to try to tame her own waves?

'You are not being asked to make a moral judgement. Frankly, your thoughts and personal feelings surrounding the breakdown of their marriage are of no use or interest to me. You are a third party. Third parties frequently have personal viewpoints. So, what I am trying to say, in effect, is you are not being put on the spot, Brenda. You are not being asked to take sides,' he finished.

'How did you manage to grow a gardenia indoors and make it flower in the middle of March?' she asked.

'Pardon?' Father Ebbs looked up from his file.

'I'm sorry.' Brenda bowed her head.

Father Ebbs looked behind him. 'Oh, that.' He laughed. 'It's a fake. My caretaker, Bill, waters it every day. I haven't the heart to tell him it's not real. He gets so much pleasure out of tending it. Looks after it like a newborn baby.'

'It looks so real!' Brenda got up, reached over his shoulder and felt the tips of the leaves. Her shoulder brushed against his cheek.

'Do you like plants?' Father Ebbs asked.

'I love them. I don't have much time for them now, though. I have been trying to grow a magnolia for three years. Every year it fails to blossom.' She sat down.

'Like my lilies-of-the-valley,' Father Ebbs raised his eyebrow. He liked the woman. She was friendly but unassuming, a nice, earthy combination. Her perfume smelt of lemons.

'Are you employed, Brenda?' he asked.

'Yes. I'm a geriatrician, I look after elderly people,' she answered.

'Really?' He was impressed. He taped the question and her answer.

'How long have you know Ruby and Eamonn Blake?' he asked.

'Since we were in school together. I have always maintained contact with Ruby. When she married Eamonn I got to know him pretty well. But I haven't had a conversation with either of them since their marriage broke down — well, not an intimate one. I really don't know how the land lies now.'

Father Ebbs held up his hand. 'That's not relevant, Brenda. We are only interested in the marriage itself, not the separation, if you understand.'

'I see.' Brenda relaxed a little. 'I think I can be of assistance there.'

'Good, very good. Did you frequent the Blake household after the loss of their baby?' he asked.

'Yes I did.'

'How often?'

'Two or three times a week.'

'That often?' He looked up.

'Yes. You see, Ruby and Eamonn hardly ever talked to each other after that. Eamonn wasn't interested any more, and Ruby turned to me. She needed me.'

'That is your opinion, I am sure. However, tell me about your visits to the house and what you observed, rather than what you felt,' he said kindly.

'That's difficult, Father,' she said honestly.

'I know. Just do your best. Think of yourself as a spectator, watching a football match.'

'Just tell the story?' she asked.

'Just tell the story,' he agreed.

★   ★   ★

Brenda recalled visiting the Blakes four months after the loss of their child. The atmosphere was tense. Long silences ensued between them. At first Brenda had tried to behave as if everything was normal, but Ruby was so on edge. She talked continuously about pregnancy and appeared to have little interest in anything else. Except for marathon cleaning sessions, and a preoccupation with germs.

Brenda had thought her behaviour was a result of the tragedy. She added that Ruby seemed oblivious to Eamonn's retreat from the marriage. When Brenda had arrived, she recalled, Eamonn had usually gone out. She had been relieved, in a cowardly way: words failed her when it came to condolences. Besides, what could one say in those circumstances? It seemed pointless to try to express compassion and sorrow for such a loss. Ruby, too, had evaded the subject, which suited Brenda down to the ground. She described Ruby's state of mind as 'obsessed'.

Then Brenda told of the evening when Ruby had attended the Round Room in the Rotunda for the open night. There, talks and lectures were given on infertility and any new treatments by the resident obstetricians. Ruby had been filled with new resolve. Brenda felt it had made her worse: her friend's mission had graduated into full-blown addiction. Nothing was going to get in her way. Not even Eamonn's lack of interest.

'I was concerned for their relationship. Ruby thought another baby would fix it. I knew Eamonn didn't care. What she thought would cure them was killing them. I tried to talk to her about it, but she fobbed me off, telling me I didn't understand anything,' she said.

* * *

Father Ebbs loved interviewing witnesses. Often they gave away fundamental information without knowing its importance, as Brenda was doing now. He held the same view as she did of this marriage, and her observations were uncannily accurate. He, too, believed that Ruby's obsession had destroyed the relationship. It was sad that she herself could not see it. She clung stubbornly

347

to the belief that she was trying to put things right. Now someone close to the couple was confirming his suspicions once and for all.

He took a deep breath and blessed himself. The end was in sight. He thanked the Lord for small miracles that came in the form of people. People like Brenda Power.

'What happened after Ruby attended the HARI unit? Did she continue to keep in contact with the Rotunda Hospital?' Father Ebbs pushed on.

'Unfortunately, she did.' Brenda sighed.

'Why do you say 'unfortunately'?' Father Ebbs enquired.

'Well, I think it only made things worse.' And Brenda endeavoured to explain why.

Ruby had eventually been sent an appointment to see the head gynaecologist of the unit. When she finally saw him he prescribed an expensive six-month course of drug treatment designed to stimulate the release of eggs from the ovaries. However, when the six months were up, Ruby had still not conceived.

Then Ruby had begged the doctor to carry out a laparoscopy.

'A what?' Father Ebbs asked.

'A laparoscopy, Father.' Brenda smiled. 'It's an internal scan of the womb, so to speak. A small camera is inserted through a tiny cut in the belly-button area. It can reveal the troublesome area almost immediately,' she concluded.

'I see. If that was the case, why didn't she have it done immediately?'

'Well, there are risks associated with the test, Father. Small risks, but Eamonn was dead against it. So was I. Apparently one in a thousand women has something go wrong. She had to sign a consent form before the operation. God, there were some rows over that,' Brenda recalled.

'Why was Eamonn against it?'

'I guess he was worried about her,' Brenda said. 'Ruby didn't see it that way. She assumed he was being difficult as usual.'

'What happened then?' Father Ebbs continued to scribble notes.

'Well, it turned out that she was the one in a thousand.'

'Dear me.' Father Ebbs sighed.

'She woke up in agony. I'll never forget it. Eamonn was ranting and raving at the doctors and nurses but they insisted it was normal to have some pain. You see, they pump gas into the womb to expand it so the camera can see more. I had only to look at her to know something was really wrong. She was sent home, but by the evening, she was doubled up in pain. We eventually got an ambulance back to the hospital. Eamonn demanded that the gynaecologist be called,' she said.

'Do go on.'

'She was in so much pain. There was even talk about morphine at one stage. The gynaecologist came in the early hours of the morning. He did an internal scan and they found she had internal bleeding.'

'I see,' said Father Ebbs.

'Anyway, it turned out they had ruptured something while the camera was in there. God, I felt so sorry for Eamonn and Ruby, all the trouble they were going through. I often wondered if it was worth it or if it was only causing a greater rift between them.'

'Why do you say that?'

'Well, the results of the test were devastating. It turned out that both Fallopian tubes were damaged beyond repair. There was nothing wrong with her eggs. The gynaecologist explained to Ruby that the ectopic pregnancy had done the damage. Ruby was beside herself with grief,' she finished.

'Well, at least they got some answers. What about Eamonn's test?' Father Ebbs was still scribbling.

Brenda looked afraid to answer, he noticed.

'Do you know the result of Eamonn's test?'

Father Ebbs repeated. It was important to have the answer on file, should the Tribunal ask.

'Am I supposed to answer that?' Brenda still seemed uncomfortable.

'You are not obliged to answer anything, Brenda. I will find out the answer from Eamonn anyway. I just wondered, did Ruby or Eamonn tell you?' he pushed.

'Yes, they did, of course.' Brenda relaxed. 'Eamonn's test came back normal. There was nothing wrong with him. I think Ruby was furious about that at first,' Brenda surmised.

'Understandably.' Father Ebbs nodded.

'It wasn't long after that that Ruby gave up the fight for a baby and the fight for her marriage,' Brenda said.

'Brenda, you have been extremely helpful. I cannot thank you enough!' Father Ebbs closed his file.

'Is that it?' Brenda asked, evidently a little disappointed. 'I don't have any more questions . . . ' Father Ebbs linked his fingers and paused. Then he said, 'Can you confirm one thing for me? Are you aware if counselling was sought by either Ruby or Eamonn?' He wanted to have this piece of information clearly highlighted on the petition. He felt it was very important.

'No, Father. I'm glad you asked. I think it's

important. I suggested it many times, but they wouldn't hear of it. They needed more than counselling, though. Especially Ruby. I do believe at some stage Eamonn asked her to go and see a psychiatrist. She was furious. I can't help feeling that a good doctor might have been able to do something for her.' She wagged her chestnut curls from side to side.

'That's most sad.' Father Ebbs tutted.

His telephone rang, and he answered it, muttering under his breath. He replaced the receiver. 'Could you excuse me for a moment?' he asked.

'Of course,' Brenda replied.

★ ★ ★

Brenda hummed quietly as she waited for Father Ebbs to return. She scanned the room for something to read. It was then she saw it.

Ruby and Eamonn's file lay on the bureau. It beckoned her to open it. She looked at it, sideways, upside-down. Some loose pages peeked out, exposed for all to see. She reached over and stuffed them in. Still, the file called to her. She willed it to go away! She prayed for Father Ebbs to return before temptation became too much.

She tried to recap on her morning with the priest. She had enjoyed the interview and found the whole process fascinating. What an interesting job it must be, listening to people's innermost secrets.

Secrets.

What secrets are in that file?

'To hell with it!' she muttered, and reached across the bureau. She opened the black file slowly, making sure not to crease or tear the paper. She took the top page, holding it between her fingertips. Then she leaned forward and read it in double-quick time.

Dublin Regional Marriage Tribunal,
Diocesan Offices,
Archbishop's House,
Dublin 9

Nullity of Marriage: Reece — Blake
J.2.254/94.

Personal and Confidential

22 March 1996

Dear Mrs Blake,

I am writing to you regarding your witness Ms Judy Rowland, who has not responded to our recent letter. As this is the third contact we have made with the witness,

353

inviting her to attend for interview regarding your application for annulment, we must assume that she has chosen not to participate. We feel it would be inappropriate to pursue this matter any further.

With kind wishes,
Yours sincerely,

Aidan Mason
Tribunal Secretary

Brenda put away the letter immediately. She waited for Father Ebbs to return. When he did, he thanked her once more for having attended: she had been of such great assistance. Then he walked her to the lift. Brenda said goodbye. She stepped into the lift and pressed the ground-floor button.

'Oh, Brenda.' Father Ebbs stuck his foot in the door. 'A tip for the magnolia . . . '

★ ★ ★

Father Ebbs gathered together his portfolio and began to list the documents it contained. He numbered them carefully. The fact sheet. The certificates of baptism and marriage. The signed appointment of an advocate. The witness sheet. The statement of the plaintiff.

The formal petition and, finally, the psychological report.

His case was ready for Rome. He sat down to write his final report, careful to avoid any lengthy emotional pleas. He told the story as he had heard it. As Auditor, he was able to add some of his own views. He was articulate and specific in highlighting what he saw as fundamental facts pertaining to the case. As he closed the final chapters, he was also closing the final chapters of his own unhappiness.

A new life awaited him. A new start. Perhaps he would meet someone. Someone like Brenda, who had an interest in the same things he did. He could hardly contain that overwhelming new feeling. Now he recognised it for what it was. It was Sean Ebbs, the man, the human being he had abandoned so many years ago. Now he held on to him with a vice-like grip. He would never again let him go.

★ ★ ★

Brenda had an early breakfast in Bewley's. She finished her coffee and walked to South Anne Street to a public phone-box. It was a Friday and she knew it was Judy's day off, that she would be at home, most likely having a much-needed lie-in. She inserted some coins and dialled her number.

'Hello?' a muffled Judy answered.

'Judy, it's Brenda,' she said sharply.

'Jesus, what are you doing phoning me so early. It's only twelve o'clock! You know I only get to sleep on for one day,' she mumbled.

'Wake up!' Brenda laughed.

'What's wrong? Has someone died?' Judy yawned.

'No. I've been thinking. I wanted to say something to you.'

'It better be good.'

'I can't believe you didn't attend the Archbishop's House,' Brenda said.

'What the hell are you on about?'

'You know quite well. You never appeared as witness,' Brenda said.

'That's none of your business. Hey? Was Ruby talking to you?' she asked angrily.

'No, she was not,' Brenda said.

'All this rubbish about an annulment. I'm not playing her game.' Judy yawned again.

'It's no game, Judy. It means nothing to us, sure, but it means a hell of a lot to Ruby.' Brenda was delighted with her newly found assertiveness. But the fact that she had opted to phone rather than call round reminded her that she still had a good distance to go in the assertiveness department.

'Well, if it means that much to her, why hasn't she contacted any of us, eh?' Judy sneered.

'She shouldn't have to,' Brenda persisted.

'Look,' Judy said, 'the last time I tried to talk to her, she was convinced I was on Eamonn's side. You know, she really believes something's going on between him and Marjory, and I got fed up trying to tell her otherwise. She won't listen, no matter what.'

'I understand that, but you and I know she's not well, Judy. Even to be thinking that way shows me just how close to the edge she is. No matter how crazy her thinking seems, she has good reason to add two and two and come up with five regarding Marjory. She still needs her friends.' Brenda wasted no more time. She had aimed her torpedo with strategic eloquence and it had slammed home. A perfect hit.

'OK, OK. I get the point,' Judy said wearily. 'What am I supposed to do?'

'I don't know what any of us is supposed to do.' Brenda pondered the question.

'Why don't we call her?' Judy suggested.

'Better still, let's just arrive unannounced,' Brenda said.

'Good idea,' Judy agreed. 'When?'

'I'll call you,' Brenda said, and hung up.

* ★ ★

At home, Brenda checked her answering-machine. The head nurse, Sarah, had left a message for her to contact the Sacred Heart Home immediately. Brenda picked up the phone to dial the number, then paused and replaced the receiver. In her kitchen drawer she kept a bag of rune stones with an interpretation book. She closed her eyes, put her hand into the bag and drew one out. She looked at it: the stone of faith. There was no need to consult the interpretation book. Brenda had a bad feeling in the pit of her stomach. She put on her coat and went straight out.

★ ★ ★

Judy rolled out of bed, moaning. Ruby's annulment had been the last thing on her mind. She knew it had been mean of her not to attend and she felt guilty. She justified her action by telling herself that the girls didn't understand her. If she had tried to explain how lonely she was, they would never have believed her. They always assumed she was fine, that she was happy. Everyone did.

She pulled open her wardrobe door, and gazed into the full-length mirror inside.

Shock! She had forgotten about yesterday and the steps she had taken to alter her appearance once and for all. She stared at the new Judy.

Oh, Jesus!
I feel sick!

24

Ruby sat gazing out of her bedroom window. She seemed to have taken up residence there. Each day she went to work, came home, had dinner then sat on the edge of the bed looking out of the window. There wasn't much of a view, just the sea and some late-evening strollers, but she seemed to need to sit and stare at nothing. She felt like a cork bobbing on the ocean.

After her outburst on St Patrick's Day, Ruby felt it was only fair to Robert to fill in the blanks. She sat him down and told him what had happened in her marriage to Eamonn. Robert was as attentive as always, rarely interrupting.

She was in emotional turmoil. On the one hand she felt enormous intimacy and connection with Robert. On the other, she felt colossal compassion and love for Eamonn. She was in her worst state of confusion to date. Every morning when she woke, she hoped one would have cancelled out the other. This did not happen. She felt guilty when she was happy to see Robert. She felt guilty when she thought of Eamonn. So she sat and stared out of the window, hoping that an answer might find her sooner rather than later.

Throughout this period of self-analysis, Ruby realised some startling truths about herself. She had an iron will, which she had always perceived to serve her well. Now, she saw clearly, it had been misused, abused, even. Had she turned her steely determination in the direction of her failing marriage, the results might have been different. Her desire for motherhood had only been one segment of her marriage, but she had allowed it to dominate everything else — their kinship, their career goals, their social life and their sex life. In her lonely crusade to conceive a child, she had lost sight of her primary purpose: to attend to her partner's needs. Ruby looked deep into her heart and was filled with self-disgust when it became obvious to her that she had abandoned Eamonn. This revelation haunted her. It visited her nightly, reminding her of the hand she had played in terminating their marriage. She had blamed Eamonn for something he had had no control over, and she had ignored the loneliness he must have endured throughout her emotional 'absence', for now she believed wholeheartedly that she might as well have left him physically, for that was what she had done emotionally. From the moment she had lost the baby, Eamonn had lost her. She had left him behind in the wild-goose chase for a child, who she had been convinced would bring her peace of mind.

But that had really been an escape from the pain, something to focus on, apart from her sorrow and loss. Now Ruby yearned for peace of mind but it was too late. She dragged herself from bed to work and back again. The days passed slowly. The nights stretched on for ever. Even Robert's kindness and understanding could not rescue her from herself.

It was early in the morning on Saturday 23 March 1996. Ruby sat on the edge of her bed. She was in no hurry to get dressed. She liked Saturdays, and not having to get ready for work, and she wondered how to spend the day.

The intercom buzzed, breaking her concentration. She was expecting Robert, but not so early. She pressed the security button to let in whoever it was and soon Brenda and Judy were standing before her, bearing a Kylemore cake bag. Ruby was pleased to see familiar faces. She needed her friends, and it was time she shared the truth with them. She owed it to Brenda especially: she had been kind, and faithful to the last. She invited them in.

'I told you she was sick.' Brenda looked around her.

'What the hell is going on, Ruby?' Judy surveyed the chaos.

'God, it's good to see you.' Ruby hugged them again. 'Whose idea was this?'

'You never call lately.' Brenda returned the hug.

'I never call you either,' Judy said lamely, 'and if it wasn't for Brenda I wouldn't have come.'

'I'm sorry too. I've been preoccupied. So much is happening. I don't know what to do with it all.' Ruby pushed her hair back from her face.

'Look, go and get dressed. I'll put on the kettle,' Brenda told her.

'We were worried,' Judy said quietly, when Ruby returned.

'I'm sorry. I just feel so . . . ' Ruby gave up trying to explain.

'Kit died,' Brenda offered, knowing Ruby never launched into her feelings without being drawn out first.

'That lovely old woman who was always calling for you?' Ruby asked.

'That's the one.' Brenda bowed her head.

'How old was she?' Judy tried to be nice.

'Ninety-two.'

'She had a good innings, then.'

'What's the matter, Brenda?' Ruby asked.

'Nothing. It's just sad. No family to visit her. It made me think,' she faltered.

'Please, I'm depressed enough already,' Judy remonstrated.

Brenda tut-tutted and glared at her.

'Have either of you seen Marj?' Ruby asked suddenly.

Brenda shot Judy a second glare.

'Em . . . no,' Judy spluttered.

'You're a hopeless liar.' Ruby laughed at her.

'It's true.' Brenda stood up for her friend.

'I haven't seen her. I think Eamonn has,' Judy added, in a muffled tone.

'How do you know that?' Ruby asked.

'Marjory makes it her business to tell me at every opportunity,' Judy said.

Ruby's face crumpled.

'Look, I didn't say that to upset you. You know he can't stay away from Jessica. I'm certain she's the only reason he calls.' Judy had regretted her last few words.

'You're so insensitive, Judy!' Brenda snapped. 'Don't you ever stop to think or does your mouth automatically take over all the time?'

'What the hell is wrong with you?' Ruby was shocked by this angry outburst from the normally placid Brenda.

'I'm so sick and tired of her. Always putting the boot in at the wrong time. Always complaining about how hard her bloody life is. As if being successful and beautiful was a chore!' Brenda said.

'It *is* a chore,' Judy responded. 'Nobody seems to understand that, though, do they? Everybody thinks, Hey, there goes Judy with her beauty. She's got no problems. She has a nice face. That means her life is plain sailing! I don't know why you all think that of me. I'm pretty! Big deal! Let me tell you it's a fucking hindrance! Men are terrified of me!' Judy was on the verge of tears.

'For goodness' sake!' Ruby frowned at her.

'It's true!' Judy defended herself.

'Oh, what rubbish! There's always someone in your life. If it weren't George someone else would be drooling all over you. They're not exactly banging my door down are they?' Brenda said wearily.

'Oh, shut up, the pair of you!' Ruby yelled. 'What about my marriage? Judy, you never even went to the Archbishop's House! You were too caught up being lonely! God, I'm sick and tired of all this moaning. Look in the mirror, for God's sake! You could be a model. You have everything but you're still not happy!'

'Looks aren't everything. You're so shallow sometimes! You think everything can be solved with enough pressure, don't you? Ruby the great Houdini! A click of your fingers and it will all fall into place! Just because Ruby says so . . . Hey presto! *And we're all fucking sorted!* I hate being beautiful! Can't either of you understand that?' she shouted.

'Well, why don't you lie down on the road and let a truck run over you?' Ruby hissed.

Judy eyed them sheepishly.

Ruby had a hunch: her stare came to rest on Judy's hat, which had not been removed since she had stepped inside. 'Why are you wearing that hat?' she asked.

Judy looked hunted suddenly, like General George Custer must have felt at his last stand, with the Indians circling, closing in.

'Judy . . . Christ . . . What have you done?' Brenda asked.

Judy pulled off her hat to reveal a closely shaved head.

'Good God,' Ruby exclaimed.

'Christ almighty,' Brenda blurted.

'Fucking Nora! She's as bald as a coot,' Ruby said.

'I think it works.' Brenda patted Judy's scalp lovingly.

Judy started to cry. 'It's awful! I've an

egghead!' she wailed.

'I thought that's what you wanted?' Ruby stared at her, horrified.

'It will grow back,' Brenda said soothingly.

'Yes. It's fashionable, you know.' Ruby racked her brains. 'To be bald, I mean. Like Sinéad O'Connor.' She looked to Brenda for support.

'Of course! And you're much prettier than Sinéad O'Connor. If you don't count the peculiar shape of your head.' Brenda's brows were knitted.

'*There's nothing wrong with the shape of your head*,' Ruby said emphatically. Although she had to admit that when you looked hard, it was a bit oval-shaped, like a rugby ball. One that had had the shit kicked out of it once too often.

'She looks like she's fresh out of a concentration camp,' Brenda observed.

Judy let out a hysterical sob. 'Shut up, Brenda!' she wailed.

'There you go again, Judy! Stop telling me to shut up! I'm not a child, you know!' Brenda retorted.

'Crikey, what's got into you two? Judy, I don't know what to say. I just never . . . ' Ruby was lost for words.

'No. But you thought it, didn't you? You thought I'd never be lonely, just like everyone else does. Beauty isn't everything.'

Ruby bowed her head, confirming the truth.

'I get so lonely sometimes.' Judy's voice quivered.

Brenda and Ruby were shell-shocked. They looked from one to the other, not knowing what to say or do. They had noticed that George had been excluded from this conversation and wondered if the drastic bald head might have anything to do with him. What had happened to the fly-by-night relationship?

They waited, not daring to ask. Then, as if she'd read their thoughts, Judy said, 'George dumped me. Yes, George, the married man, dumped me. He said I was too good-looking! Yes! You heard me! He said he couldn't go out with me because other men would be staring at me all the time and he wouldn't be able to handle it. So he dumped me!' she cried.

'Oh, God, what a jerk!' Brenda went to her and hugged her.

'The bastard!' Ruby said.

'I never get asked out. I'm too much of a threat to guys. I'm so lonely all the time. You've no idea how lonely I am. You wouldn't believe what I did this week,' she confessed.

'What? What on earth did you do now?' Ruby asked.

'I put an ad in the newspaper . . . the personal column.' She eagle-eyed them forlornly.

'You what? You advertised in the paedophile, sexmaniac and couple-swapping column?' Ruby stared at her in disbelief.

'Oh, God, Judy, what did you do that for? That's strictly for hopeless cases. People like me.' Brenda smirked. 'I'm really sorry,' she added.

'Stop saying sorry, Brenda,' Judy begged.

'I'm sorry I'm always saying sorry,' she returned.

Ruby felt guilty for not calling her friends. She had forgotten about everything and everyone. Suddenly, Judy's absence from the Archbishop's House didn't seem to matter. None of it mattered. She no longer knew who was right or wrong, or even what it was all about. Perhaps Judy's absence might even speed up the case a little. 'Can we please sit down and have a cup of tea?' she suggested.

'I'm sorry, Judy. I *have* tended to think you'd got it all. What problems could you possibly have? You run your own business. You've a luxurious apartment and you're intelligent and beautiful! I never imagined you being lonely. Never.' Brenda wagged her head from side to side.

'Me neither,' Ruby said.

'We've all got our problems,' Judy said, 'and *everyone* gets lonely from time to time. Even me.'

Ruby stared at the wall for what seemed an eternity, her mind racing as she imagined Eamonn with Marjory. 'Brenda, what do you really think of Eamonn?' she blurted out.

'What do you mean?'

'It's just that sometimes friends aren't honest, you know? I really want to know what you think of him. You too, Judy. Don't tell me what you think I'd like to hear. I want the truth . . . '

'Christ. You know what I think of him!' Brenda said, astonished.

'Tell me,' Ruby insisted.

'He's the best.' Brenda turned to face her. 'What do you want me to say? He's a bastard? Just because you've split up? Hey! I can't take away from Eamonn's character. I'd give my right arm for a man like him,' she replied honestly.

'So would I.' Judy nodded in agreement. 'I'd probably go as far as giving him my left arm as well. I might even throw in a few other limbs.'

'Are you just saying that because I married him, and you feel you have to like him?' Ruby implored.

'No, Ruby, I am not! I'm not doing that

any more. No more people-pleasing! I am sick and tired of always having to get it right. I'm fond of Eamonn. He's a terrific guy. Sorry to disappoint you, but it's the truth. You couldn't have done better.'

'Do you think he loved me?' Ruby whispered.

'Oh, for fuck sake!' Judy burst out laughing.

'Please, I know it sounds stupid. I just want to hear it from someone else.' Ruby's brown eyes pleaded with them.

'Did he love you? Past tense? Are you for real? That man is positively crazy about you. If you don't believe me, why don't you ask him yourself?' Judy was peering out of the window.

'Don't be ridiculous. You know he won't talk to me.'

Judy grabbed her hat and put it back on. 'I'm not so sure about that. He's outside your front door, with Marjory.'

25

Ruby paced the floor, talking to herself. Any loving thoughts about Eamonn had taken flight at the mention of Marjory's name. Now she was at the door, with him in tow. The humiliation! She annihilated any softness inside herself, and castigated herself for being so foolish as to believe that Eamonn still loved her. The previous conversation with the girls didn't matter: this was the ultimate proof that she had been living in denial about the whole situation. She forgot about forgiveness, healing, and anything remotely spiritual.

'What the hell is Marjory doing with him?' she ranted.

'Calm down, for Christ's sake!' Brenda tried to soothe her.

'Why did he have to bring her?' she raved.

'Moral support,' Brenda tried.

'Blatant antagonism, more like. Watch her, Ruby. She's up to something,' Judy warned.

Ruby ran to the bathroom. She tore wildly at her hair. They weren't going to get the better of her! The intercom buzzed. She heard voices. 'Bloody hell!' she muttered, under her breath. Then she took herself in hand, and sauntered into the sitting room, head held high. 'Well. This is a surprise.' She glared at Marjory.

Eamonn stood in the centre of the room, refusing to sit down. Marjory stood at the window, going up and down on her toes. Brenda stood at the front door, looking as if she needed to know she had an escape route. Judy had disappeared into the kitchen.

'Hello, Ruby,' Eamonn said softly.

Ruby blushed. He stood tall and elegant in the centre of the room. He wore a green suit with a white shirt, and a faint hint of aftershave floated in the air. Ruby was shocked by how tall he was. She had forgotten. He looked handsome and elegant.

Marjory smiled at her, as if it were all perfectly innocent.

'Hello, Marjory. To what do I owe this honour?' she asked smartly.

'Ruby, we came to talk to you,' Marjory said quietly.

'We?' she swung around.

'We?' she repeated, looking straight at Eamonn.

'Excuse me, but is this Confront Ruby Day, or what? This is worse than the bloody Tribunal,' Ruby said.

Judy slammed a teapot on the table.

Brenda made a half-hearted search for

extra cups. 'I didn't know they were coming, I swear!' She panicked. 'Ruby, c'mon, we're all friends here. Anyone want a Kylemore cake? They're fresh from the — ' Brenda was interrupted.

'I didn't come here to exchange sponge recipes,' Eamonn snarled.

'What in God's name is going on?' Judy beseeched.

'You tell me.' Ruby returned with a dripping mug. She stared at Eamonn and then at Marjory. 'If you wanted to talk to me, you didn't need to bring an army. What's she doing here?' She gestured at Marjory.

'It's about time we all expressed ourselves. This has gone on long enough. Everybody in this room is being affected,' Eamonn said.

'You're talking through your backside,' Ruby rubbished him. 'The only people being affected are you and me!'

Eamonn's mobile phone rang. He answered it with obvious agitation. 'Hello? Hello? Mam? Not now, Mam! I'm in the middle of something!' he shouted.

'See? We can't even end our marriage in peace.' Ruby was exasperated.

'For God's sake, calm down. Take deep breaths,' Brenda advised.

'Belt up, Brenda. They need this.' Judy surprised everyone.

'I agree,' Marjory piped up.

'And what would you know, Marjory? What has any of this got to do with you?' Ruby paced the floor angrily, chewing a nail and looking nervously out of the window.

'It has everything to do with me. You dragged us all into your marriage. You have *both* placed me in a terrible position. I don't know what to do or say any more!' Marjory pouted.

'You're loving every minute of it,' Judy said flatly.

'I go along with that,' Brenda said, surprising even herself.

'I never asked you to do anything!' Eamonn turned on Marjory.

'Yes, but what if you had? What would I have done? No matter what I did I would have been betraying the other party.'

'Excuse me, do you mind? This is my flat. Frankly, I've had enough lunacy for one day and I would appreciate it if you all left. Like right now.' Ruby's patience had reached its limits.

'I'm not finished,' Eamonn said coldly. 'I'm not leaving until this thing is settled.'

'I have nothing more to say.' Ruby tried to usher them towards the door.

'You haven't apologised.' Marjory stepped on to the high moral platform.

'Apologise! For what? All I asked of any of you was that you tell the truth!' Ruby said.

'Oh, that's fucking choice coming from you!' Eamonn started to lose his temper.

'What's that supposed to mean?' she shouted back.

'You expected all of us to be honest. How honest were you, Ruby?' Marjory slammed the point home.

'Exactly!' Eamonn agreed.

'Eamonn, are you blind? She's playing you like a violin!' Brenda said.

'Nice turn of phrase. The next time I visit I must remember to bring a thesaurus,' Marjory sneered.

'Thesaurus? I thought they were extinct.' Brenda looked around her.

'Brenda, did someone drop you on your head when you were born?' Eamonn enquired.

'Maybe, but if you can't see what Marjory is at, perhaps someone took a whack at yours too,' she threw back.

'Too bloody true! Who the hell do you think you are to judge my marriage, Marjory? I'm surprised you didn't throw a party when we broke up!' Ruby exclaimed, finally unleashing what should have been expressed years earlier.

'At least I have some dignity. I had the

376

decency to wait until the annulment was concluded. I didn't start shagging some old lady from the waiting room.' Eamonn interrupted.

The intercom sounded again.

Ruby remembered Robert. She opened the door and in he stepped, grinning from ear to ear. His face froze when he saw the gathering. He turned on his heel to leave.

'*I rest my case!*' Eamonn screamed.

'Robert, wait.' Ruby pulled him back.

'Yeah, not so fast,' Eamonn joined in. 'Come on in and join the party!'

'Everybody, this is Robert. My . . . my friend.' Ruby struggled: she didn't know how to describe him.

'I don't think I belong here,' he said.

'Of course you do.' Eamonn led him by the arm and plonked him down on the couch beside Judy. 'Now, where were we?' he hissed.

'This is crazy.' Marjory laughed. 'This is just insane.'

Robert tried to stand up. Eamonn laid a hand on his shoulder and violently pushed him down again. 'What's the hurry, mate? We're only just getting warmed up. Why don't you fill everyone in, Ruby? The girls are dying to know all about your *friend?*'

Ruby could see that Eamonn was enjoying her discomfort. He revelled in control. 'Stop it!' she warned. 'He has nothing to do with this and you know it.' She walked towards Robert and stood behind him. Robert removed his hat, wiped the top of his head, then replaced it awkwardly.

'At least we have something in common,' Judy pulled off her scarf.

'Very nice,' Robert remarked.

★　★　★

He felt as if he had walked into a minefield.

The scalped woman kept smiling at him. Perhaps she wasn't the full shilling. She looked like an extra from One Flew Over the Cuckoo's Nest.

'Ruby and I are just friends,' he said. 'We talk, that's all.'

'Sure you're friends! Robert here attends the Archbishop's House too. Imagine that? Ruby and Robert have a lot in common. They're very, very good friends. They have a lot of things to discuss. In fact sometimes, when there's a lot of talking to be done, Robert has to stay overnight in Ruby's flat! After all, such lengthy discussions would tire anyone out.' Eamonn's face burned with rage.

Robert put his head into his hands.

'Enough is enough!' Ruby yelled. 'Let's

settle this thing once and for all, shall we? That's what you came here for, Eamonn, isn't it? It's true, OK? I have been seeing Robert for some time now, but not in the way you think. Isn't it typical of you to assume that we're romantically involved? It's none of your bloody business anyway. It's nobody's business but mine. We've been separated for two years, remember? Now, all of a sudden, you're behaving like I'm your wife and I've been unfaithful to you. How ironic. I was always the faithful one!' she shouted.

'Don't, Ruby.' Robert laid a hand on her arm.

'Who are you to judge me?' Ruby railed. 'What did you think I was going to do with my life after you? Huh? Become a nun, and grow prize courgettes on the top of a mountain or something? I'm entitled to see whoever I want, whenever I want! I never went behind your back, which is more than I can say for you and Mother Teresa over there!' She glared at Marjory.

'I was never unfaithful to you!' Eamonn declared indignantly.

'Oh, yeah? I saw you buy flowers for someone on Valentine's Day. I saw you! Now you're treating me like I had a head injury! I wasn't born yesterday!'

Eamonn scratched his head. 'Why all this

fuss about a bunch of flowers?' Eamonn seemed genuinely confused.

'I think I can explain that.' Marjory stepped up to Eamonn and purred like a kitten. 'They were for me,' she said, with utter certainty.

'Jesus.' Brenda looked her up and down.

'What? I never gave you flowers!' Eamonn insisted.

'That's true. But you wanted to, didn't you? You hadn't the courage to do it. Now is the time. Now is the time, Eamonn, to let everyone know that you're in love with me.' Marjory swung round to face them all.

'This just keeps getting better and better,' Judy howled with laughter.

'I haven't the faintest idea what she's on about.' Eamonn stepped back from her, as if she had terminal bad breath.

Ruby had gone white. She walked up to him, shaking from head to foot. 'Is this true?' she asked. Her anger had dissolved only to be replaced with a gnawing sense of dread.

'Of course it's not true!' he said angrily.

'They were red roses.' She stared right into his eyes.

Their faces came closer together.

Nobody dared to move.

'They should have been white!' Eamonn fumed. 'I bought them for our . . . I was

380

going to . . . ' His voice broke.

Everyone held their breath.

'I was going to . . . ' Eamonn tried again.

'Stop it, Eamonn. You're only hurting yourself!' Marjory jumped to his defence.

'Sit down, you fool,' Robert piped up.

Marjory sat down, looking shocked.

The others stared at the floor.

'I was thinking of Genevieve. I wanted to bring them to you. I wanted to . . . acknowledge her in some way, through you . . . I was going to give them to you . . . I couldn't do it. I left them in a church instead.' Eamonn stood arms outstretched, his voice quaking with emotion.

Brenda burst into tears. Judy pulled out a small bottle of whiskey. She took a long slug, then passed it to Robert who passed it to Marjory, who spluttered and coughed as the strong liquor hit the back of her throat.

Ruby swayed on her feet. Her eyes locked with Eamonn's. His hands remained poised in mid-air. She wanted to reach out and pull them down to his sides. She couldn't move an inch.

'Maybe we *should* call the priest?' Brenda suggested — for her own selfish reasons, although the others were not to know this.

They all turned to look at her.

'Just a suggestion.'

'None of us should be here,' Judy remarked.

'My thoughts entirely.' Robert stood up.

★ ★ ★

Marjory had begun to panic, to lose control. She had to do something fast to save face. She decided to treat herself to a large dose of BSE (Blame Someone Else). It was a long shot, but it was her only recourse.

'You led me on, Eamonn!' she exploded. 'All those times you kept calling on me, complimenting me, playing up to me. You lied to me!'

'I never did any such thing!' he shouted. 'I called to see Jessica! I never gave the impression that I wanted a relationship with you.' He looked at her with disgust.

'I think we should all leave,' Robert said, with authority.

Everybody watched Marjory with disbelief. She gathered her things, her fury at volcanic peak. 'Is that it?' She walked towards Eamonn and laid a hand on his arm.

'Leave me alone,' Eamonn said sharply.

Marjory glanced at Ruby and threw her a now-look-what-you've-done look.

'Get out. All of you. Now!' Ruby demanded.

When everyone but Eamonn had left, Ruby was wheezing. But she hadn't finished. She had opened the door just enough to let out past insecurities have their final say. 'She was always between us. Right from the beginning, wasn't she?' she began.

'Who?' he asked.

'Marjory. Even on our wedding day she managed it. Giving you that letter. Remember? The letter you told me was a card? Why did you do that? I trusted you. You'll never know how much I suffered because of that lie. Then you had to drag her into the hospital when I lost . . . and it didn't stop there, did it? Since we've split up she's been like a moth to a flame, warming up to you, using you,' she muttered.

'I never felt anything for Marjory. You know that. I never made any fuss about that letter because I thought it would upset you. That was all I cared about, not the silly gesture that it was. I never took it seriously. You did. I'm sorry if I chose the wrong way to deal with it. Seems like I always choose the wrong way to deal with things,' he said dejectedly.

'Yes, you do deal with things the wrong way, Eamonn. You're still doing it, even now. Did you think flowers were going to bring *her* back? That it was that simple?' Ruby pounced on him. It was the first time in four years that she had accepted his invitation to talk.

'No,' he whispered.

'Then what?' she begged.

'I thought it would . . . bring you back,' he choked.

An awesome silence filled the room. They stared at each other, bewildered.

Ruby was stunned into muteness. With just a couple of words he had made mincemeat of her steely resolve. She fought for air. She fought to break free. There was only one way out.

Within seconds she had shifted emotional gears. She grabbed a cloth from the sink, dragged a chair over to the window, stood on it, and began to wipe down the Venetian blinds.

Eamonn stared at her. 'What are you doing?' he asked.

'I'm cleaning the blinds. What does it look like?' Frantically she ran the cloth backwards and forwards.

'Why can't you say her name, Ruby? Try it, just once.' Eamonn pleaded.

Ruby was gathering speed with the cloth.

'It's not anybody's fault, Ruby. Not yours. Not mine. Not the Church's, not the baby's.' His voice shook.

Ruby wanted to hear — didn't want to hear.

'We did our best. Do you hear me? It's not your fault,' he tried again. 'You have to forgive yourself.'

'I can't!' she said, through gritted teeth.

'You must!' Eamonn commanded. 'Ruby, you can clean and scrub and scour all you like, but you will never wash it away, do you hear me? You will never wash away the bad feeling. You can't wash Genevieve away!'

Ruby turned swiftly. '*Nor can she be replaced by someone else's daughter!*' She wheezed from tension.

The words echoed in the silence. Eamonn hung his head. Ruby knew that they had gone through him like a poisoned dagger.

'I was wrong,' he said. 'I just wanted to feel closer to Genevieve. Every time I see Jessica I feel closer to her. I see the life Genevieve didn't have a chance to experience. I'm sorry.' He broke down, putting his head in his hands. Tears rushed forth.

Ruby remained motionless. Her heart broke as she saw, for the first time, Eamonn's suffering. She couldn't bear it. She couldn't bear any of it any more.

'I'm sorry!' she wailed. 'I'm sorry! I'm sorry I left you alone and sad. I am sorry I abandoned you, Eamonn!' She stared at the cloth in her hand, as if it was some foreign object, and stepped down off the chair.

'I am just as guilty.' Eamonn sighed. 'I abandoned you too. I forgive you. You must forgive yourself. If you can find room in your heart, it would help if you forgave me too.' He dropped his head.

Ruby was speechless.

Eamonn was reversing towards the door.

Please don't go, she begged in her head.

'I'm leaving now.' His eyes were on her as he backed away.

Eamonn, look at me! Please see me.

He stepped out and closed the door.

Don't leave me here with myself!

Ruby fell to her knees sobbing. She had needed him to move towards her — a touch, even a step in her direction would have made all the difference. Some gesture that would have left no question mark over his commitment to her. With the annulment still pending and feeling so distraught, she had not been able to reach out. She wiped her cheeks with the back of her hand. She had needed Eamonn to forgive her — for what, she was not sure. Now she understood how great her need for compassion was.

She had none to give herself. She had found herself guilty of a crime she *knew* she hadn't committed. Yet she had to carry the ball and chain. Eamonn's words had served as an acquittal. The freedom reduced her to uncontrollable tears.

Still on her knees, she began to pray for forgiveness. She prayed for her broken family. She prayed for peace. She prayed for her daughter's soul to be set free. She prayed for acceptance. She talked to Genevieve. She prayed to her. She asked her to help them. She begged her to let her know that she was OK. That she forgave her mother for killing her.

Please, darling, forgive me.

She cried, convinced she had caused her daughter's death and that she was being punished here in the mortal life. Her hell was a place called Planet Earth. Words tumbled from her mouth. Like a mantra, she repeated them until she felt as if her mind had evacuated her body.

It felt good, to be floating out there, a stone's throw from nowhere. She felt weightless, dizzy with concentration. She imagined Genevieve's face, all soft and sweet and filled with love. She smiled as the image drew closer. She felt encompassed in its warmth. Its purity washed over her, cleansing her sins.

The scent of white roses suddenly filled the room. Ruby inhaled the aroma. A soft breeze kissed her cheek.

You're never alone, Mam. I will always be here . . .

'Oh, darling, thank you! Thank you! Thank you!' Ruby cried into the silence.

26

Ruby had emerged from the deep. She felt lighter. She felt relieved. She felt hope. She felt the first flutterings of faith. She believed that, somewhere out there, her daughter was alive and well. At first she worried that she had lost her mind. Then she knew she had found it again.

She no longer felt the incessant need to clean the flat. It hadn't completely disappeared, but she started to take note of the times when it drove her. She began to record the moods that led to a cleaning binge, and the first thing that struck her was that she was almost always thinking of Eamonn and the marriage break-up.

She tried not to give in to the urge. She deliberately left dishes unwashed, and stopped herself Hoovering twice or bleaching the bathroom several times.

She had retrieved her sense of self, rescued it from the clutches of a thwarted evil. The evil was the *twisted* past. Ruby understood now. She had unravelled its thorny stems. She had weeded out the illusions. New shoots of reality were pushing bravely through the fresh earth. Truths had begun to blossom. The garden of life was springing forth. Confusion and misunderstanding had been wrenched out.

The garden begged for water and light, for new seedlings. Robert was the first to plant. Ruby tended their relationship, as if it was a prize-winning rose.

'Robert? I've been calling you all day. Why didn't you ring me?' Ruby asked concerned.

'I've only just come in.'

'I would have called round, only I didn't want to seem rude.' Ruby wondered why he had kept her at bay for so long. She had never been invited to his home and often wondered if some great big secret lurked within its walls. 'Can we meet?' she asked.

'Of course,' Robert replied.

★　★　★

Robert arrived at Ruby's flat minus a hat. It was early May and the sun was shining. Ruby was immersed in Baby Bio plant food and watering-cans. 'I didn't expect you so soon,' she said as she let him in.

'How are you feeling today?' he asked.

'Do you know what? I feel pretty damn good!' Ruby gleamed.

Robert was suspicious. Ever since that

awful confrontation Ruby had been transformed. She glowed with peace and serenity. He couldn't help thinking that something had happened between her and Eamonn. Had they rekindled their love? What had happened after he had left? He stared at her, unsure how to word his questions.

'What's wrong?'

'Nothing.' He smiled. 'I guess I just wanted to talk . . . '

'We never stop talking, Robert,' she said.

The white flesh above her breast exposed itself, sending desire soaring through his veins. He dragged away his eyes, willing his manliness to stand down.

'I wanted to ask you something,' he said. 'I'm a little anxious, I guess. You haven't told me, you know, what happened that day Eamonn arrived. You seem happier. I don't understand why. Did something happen? I need to know where I stand.' Robert grimaced as he choked on the chunk of pride making its way slowly down his gullet. He picked up a packet of pansy seeds and fiddled with it.

'I see,' she said, nodding. 'You're worried that something happened between me and Eamonn, and that that's why I have been better lately?' she whispered.

'Well, not exactly.' Robert tried to remain

calm, but the pride had reached his stomach. It jostled for space with anxiety and stubbornness, who made room for the new tenant.

'I've been very selfish,' Ruby apologised. 'It's just that I haven't felt so peaceful for such a long time. I was hogging it for a while. Enjoying it, wallowing in it. I'm sorry. I never thought to share it with you.' She turned his face towards hers. 'Yes. Something did happen with Eamonn. We talked. At last. We tried to confront those old ghosts, the problems of the past. It's not completely resolved but it's a start. I think we needed that more than anything else. Do you understand?' She looked seriously into his doubtful eyes.

He nodded. 'Do you still love him?' he mumbled, horrified by the sound of his own voice. It seemed perverse to ask her such a thing.

'Yes. I will always love Eamonn,' she answered clearly. 'How can I stop loving the man who married me and went through all that pain with me? I realise now how much I made him suffer. Eamonn was not at fault. Remember when you told me to take blame out of my life?'

He wished he had kept his mouth shut.

'That's what I did. I did it for Eamonn as

much as for myself. From that day onwards I have felt such . . . such . . . *compassion* for him. I will always love him for trying, do you understand? We are intrinsically linked because of our past. Don't you love Mary?' she asked.

'Yes, I do, but not in that way. I would always be there for her. I think I am beginning to grasp what you mean.' Robert tried to be objective and understanding. 'You see, I need to know, Ruby, is it *that way* with us? Are we an item?' He moved closer to her and cocked his head sideways, keeping his eyes firmly on her lips. He willed her to show him. It was now or never.

Ruby moved backwards, slowly putting distance between them. No words came. However, they were not needed: her inaction told him everything. 'I'm sorry, I just am not ready to go any further right now,' she blurted.

'I'm sorry too.' Robert sighed. 'And it's more than that, isn't it? You're still *in love* with Eamonn, aren't you?' Robert hoped she would spare him the answer.

Ruby didn't reply. That spoke in volumes. There was nothing more to be said. Robert put his hand into his inside pocket. 'For you,' he said. 'to make up for Mother's Day,'

Ruby took the package.

'It's your story, Ruby.'

He straightened himself up and made to leave. He was glad he had not had to tell her about the annulment. It wouldn't have made the slightest difference anyway.

'Thank you,' she said. 'I don't know how to express my gratitude to you. You've helped me so much. Can we remain friends, Robert? It would mean so much to me.'

'We will always be friends, Ruby. That I promise.' And with that he left.

27

102, Howth View,
Sutton,
Dublin 13
26 June 1996

Dear Judy,

This is an official invitation extended to you and Brenda, for dinner on Friday 28th around 8 p.m. Now, you have absolutely no excuse for not turning up! We have a lot to catch up on. I look forward to seeing you.

Love,
Ruby

PS Bring something to drink.

At eight p.m. on Friday Ruby was putting the final touches to the table in the main room of the flat. She had had to borrow an extra chair from a neighbour. She studied the overall effect, and was pleased. She had gone to a lot of trouble. The prawn cocktails looked delicious. She perched a slice of lemon on the side of each glass, then dipped her little finger into the dressing and licked it off.

She took the ice-cream from the freezer and placed it in the fridge. Judy hated frozen ice cream, and it would be nicely soft when they were ready for dessert. She opened the oven to check the lasagne. She had made it herself, and it looked wonderful. The crispy cheese topping crackled and the pungent aroma of the garlic bread pervaded the room.

The intercom buzzed. Ruby almost tripped over herself in her hurry to answer it. She opened the door and her two best friends stepped in. Brenda hugged her and handed her a bottle of wine.

'He's not here,' Judy said.

'Who's not here?' Ruby asked, confused.

'Robert. I thought you were going to introduce us. Properly, I mean. Why did you invite us over? Wow! Mateus rosé, my favourite!' She picked up the rounded bottle.

'You frightened him away with that head of yours. He thinks my friends are all patients on leave from St Brendan's.' Ruby patted Judy's head, from which soft bristles had begun to sprout.

'I'm kind of getting used to it.' Judy smiled.

'Yeah. It grows on you,' Brenda quipped.

'It had better.' Judy punched her arm.

'Hey, you got the scented candles I love!' she added.

They sat down to eat.

'What's going on?' Judy probed.

'Since when did I have to have a special reason to invite my friends over?' Ruby placed the garlic bread in a basket.

'You look so . . . so . . . '

'Suspiciously happy!' Brenda finished for her.

'Yeah. What's going on, Ruby? Are you shagging the old man?' Judy lowered her wine in one gulp.

Brenda tried not to laugh. 'No. I am not *shagging* him. I hate to disappoint you both. In fact, whatever was going on with us has finished,' Ruby divulged, which was highly irregular for her. 'It was only ever a friendship anyway.'

'God, how boring,' Judy remarked. 'But I guess we're in that league now. Looking for friendship, you know, companionship instead of sex. We're getting old. It's all so . . . so . . . scary.'

'Why didn't you tell us about him?' Brenda demanded.

'Look, I have to apologise. I've wanted to tell you things but I just couldn't. I hadn't come to terms with anything. Then I applied for the annulment. That changed everything.

That was when I met Robert, but I was still hurting over Eamonn and, well . . . It's really hard to explain. It takes time to be able to express things. I know you won't understand fully what I'm trying to say.' She wondered how to pack the past year's events into one evening.

'I thought I could handle it all alone, you see. I'm so glad I applied for the annulment. It has helped me understand what happened to our marriage so much better. Things make sense now that didn't then. I was so enraged about being infertile. Poor Eamonn, I made him suffer so . . . ' She drifted off.

The girls waited with bated breath, but Ruby continued on a different track. 'Then Robert came along, and he never judged me or told me what to do, and for the first time ever I felt I could just come to terms with things alone, without having to consider anyone else's feelings. I hadn't been able to focus on me at all. He's such a good friend.'

'Well, he has obviously had a good effect on you.' Brenda glanced around the untidy apartment.

'Unlike Marjory,' Judy sneered.

'Don't be so hard on her.' Ruby tried to be the Good Samaritan. 'I feel sorry for her.'

'How can you forgive her so easily? Aren't you angry with her?' Brenda asked.

'No,' Ruby replied, knowing that she was but that the anger had been misdirected and was a complete waste of energy. She knew that in time it would dissipate if she reminded herself of the facts. 'What's the point in being angry with her? Even if he was seeing her, what business is it of mine now, anyway?' She tried to persuade herself that she was being mature and adult about it. 'I'm only sorry I couldn't have handled things better. I was always looking in her direction. The wrong direction. Marjory was only a threat because I made her into one. As long as I focused on her, I could avoid looking at me.'

'Have you contacted her since?' Brenda wanted to know.

'No, but I will. When I'm able,' Ruby replied.

'How could she have thought Eamonn was interested in her?' Judy wasn't satisfied.

'Well, he was spending a lot of time over there. Maybe he gave the wrong impression,' Brenda answered.

'Jessica and Ben were his reason for being there,' Ruby answered softly.

'God, he adores Jessica,' Judy commented.

'Yes, he loves children,' Ruby said, with a tinge of sadness. 'He would have made a damn good father.'

'Your annulment has affected us all in

some small way,' Brenda remarked. Judy nodded in agreement. 'At first I thought it was tearing us all apart, you know, with all the arguing and ill-feeling between us. But it has actually affected me in a positive way. I'd been living in other people's shadows. When I went to see Father Ebbs I began to think about how important it was for me to be there. I had a purpose. I decided to stop regarding myself as so unimportant. And when Kit died, I decided to get a life. I'd make an effort. It was time to stop being so bloody sensible. I've signed up with a mountain-climbing group. It's something I've always wanted to do. We meet every Sunday afternoon. I love it. The wind, the steep hill . . . The instructor,' she threw in shyly.

'Go on,' Ruby urged her.

'Well, he's drop-dead gorgeous, single and — '

'Dark and mysterious?' Judy interrupted.

'OK, it might sound trashy. Think, though. Had I not gone to the Archbishop's House, I would never have met Father Ebbs. Had I never had that experience I wouldn't have joined the class. Now I have a whole new bunch of friends. I keep fantasising that the instructor might ask me out. We could go to Slattery's pub after the walk, have a few drinks, and then, well, who knows?' She blushed.

'Jesus. Our Brenda.' Judy poured herself another drink. 'Why wait for him to ask? I dare you. For once in your life, Brenda, go for it,' she encouraged her.

'I'll think about it.'

'The annulment affected me too,' Judy added, serious now.

The others were intensely curious. They couldn't imagine *anything* having an effect on Judy.

'What? Don't stare at me like I belong in the Puzzle Factory.' She waved her hand at them. 'It did! I swear it did! I never went to see the good Father Plebs,' she slurred.

'Ebbs,' they corrected her.

'Plebs, Ebbs, Shlebs, whatever! I should have gone, but I didn't. I was a coward. It was wrong of me, but you know what? Because I didn't go I felt guilty, and I hate it when I feel guilty, and that's why I called over to you that day. Christ, when I saw Eamonn and then Marjory . . . ' The girls giggled and refilled their glasses.

'Never mind that. You stole the show when you exposed your shaved head indecently.' Brenda giggled.

'OK, girlies, I think that joke has been long exhausted. Seriously, though, it forced me to think about friendship. None of us is getting any younger, you know, and I need my buddies. I'm sorry, Ruby. I'm sorry I didn't go. Perhaps I wasn't meant to, after all,' Judy concluded.

'I'm glad you didn't keep that appointment. Imagine the look on Father Ebbs's face. You hardly look like a credible witness with a scalped head. You might have given him a heart-attack!' Ruby laughed.

'Yeah. Try explaining that.' Brenda giggled.

'No problem. I had it covered. I'm recovering from cancer, you see. It's a chemo thing,' she said.

'That's shameful,' Ruby scolded her.

'Any better suggestions?' Judy eyed them.

'You could be joining the Cistercian monks?' Brenda proffered. 'Or auditioning for a part in *Last of the Mohicans: The Sequel?*'

Ruby laughed. She was fascinated by her friends' confessions. She had started the evening feeling guilty.

Now her annulment process had turned out to be a blessing in disguise. How ironic.

The can of worms had been opened, along with the bottles of wine, and the occupants slithered across the table rampant in their newly found freedom.

'What about you, Ruby? How has it affected you?' Brenda asked.

'Well, I was very bitter after the break-up. I had myself convinced that Marjory was a part of it. I realise now I was just looking for someone to blame. I found out how vulnerable men are too, how soft they are underneath,' she said wistfully.

'You know something? You're beginning to sound like Brenda,' Judy remarked.

'What's so bad about that?' Brenda asked. 'And what about Eamonn and you now?' She had taken the bull by its treacherous horns.

Ruby rubbed her eyes. 'Do you mean, is there a chance that we will get back together?' she asked.

'Well, where do you two stand now regarding the annulment? What's the story?' Judy had grabbed a horn for herself.

'I don't know what stage it's at. I imagine it's ready to be sent to Rome. God knows how long after that it will be before it goes to the Tribunal court.' She gazed into her empty glass.

'How do you feel about it now?' Brenda continued her line of enquiry.

'Different,' Ruby answered.

The girls waited for her to elaborate.

'What is a marriage, eh? If a couple are committed, really committed, and they try very hard against all the odds, does that mean their marriage should be rendered invalid?

What's really important is that those two people really love each other and stick it out to the end.' She listened to her own words and wondered if Eamonn felt the same way.

'Personally, I think your marriage to Eamonn was a damn sight better than anyone else's I know,' Judy said.

'He still loves you,' Brenda said.

'I don't know if he does.' Ruby's concern showed in her tone.

'He's afraid. That's all. Men are terrible cowards. They lose everything when a marriage breaks down. Let's face it. The woman regains her name, keeps her home and the children. If there are any.' She paused. 'What does the man get? A bedsit and a maintenance order.'

'That only applies to some men. Be honest. You couldn't call Eamonn's place a bedsit. He has no maintenance to pay either. But he's bloody miserable without you.' Judy poured herself the dregs of the wine, almost squeezing the bottle to get at the last drops.

'His pride is killing him. He could have any woman he wants. He needs children, a home, a woman about the place. He just can't face what he considers to be a failure. His failure. It wasn't his fault. It wasn't mine. At least he has agreed to that now. That's progress.' Ruby was talking to herself more than to anyone in the room.

'Who are you trying to convince?' Judy jeered.

'What do you mean?' Ruby asked, confused.

'We know he still loves you,' Brenda insisted. 'Do you remember Jessica's birthday party, Judy?'

'How could I forget?' Judy slurred.

'Marjory asked me to go and collect the cake. Eamonn handed me a lottery slip and asked me to do it for him in the newsagent's,' Brenda said. 'Well, I had a sneaky look at the numbers. The first two sets were your birthday and his birthday. He's still using them,' she said.

'He is?' Ruby tried to hide her interest.

'He still loves you,' Judy confirmed, 'and you still love him. What a pair of complete eejits you are.'

'Don't be silly. It would take more than a lotto slip to convince me. Old habits die hard.' She laughed, hoping *she* wasn't a habit. She wished they would stop putting ideas in her head. If Eamonn loved her, why wasn't *he* telling her?

'You just hold on, Ruby. It's never too late. He'll be back. Hey, look at me? I'm teetering on the menopause and only starting to date.'

Brenda fiddled with a chestnut curl.

'What about me? Since I shaved my head I've had more dates than I care to remember! In fact, I think I'll stop cleansing and toning my face. Some spots wouldn't go amiss. I'm still working on the flabby tummy, but I'm hopeful.' Judy joked.

'Women would have killed for your long hair. They pay through the nose for extensions, you know.'

'They'd have been welcome to it.' Judy hiccuped.

★   ★   ★

When the girls had left, Ruby wandered around the flat. The dirty plates were calling her, but she had promised to stop indulging her cleaning obsession. Their seductive powers forced her to run out of the kitchen. She removed her makeup and put on her nightdress. As she got into bed, she remembered Robert's gift. With the drama of the evening, she still hadn't got round to opening it.

It was in her bedside drawer, in pretty wrapping paper, which she was careful not to tear. Inside was a book. Ruby laughed when she read the title: *Sleeping Beauty*. It was beautifully illustrated. Ruby remembered buying books for her daughter, in the hope that some day she would read them to her at night. *Sleeping Beauty* had been among them. She flicked through the pages and wondered why Robert had chosen such an unusual item as a gift for her. She read the large print on each page. All of a sudden, she realised why he had wanted her to read it. She herself had been in a deep sleep . . . Robert had kissed her and made her realise that her prince had been Eamonn all along.

28

Ruby awoke with the solution dancing on the tip of her tongue. She would not go to work today: a far more urgent matter called for her immediate attention. She rang in sick, then set out on her journey through the early-morning traffic. Irate drivers beeped and cursed as they inched their way through Fairview. Ruby turned off and headed towards Ballybough, hoping to escape the heavy congestion, but it was no better. What's the hurry anyway? she thought. She switched on the radio and listened to the nine o'clock news.

She turned off the Drumcondra Road, having being stuck in the same spot for fifteen minutes. Had she walked she would have got there quicker. She drove up the ramp, taking note of the splendid gardens that were in bloom, in stark contrast to the greyish blanket that had covered the land on her previous visits. The flowerbeds exploded with colour and the sun streaked through skyscraper trees.

She parked the car, and seconds later was in the lift on the way to the third floor.

The doors opened and the receptionist looked up. 'I would like to see Father Ebbs,' Ruby said.

'Have you an appointment?'

'I'm afraid not. It's an emergency. I'm sure he will see me if you ask. I won't take much of his time,' she pleaded.

The receptionist dialled his office, looking put out.

'He will see you presently,' she said coolly. 'He is in his office,' she added.

Ruby walked directly to the interview room, her stomach doing double-somersaults as she listened to the loud click-clack of her heels. She rapped lightly on the door.

'Come in!' a strange voice called. Ruby pushed open the door. Father Ebbs was standing in the middle of the room surrounded by complete and utter chaos. His sleeves were rolled up and he appeared to be packing things into tea-chests. He greeted her with warmth and cheer.

'Mrs Blake! How nice to see you again!' he said.

Ruby leaned over boxes and bags and shook his hand. She had come to like Father Ebbs too. In a way, he was responsible for the recent changes in her life. He had played a huge part in getting her on to the right track. She was grateful to him.

'I'm sorry I didn't call,' she said, surveying the deluge. 'What on earth are you doing?'

'I'm moving,' he said, in a low, soft, knowing voice.

Ruby waited for elaboration. It wasn't forthcoming. 'I see,' she said, deciding not to pursue the matter further. After all, it was none of her business. Besides, she was here on a serious mission. She got straight down to it. 'Father, I came because I have changed my mind.' He continued to stack magazines and papers.

'I have been thinking a lot about the annulment, you see, and, well . . . I realise that . . . I feel that . . . our marriage *was* valid, Father.' She paused, waiting for a response.

Father Ebbs moved on to his desk and pulled out the contents.

'I know it sounds strange, but I really feel that the annulment process has helped me to see that just because we couldn't have children, and we were unable to deal with that at the time, it does not invalidate our marriage. When we married, we committed ourselves in good faith. We had no idea what the future held. While I know our marriage is in trouble and may never be repaired, I can accept that, Father. To say it never existed is another matter entirely. Why it's pure . . . insanity!'

Father Ebbs threw her a wry smile. 'Oh dear. I'm afraid you're too late, Mrs Blake,' he said.

'What do you mean?' Ruby asked, nonplussed.

'I have already submitted your application to Rome.'

Ruby's face reddened with a mixture of embarrassment and rage.

'I'm sorry, really I am,' he added.

'Can't you get it back? I mean, can't you withdraw it?' She looked at him with desperate eyes.

'No, I'm afraid I can't. Once it's submitted the wheels are set in motion. I'd imagine a response from the Tribunal won't be long in coming,' he replied.

'Oh, God, I feared this would happen,' she murmured. 'What should I do? There must be some way to stop it!'

'You will just have to wait,' he said. He stretched his back and put his hands on his hips.

'Wait? I can't wait. Don't you understand?' She had raised her voice.

'Mrs Blake, you came to me with an application. I processed it at your request. I cannot do any more. Had you come to me earlier I might have been able to stop it. I'm deeply regretful but it is out of my hands. I wish there was something more I could do for you.'

'I'm afraid I don't understand that. That's my problem with the Church. Understanding it, that is!' she said.

'I'm afraid I don't follow you, Mrs Blake.' Mechanically Father Ebbs continued packing and stacking.

'It has never changed, has it?' She said upset.

'What has never changed?'

'The Church! The holy Catholic Church! It's never changed, has it? There's still no room for mistakes! We can't make a simple mistake, can we? We're only human beings, you know. We all make mistakes, even the priests and the bishops! But no! We have to pretend. No mistakes allowed!' she challenged him.

'I think I'd better refrain from commenting on that,' Father Ebbs replied sternly. 'I must point out to you that you were repeatedly informed of the seriousness attached to applying for an annulment. I did emphasise that, Mrs Blake.'

'Yes, I know you did, Father, but things have changed! Why can't the Church abide the word 'change'? It's a dirty word — like sex! A thing deemed almost evil. Even to dream of change is a mortal sin. Why?' Ruby had pinned him into a corner although she could see from his face that he had tired of the debating society.

'Mrs Blake! Am I being led to believe that you are suggesting *I* am the Church?' he asked.

'You bloody well are to me!' Ruby insisted.

'Not any more!' Father Ebbs said flatly.

They stared at each other.

Then Ruby noticed the absence of his cassock and his collar. Slowly it dawned on her. She was witnessing his desertion at first hand. Her hand flew to her mouth. Father Ebbs continued, unperturbed, with his work.

'You're leaving for good, aren't you?' she asked, not caring if it was an impertinent question.

'Yes,' he answered, apparently not caring if it was an appropriate response.

'And because you're leaving, I'm no longer your case, is that it?' she said.

'Yes and no. I'm no longer responsible for the outcome, but I do care about your case.'

'As far as I am concerned, I came to you, Father Ebbs! You represented the Church to me. Am I to believe that because you are leaving the priesthood you are no longer valid in my life? *Are you now 'Null and Void' also?*'

Sean Ebbs smiled. He couldn't help it. He was responsible for this shift in attitude. Mrs Blake had grown indeed, but she was no match for his theological expertise.

'How do you know you're not making another mistake?' He aimed the question with precision. It was based on a shoot-to-kill policy.

'*How do you know you're not making another mistake?*' Ruby pointed to the packing exercise.

He let out a reluctant laugh. 'I don't,' he said.

'Exactly.' Ruby nodded.

'I'm sorry I can't help you any further, Mrs Blake,' he said, softer now that he had broken the news.

'I'm sorry too,' Ruby said.

'For what it's worth, I believe your marriage is valid. I can only hope that the Tribunal in Rome takes the same view. I also want you to know that what was discussed between us shall never pass my lips.' He was trying to reassure her.

'I trust you mean that.' Ruby sighed.

'Father, I wish I'd known back then what I know today. I made a terrible mistake. You're not to blame, I know that. If anything, you've helped me greatly.'

'I have?' The priest looked up. For the first time he took in her general demeanour. Ruby Blake had been transformed: she was dressed plainly, her face without makeup. If anything, she looked more beautiful, more peaceful, serene. Her eyes looked softer, her features less sharp. She was almost childlike and vulnerable.

'You made me look at things from a different angle. But for you, I'd never have realised that I married a good, decent, honest man.' She smiled at him.

Father Ebbs was curious as to how that realisation had brought her peace. He was bewildered, but pleased. 'I'm most grateful for your kind remarks, Mrs Blake. You in turn have helped me to re-evaluate my own principles,' he told her. 'And now I must leave you. I have many things to attend to. I wish you well.' He stuck out his hand.

'I wish you well too, Father.' Ruby clasped it in hers.

'Sean,' he replied.

'Sean,' she repeated. Suddenly she darted forward and kissed his cheek.

He blushed, flattered by her display of affection.

'They're making a terrible mistake in letting you go. The Catholic Church needs

415

more people like you, Sean. People wouldn't be so discouraged if they felt the human touch more often.'

'It is my choice. The Catholic Church has done nothing wrong,' he said.

★   ★   ★

He smiled at her. He looked so different, Ruby thought. There was a sparkle in his eye that advertised what was going on inside. He looked ten years younger all of a sudden. And there was something else. What was it? Then it dawned on her. He was no longer Father Sean Ebbs, the priest. She was seeing him as a *man*. How strange.

He left the room. Ruby stood still for a moment, wondering what to do. Then the door was flung open and Bill, the caretaker, entered. 'Sorry, ma'am, I didn't realise anyone was in here.'

'Quite all right. I was just leaving,' Ruby replied.

The caretaker walked over to the beautiful gardenia plant behind the bureau. He lifted it up and, without hesitation, dumped it headlong into a black rubbish bag.

Ruby looked on in horror. 'No worries.' He'd noticed her expression. 'It's a fake. I never had the heart to tell poor Father Ebbs.

He's off now, so makes no odds,' he confided, in a sorrowful tone.

★ ★ ★

Outside the Archbishop's House, Ruby ambled towards the car. Thinking, thinking. She started the engine. Still thinking, thinking. By the time she had hit the Drumcondra Road she had made up her mind. She glanced at her watch. Eamonn didn't start work until ten a.m. If she hurried she might catch him before he went to the office.

The car seemed to agree with her. It took on a life of its own. Like Chitty Chitty Bang Bang, it spread its wings and veered in the direction of Eamonn's apartment block.

★ ★ ★

Sean Ebbs knelt in the oratory, his head bent, his carriage humble. It was peaceful and quiet. He joined his hands and prayed for the first time in months. At last, something had happened. He had something important to pray about. He spoke to God with ease and sincerity.

He thanked him for Ruby Blake's visit. For months he had felt he was harming more than healing her. Today, he had seen that Ruby had come full circle and a new Ruby had risen up. She was a stronger woman. A better person had emerged. He had helped her.

His vocation had not been in vain, after all. Yes, he had decided to leave, but at least he knew now that he had contributed to another person's well-being. At the end of the day, that was all that mattered.

29

Eamonn played idly with the morning's post. He had enjoyed a good night's sleep. He sipped his coffee as he sifted through the various envelopes. Visa bill. Another rise in mortgage interest. ESB credit facilities. A South African missions appeal, and a free sample of Lenor fabric softener. He flung them down haphazardly. A plain white envelope slid across the table, and landed in his lap. It bore the stamp of the Catholic Marriage Tribunal Office. He froze. It could mean only one thing.

Eamonn had had his share of ups and downs since his meeting with Ruby. He had found himself asking questions that he did not want to answer. That day he had seen something in her face that had made him stop and think. Initially, he had thought it was Robert Ryan who had put the new look into her eyes, but when they had spoken, he had realised, with great sadness, that he was seeing Ruby's ghosts. Her eyes had been filled with want: for freedom, forgiveness, acquittal. He felt such overwhelming compassion for them both. Perhaps enough time had passed for them to see each other in a full, uncut version of humanity: the flaws, the shortcomings, the merits, the liabilities, the weaknesses. Ruby's strength shamed him. He wanted to tell her how much bigger a person than himself she was. He wanted to reach out and touch her hand.

He had held the truth captive, a hostage, a prisoner, but it had broken free anyway. The truth will set you free, he thought. Yes, it did, but it sure as hell hurt too. He thought back to his wedding day, and examined his reason for withholding the letter from her. Partly it was because he had felt flattered by it. It had fed his ego. But he didn't need nourishment other than Ruby's love. Why was I so stupid? Was I born dumb or what? he castigated himself. He recalled phoning Marjory from the hospital and cringed, realising now how that must have made Ruby feel. Of all the times and places to do such a thing! Yet at the time he had not known how offensive it would seem.

Eamonn acknowledged that he had not handled things well. His pride had prevented him considering Ruby's struggle. All he had chosen to see was her bitterness, her lack of compassion and disinterest. Had he looked into her eyes, asked her some questions and listened to the answers, maybe the whole thing might have been sorted out. He now saw quite clearly that, yes, she had displayed these things, but she had also displayed the other side of the coin. Eamonn had not wanted to admit to that. He wanted her to be bitter, resentful and angry. It had suited him that way. He could deal with that. That was what he had expected that day, when he had arrived with Marjory. Not the soft eyes. Eamonn had taken those eyes home with him. He hadn't been given a choice this time. They would live in him. They would take up residence in his apartment.

He had refused to comfort Ruby. His cruelty made him feel sick. He loved her. He had always loved her. How much more deeply he loved her now.

He thought about Marjory and had to confess to himself that he had used her. He had known it would push Ruby's buttons. He had known how to play that ace!

He had even enjoyed Ruby's jealousy, with a perverse pleasure.

Up to a couple of weeks ago, he had had no idea where to start on rebuilding his life. He had been suspended in mid-air for two years — afraid to go back, afraid to go forward. He had forced himself to take a few steps: with or without her, he had to start living again. He had visited the nearest plant nursery and purchased some pretty window-boxes. He also bought some hanging baskets. Slowly his home took on a softer aspect. He hung some watercolours on the wall. He bought a decent cookbook. He listened to a new CD. He hated it so he threw it out. That didn't matter. He was determined to join the human race again.

During this period of one step forward and two back, Eamonn found that one thing did not change with his moods. Something that had been hanging around the recesses of his mind for quite some time. He had found himself repeatedly returning to the theology file under his bed and reading bits, a page, a chapter, a question. His hunger for study was returning. He read, and re-read, his answers to questions that he now realised he hadn't understood. He corrected his own work.

Then, one evening, he found himself passing All Hallows' College on the Drumcondra Road. Before he could change his mind, he parked the car, walked into the reception area and signed up for the first trimester in 'Theology and Theory'. He would start at night school in September. He was excited and felt the first flickering of renewed hope.

Now he held up the white envelope and

placed a sharp knife in the corner. He heard a car pull up outside. An alarm, two beeps. A click-clack of heels. He peered out of the window. The familiar gold hair was approaching his hall door. He put down the envelope, still sealed, and went to open the door. Ruby stood before him with a tear-stained face.

She must have had the letter too, he thought. He couldn't decide whether it had been good or bad news.

'I know you're on your way to work, Eamonn, but I need to tell you something. It's really important.' She sniffed.

'Come in,' he said, guiding her by the arm. 'Sit down. I'll phone in and tell them I'll be late.'

Eamonn dialled the number, keeping one eye on the envelope lying on the kitchen table. He thought of Robert Ryan. Was she still seeing him?

Ruby reached across the counter and pulled a tissue out of a pretty blue box.

'Ciara, it's Eamonn. I'm running late. Carry on without me. Should be there in an hour or so. 'Bye.'

'Answering-machine,' he said nervously. 'I'm afraid I have no decaff coffee.' He rummaged through the presses.

'Any tea?'

Ruby had surprised him. 'Yes. Earl Grey. I

thought you didn't like — '

'Twining's?' she interrupted.

'The very one.' He looked at her with disbelief.

'That will do. Thanks,' she said.

Eamonn didn't know what to do. He stood still, arms folded, feet apart. He tried hard not to stare: Ruby wore no makeup, and had on a light tracksuit. The lack of makeup brought up her dimples even more. She tucked her hair behind her ears.

Eamonn put a cup of tea in front of her. She lifted it and drank it. She showed no interest in what it was, how it was made or what he had put in it.

'Eamonn, I went to see Father Ebbs this morning,' she started, 'or Sean, I should say.'

Eamonn looked over his shoulder as he fiddled with the tea caddy. 'Sean?' he asked, bemused.

'Never mind.' She waved her hand. 'That's another story. I went to ask him to retract the application.'

Eamonn smiled so hard that his face begged him to stop.

'I realise it was a mistake. It is an insult to both of us to suggest we were never married.'

★　★　★

He just kept smiling that silly, stupid grin. He was making her nervous. She was determined to remain dignified. She willed her pride to step down, to leave her alone.

'Eamonn, I don't know how to apologise for everything I did and said. I was angry, hurt. I felt like a freak. I only want us to be happy and free. We should not have to pay this terrible price any more,' she said, with great sadness.

'Look, you have nothing to apologise for, Ruby. I've thought long and hard about all this. It wasn't your fault.' He stood awkwardly, sipping his tea. Still grinning like a Cheshire cat.

'Why are you grinning?' she asked.

'You've no idea how much it means to me to hear you say that our marriage was valid. It's the most important thing in my life,' he said.

'But, Eamonn, it cannot be taken back. The application was sent to Rome!' She started crying again.

'I know.' He held up the white envelope.

'Oh, God.'

They sat in silence staring at the letter as if it contained a bomb and was about to explode.

Tick. Tick.

'Look, I have only one thing I want to ask you,' Eamonn said suddenly. 'Look at me,' he implored her.

She looked him straight in the eye.

'This is important. I want you to think hard before you answer me,' he whispered.

Ruby nodded.

'No matter what it says on that piece of paper, promise me that our marriage is valid. Promise me that we agree to that, no matter what the Church's view is.'

Ruby concentrated hard on the words, keeping her eyes on his. She saw a hint of laughter. Or was it love? 'I like the idea,' she said, smiling now.

'Do you promise, Ruby?'

'Yes. I promise,' she answered, feeling elated by their dual consent.

'You mean it?' he checked.

'I promise,' she repeated.

He went to her and hugged her tightly. 'Now it doesn't matter any more.' He rocked her lovingly.

'No, it doesn't.' She laid her head on his shoulder.

Eamonn tossed the white envelope over his head. It floated featherlike, backwards and forwards, until it landed with a soft thud in the bin.

Ruby was reluctant to move. She knew she should move. She would move, any minute now.

* * *

Eamonn could smell her perfume. It had been so long since he had held her. He knew he should move. He decided he would move soon. He would move now, in a minute. He rested his hand on the back of her hair and closed his eyes. If he kissed her, would she pull away? He kissed the top of her head. And waited. Ruby remained in his arms.

He kissed her hair again, this time stroking it with the palm of his hand. And still she remained in his arms.

'Ruby,' he whispered, in her ear.

She turned her face sideways, her brown eyes meeting his. They spoke in volumes. She kissed his lips. A hesitant kiss, the type that needs a reaction. He reacted immediately. He knelt before her and lifted her sweater. His mouth found her nipples, and she moaned with pleasure. He teased them nibbling, licking. Their clothing was dismantled, messily strewn across the room as they moved towards the bedroom.

Her hands became entwined in his trousers. His hands became entangled in her hair. Ruby lay on her stomach, and Eamonn lay on top of her.

Eamonn parted her legs, inching his way into the curves of her flesh, as Ruby showed him the way. She cried out as he drove into her, unleashing a million years of starvation, deprivation and loneliness. A few minutes later, they lay together, their bodies wet with perspiration. Eamonn's nose was buried in Ruby's armpit. He couldn't breathe. If he didn't move he would smother. Suddenly the intensity of their lovemaking made him want to explode with laughter. He lifted his head and gazed at their contorted position.

His left foot was caught in the quilt; he tried to wriggle it free. Ruby raised her head and looked over his shoulder. She started to giggle. He giggled with her. Eamonn slid down the side of the bed to retrieve his foot, and tumbled noisily on to the floor. He was trying to stop laughing so that he could catch his breath. Ruby was hysterical, arms flailing wildly. Each time she managed to control herself, Eamonn started again. She pulled herself upright and held her arms across her breasts.

'It's a bit late to be modest now,' Eamonn commented, crawling around the floor, picking up their clothes as he went along.

'Speak for yourself.' Ruby laughed. 'Your knickers are on back to front,' she noted.

'Move over.' He squeezed in beside her. 'Thank God, I found you again,' he muttered, serious now. 'Ruby,' he whispered. 'You know I love you.'

There. It was out. There was nothing else to be said.

'I really do. You know there couldn't have been anything between Marjory and me, don't you?' he said again, his lips turning up into a radiant smile. Now he wanted her to banish Robert Ryan.

'I know,' she said. 'I love you too,' she whispered. Those were the words she had sworn never to utter again. 'Yes, I really do!' she repeated, almost as if she wasn't sure that she had heard herself correctly. It sounded right. It felt right.

'What are we going to do?' she asked.

'Do we have to do anything?' Eamonn asked. 'Can't we just 'be'?'

'What if you feel different tomorrow?'

'Every morning for the last ten years I've woken to the thought of you. Why should it be any different tomorrow?' He smiled lovingly at her.

'What about the children?' Ruby said sadly.

'Ruby! For goodness' sake. Marriages are not made up of children alone. What we've got is a blessing, children or no children,' he said.

'You don't mind . . . having no children?' she asked.

'No. I don't mind. You scared me there. For a minute I thought you were going to suggest

IVF treatment or adoption or something.' He laughed.

'Well, now that you mention it . . . ' She gave him a broad grin.

★ ★ ★

Mr Sean Ebbs sat in a small, two-bedroomed cottage just outside County Meath. He took in his new surroundings, then went to wash his hands, which were caked in muck. He had just planted his beloved lilies-of-the-valley and had a hunch that, finally, he would see them blossom. He would live to see it all blossom. His flowers, his manhood, his life.

He had read the Tribunal's response with glee. His last assignment as a priest had been a success. He had done his job well.

He blessed himself and prayed for the Blakes. They would never know what they had given him, or the part they had played in his being set free.

At least he had returned the favour. He saw the irony. He had had no say in the final outcome. He laughed out loud.

Perhaps there was a God, after all . . .

Dublin Regional Marriage Tribunal,
Diocesan Offices,
Archbishop's House,
Dublin 9

Personal and Confidential   28 July 1996.

Marriage: Eamonn Blake and Ruby Reece

Place: St Fintan's Church, Sutton, Dublin 13

Date: 14 February 1988

RE: APPLICATION FOR ANNULMENT
ON THE GROUNDS OF LACK OF
KNOWLEDGE

I submit that the presumption of validity in
this marriage should be upheld.

By Direction of the Presiding Judge

We do hope that you have enjoyed reading this large print book.

Did you know that all of our titles are available for purchase?

We publish a wide range of high quality large print books including:
Romances, Mysteries, Classics
General Fiction
Non Fiction and Westerns

Special interest titles available in large print are:
The Little Oxford Dictionary
Music Book
Song Book
Hymn Book
Service Book

Also available from us courtesy of Oxford University Press:
Young Readers' Dictionary
(large print edition)
Young Readers' Thesaurus
(large print edition)

For further information or a free brochure, please contact us at:
Ulverscroft Large Print Books Ltd.,
The Green, Bradgate Road, Anstey,
Leicester, LE7 7FU, England.
Tel: (00 44) **0116 236 4325**
Fax: (00 44) **0116 234 0205**

Other titles published by
The House of Ulverscroft:

ELEGANCE

Kathleen Tessaro

Browsing in a second-hand bookshop, Louise Canova stumbles across a faded grey volume. Written by the formidable French fashion expert, Madame Genevieve Antoine Dariaux, *Elegance* is an encyclopaedia of style that promises to transform plain women into creatures of grace and poise. And there's nothing Madame can't advise upon — including inattentive husbands, false friends, and the powerful bond between mothers and daughters. When Louise vows to follow Madame's advice, her life is transformed. Within the book's pages lie clues to her own past, and as she begins to unravel them, she discovers a courage she never dreamt possible. However, everything — even elegance — has its price.

TOO LATE FOR LOVE

Lisa Andrews

When Gemma Davenport hears that Blake
Adams is going to buy her glass company,
her heart sinks. Ten years ago they had a
passionate affair which left Gemma
broken-hearted and with a permanent
reminder of Blake. As soon as she sees him
again, it is clear that Blake is enjoying
every moment of the take-over. He makes
it apparent that he has never forgiven her
for what he sees as her 'betrayal' in
marrying another man. Gemma is soon
wondering (and hoping?) if Blake is so
intent on getting his own back that he's
trying to rekindle their once 'fatal
attraction' . . .

GRABBING THE FAMILY JEWELS

Gaby Hauptmann

Anno Adelmann — survivor of two heart attacks — is a wealthy widower, and his four scheming daughters all have designs on his inheritance. Anno, who refers to them variously as hyenas and piranhas, decides to have a bit of fun at their expense. But what starts as a joke soon becomes much more serious, and the family finds itself dealing with kidnapping, blackmail and even attempted murder. Vanity is mocked and bad behaviour deliciously punished as the four sisters learn some uncomfortable lessons in sibling rivalry.

THE MIDDLE AGES

Jennie Fields

An architect with a prominent New York City law firm, Jane Larsen designs bank branches and supermarkets, yet is rarely allowed to indulge in her one passion: designing houses. Divorced and focused on her teenaged daughters, Jane isn't even interested in finding Mr Right. Still, her life has begun to feel empty, and she's lost track of the dreams she once had. Then she decides to look up an old boyfriend with whom she's lost contact — the love of her life. Before long, she has a long-distance relationship brewing, and she's alive in a way she hasn't been for years.

GRAMERCY PARK

Paula Cohen

Mario Alfieri is the world's greatest tenor. He is also rumoured to be the world's greatest lover. When he arrives in New York in 1894 to prepare for his first season at the Metropolitan Opera House, all Manhattan is aflame with excitement. Success, it seems, is assured — until he meets Clara Adler. This bewitching orphan lives in the mansion of her late guardian, penniless and alone except for the unwelcome attentions of Thaddeus Chadwick, the lawyer who controls the estate. Mario and Clara fall hopelessly in love. But Chadwick is determined to keep Clara for himself and will stop at nothing to destroy all that Mario and Clara hold most dear . . .

JULIE AND ROMEO

Jeanne Ray

Julie Roseman, a divorcee and Romeo Cacciamani, a widower, own rival flower shops in Boston. They don't know what started the family feud generations before, but they have never questioned it — until the fateful day when these two vital, lonely people see each other across a crowded lobby at a small business owners' seminar and an intense attraction blooms. But the path of true love never did run smooth, and with Romeo's feisty, octogenarian mother and a pack of fierce children coming between them, it looks like Julie and Romeo's tale will not end happily.